P...

Peaches and Scream

"Cozy readers will savor every word of this peach of a mystery. Ms. Furlong's turn of phrase is delightful, her characters are endearing and the mystery will keep readers guessing until the very end. The Georgia Peach Mysteries are loaded with Southern charm, sassy characters and tantalizing recipes—a pure delight!"

—Ellery Adams, *New York Times* bestselling author

"Georgia belles can handle anything—including murder—as Susan Furlong proves in this sweet and juicy series debut."

—Sheila Connolly, *New York Times* bestselling author

"This wonderful series is going to have you humming 'Georgia on My Mind' and have your mouth watering to try the five peach-inspired recipes included in the back of the book! This series has everything a cozy mystery lover could want: loyal family, fantastic friends, a wonderful juicy story line and a dog called Roscoe." —A Cup of Tea and a Cozy Mystery

Berkley Prime Crime titles by Susan Furlong

PEACHES AND SCREAM
REST IN PEACH

Rest
in Peach

SUSAN FURLONG

BERKLEY PRIME CRIME, NEW YORK

**BERKLEY
PRIME
CRIME**

**An imprint of Penguin Random House LLC
375 Hudson Street, New York, New York 10014**

REST IN PEACH

A Berkley Prime Crime Book / published by arrangement with the author

Copyright © 2016 by Susan Furlong-Bolliger.
Penguin supports copyright. Copyright fuels creativity, encourages diverse voices,
promotes free speech, and creates a vibrant culture. Thank you for buying an authorized
edition of this book and for complying with copyright laws by not reproducing, scanning, or
distributing any part of it in any form without permission. You are supporting writers and
allowing Penguin to continue to publish books for every reader.

BERKLEY® PRIME CRIME and the PRIME CRIME design are trademarks
of Penguin Random House LLC.
For more information, visit penguin.com.

ISBN: 978-0-425-27856-7

PUBLISHING HISTORY
Berkley Prime Crime mass-market edition / April 2016

PRINTED IN THE UNITED STATES OF AMERICA

10   9   8   7   6   5   4   3   2   1

Cover illustration by Erika LeBarre.
Cover design by Sarah Oberrender.
Interior text design by Laura K. Corless.
Interior map copyright © by Nurul Akmal Markani.

This is a work of fiction. Names, characters, places, and incidents either are the product of
the author's imagination or are used fictitiously, and any resemblance to actual persons,
living or dead, business establishments, events, or locales is entirely coincidental.

PUBLISHER'S NOTE: The recipes contained in this book are to be followed exactly as
written. The publisher is not responsible for your specific health or allergy needs that may
require medical supervision. The publisher is not responsible for any adverse reactions to
the recipes contained in this book.

If you purchased this book without a cover, you should be aware that this book is stolen
property. It was reported as "unsold and destroyed" to the publisher, and neither the author
nor the publisher has received any payment for this "stripped book."

Penguin
Random
House

For my husband, Nyle.
Thank you for your love and support.

Any woman who's had the privilege of growing up below the Mason-Dixon line understands the history and tradition of a debutante ball. My mother was no exception. From the time I could walk, she started grooming me for my debut to polite society. I can still remember her little bits of advice to this day—tips she called her Debutante Rules. Of course, some of them were a little offbeat; but they did encourage me to become the best woman I could be. You see, my mama's advice taught me that being a debutante is less about the long white gloves, the pageantry and the curtsy, and more about a code of conduct that develops inner beauty, a sense of neighborly charity and unshakable strength in character that sees us women through the good times and the bad. Later, as I traveled the world, I came to learn that these rules of hers transcended borders, cultures and economic status. In essence, my mama's Debutante Rules taught me that no matter where you're from or who your people are, becoming the best person you can be is key to a happy life.

—Nola Mae Harper

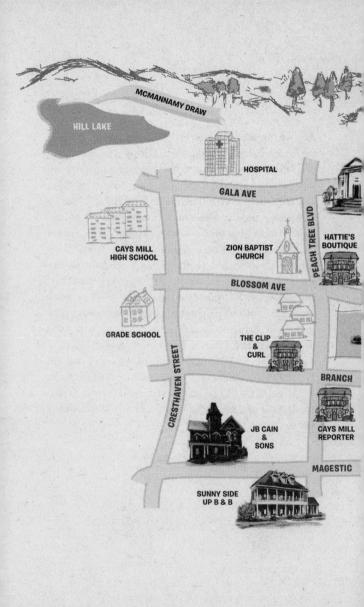

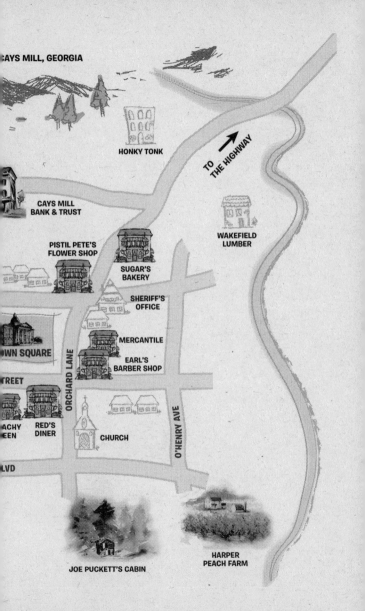

Chapter 1

🍑

Debutante Rule #032: Like a magnolia tree, a debutante's outward beauty reflects her strong inner roots . . . and that's why we never leave the house without our makeup on.

Frances Simms's beady eyes were enough to make my skin crawl on any given day, but at that particular moment the presence of the incessantly determined owner and editor of our town's one and only newspaper was enough to frazzle my last nerve.

"Can't this wait, Frances? I'm right in the middle of something." I turned my focus back to my project. Truth was, I could have used a break; my arm was about to fall off from all the scrubbing I'd been doing in my soon-to-be new storefront. Still, I'd suffer through more scrubbing any day if it meant I could avoid dealing with the bothersome woman. And today, of all days, I didn't need her pestering presence.

Frances persisted. "Wait? I'm on a deadline. Especially if you want the ad to run in Tuesday's issue." The *Cays Mill Reporter*, the area's source of breaking news—or rather, reputation-breaking gossip—faithfully hit the usually hot Georgia pavement every Tuesday and Saturday. Since I was a new business owner, Frances was hoping to sign me on as a contributing advertiser. For a mere $24.99 a month, I could reserve a one-by-one inch square on the paper's back page, sure to bring in hordes of eager, peach-lovin' customers to my soon-to-open shop, Peachy Keen.

"This offer isn't going to be on the table forever," she continued. "I'm giving you a ten percent discount off my normal rate, you know."

My friend Ginny spoke up. "Oh, don't go getting all bent out of shape, Frances." Having a slow moment at Red's Diner next door, which she owned with her husband, Sam, Ginny had popped over to check my renovation progress. "This is only Saturday," she went on. "Besides, Peachy Keen doesn't officially open for another few weeks."

Over the past nine months since my return to Cays Mill, what started as a little sideline business to help supplement my family's failing peach farm had grown into a successful venture. From that first jar of peach preserves sold at the local Peach Harvest Festival to a booming online business, Harper Farm's Peach Products had been selling like crazy. Unable to keep up with the demand, I had struck a deal with Ginny and Sam: For a reasonable percentage of profits, I'd get full use of their industrial-sized, fully licensed kitchen after the diner closed each day, plus a couple hours daily of Ginny's time and expertise in cooking. Since the diner was only open for breakfast and lunch, we could easily be in the kitchen and cooking by late afternoon, allowing Ginny enough time to be home for supper with her family. Then, Ginny offered to rent me their small storage area, right next to the diner, for a storefront—a perfect location—which now stored much of my stock until we could open. The deal worked for both of us: I needed the extra manpower, and Ginny needed the extra money. Especially with one child in college and her youngest, Emily, finishing her senior year in high school.

Frances was pacing the floor and stating her case. "That may be true, but space fills up quickly. My paper's the leading news source for the entire area."

"Oh, for Pete's sake, Frances," Ginny bantered, "it's the *only* news source in the area. Besides, that quote you gave Nola is five bucks higher than what I pay for the diner's monthly ad."

I quit scrubbing and quirked an eyebrow Frances's way. "Is that so?"

"Well, I've got expenses and—" She started to explain but was cut off mid-sentence when the back door flew open and Emily burst inside.

"Mom!" Emily cried, her freckled face beaming with excitement. She snatched up Ginny's purse and held it out. "The delivery truck just pulled in front of the boutique. The dresses are in!"

Ginny let out a little squeal, cast a quick glance toward the window and reached into her bag. "Okay, okay. Just give me a minute to freshen up." She pulled a compact out and started touching up her lipstick, a shocking red tint that looked surprisingly fabulous with her ginger-colored hair. "Oh, I can hardly wait! Emily's cotillion dress. Can you imagine!" she gushed and glanced my way. "Come on, Nola. You said you'd come with us, right? You've just gotta see the gown we ordered."

I peered anxiously at the stacks of lumber for the unfinished shelving, the loose plaster and the wood floors that were still only half refinished. Knowing the renovation was too much for me to handle alone, I'd hired my friend, Cade McKenna, who owned a local contracting business, to help me transform the storage area into a quaint shop. One of the interior walls sported exposed red brick and would add the perfect touch to the country-chic look I wanted. But my vision and reality didn't mesh easily; I'd been scrubbing loose mortar from that wall for hours already. Cade said the loose stuff really needed to be removed before he could seal the rest. I threw a quick glance through the window. I'd already known my work would be interrupted later today when the delivery truck arrived; I'd been dragged into my dear friend and her daughter's excitement since the get-go. But, truth be told, I almost preferred flaking mortar to facing up to the debutante issues I knew would soon erupt into a community-wide frenzy. "I'd love to go, but I really should keep at it."

Ginny waved off my worry. "You've been at it all morning. You need a break."

"Hey!" Frances turned her palms upward in protest. "I wasn't done discussing the ad."

"Oh, shush up, Frances," Ginny said to shut her down. She reached back into her bag, this time pulling out a small bottle of cologne and giving herself a couple quick spritzes behind the ears.

"You're fine, Mama," Emily interrupted. "Let's get going. I'm dying to try on my dress."

Ginny finished primping and shouldered her bag. "All right, sweetie. Let's go." She squeezed her daughter's arm, her eyes glistening. "I just know you're going to be the most beautiful debutante at the cotillion!" Then turning to me, she added with a mischievous grin, "Are ya coming with us, or do you want to stay here and discuss *the ad* with Frances?"

Since she put it that way, I decided I could use a little break and proceeded to rip off my apron and remove the bandana covering my cropped hair. I ran my hand through the short strands, trying to give it a little lift, the extent of my personal primping routine, as I made my way to the back door. Opening it wide, I shrugged toward Frances, who was still standing in the middle of my would-be shop, a befuddled look on her face. "Sorry, Frances. Guess we'll have to talk about the ad some other time."

She opened and shut her mouth a few times, but all that came out was a loud huff. Finally relenting, she threw up her hands and stormed out the door. I couldn't help but stare after her with a grin on my face. Usually I didn't take so much delight in being rude, but ever since Frances's paper ran a smear campaign on my brother-in-law last August, I'd had a hard time being civil toward her. Who could blame me? At the time, she'd relentlessly pursued, harassed and tried to intimidate information from not only me, but my then-very-pregnant sister, Ida. And, when Frances found she couldn't coerce information from us, she printed libelous half-truths about Hollis—on the front page, nonetheless!—that all but landed him a lifetime prison sentence. Thank goodness all that misery was behind us now. What a relief knowing the only thing Frances could hound me about these days was a silly display ad for the back page of the paper.

Emily was right; Hattie's Boutique, owned by my childhood friend Hattie McKenna, was already teeming with a small but enthusiastic pack of giggling debutantes and their equally excited mothers. They were pressing against the main counter like a horde of frenzied Black Friday shoppers while Hattie pulled billows of white satin and lace from long brown boxes. Carefully, she hung each dress on a rack behind the counter. "Ladies, please!" she pleaded. "Take a seat in the waiting area. I just need a few minutes to sort out the orders."

One of the mothers, Maggie Jones, the preacher's wife, was at the head of the pack sticking out her elbows like a linebacker in hopes of deterring the other gals from skirting around her in line. "Did the dress we ordered come in? Belle would like to try it on."

Hattie smiled through gritted teeth, once again pointing across the room toward a grouping of furniture. "I'm sure it did, Mrs. Jones. If y'all would just take a seat, please, I'll be right with you." She lifted her chin and kept her finger pointing across the room, making it clear she would not unpack one more dress until we complied.

With a collective sigh, the group, including Ginny, Emily and me, sulked to the waiting area. The mothers politely settled themselves on the flower-patterned furniture while the girls huddled off to the side to discuss the latest debutante news. It was a wonder they never tired of the topic. I, for one, could hardly take much more. For months, I'd been hearing constant chatter about our town's spin on a high society debut: the presentation, what would be served at the formal dinner and, of course, all about how elegantly Congressman Wheeler's plantation would be decorated for the Peach Cotillion. Usually the whole shindig was held up north at some ritzy country club, but this year, thanks to the generosity of one of our outstanding residents, congressman Jeb Wheeler (who just happened to be up for reelection), the cotillion was staying local with the ball taking place at his family home, the historic Wheeler Plantation.

"Maggie Jones is awful pushy for a reverend's wife, don't you think?" Ginny whispered.

Leaning back against the cushion, I inwardly moaned. That's why I hadn't wanted to come; Ginny was taking this cotillion stuff way too seriously. As a matter of fact, the pending cotillion and its accompanying affairs seemed to be bringing out the worst in all the town's ladies. Like the well-dressed woman across from us who sported an expensive-looking beige leather handbag and an all-too-serious attitude. She was seated with ramrod-straight posture and legs folded primly to one side, a proud tilt to her chin as she impatiently—and imperiously—glanced around the room.

"Who's Miss Proper over there?" I quietly asked Ginny.

She glanced over and quickly turned back, her face screwed with disgust. "That's Vivien Crenshaw. You know, Ms. Peach Queen's mama." She nodded toward the group of girls where a tall blonde with dazzling white teeth stood in the center of group. She was gushing dramatically about her date for the dance while the rest of the girls looked on in awe. "Her name's Tara," Ginny continued. "Emily says she's the most popular girl in high school. Top in everything: lead in the school play, class president and head cheerleader . . . you know the type."

Yeah, I knew the type. A picture of my own sister's face formed in my mind. Ida, the star of the Harper clan, always exceeded everyone's expectations, whereas I always did the unexpected, keeping my family in a continuous state of quandary. Even to this day, there were things I just couldn't bear to tell my parents, for fear it would put them over the edge. I shook my head, telling myself not to think about all that right now.

Luckily, a movement outside distracted me from my downward spiral. Adjusting my position to get a better look, I gazed curiously at the young girl washing Hattie's windows. She was dressed in sagging jeans and a too-tight T-shirt topped off with shocking black hair that shadowed her features. This must have been the girl Hattie mentioned hiring for odd jobs. She was nothing like the other girls in town. I felt an instant connection to her. As I continued to look on, the girl paused, reached into the pocket of her jeans and extracted a hair band. She pulled back her hair, exposing several silver hooped earrings running along the rim of her ear and topped off with a long silver arrow that pierced straight through to the inner cartilage. *Ew.* That must have hurt! I felt no connection now. But still, it was fascinating. It reminded me of some of the extreme piercings I'd observed in the remote African tribes during my days as a humanitarian aid worker.

I was about to ask Ginny if she knew the girl when Hattie called out from the other side of the room. "Okay, ladies. I think I've got everything straightened out. Now one at a time. . . ." She held up the first dress. "Belle Jones." The preacher's wife and her daughter scrambled to grab the dress before heading off toward the dressing rooms. "And, this one's for Sophie Bearden," Hattie continued, handing out the next dress to a squealing brown-haired girl.

Just as Hattie was reaching for the next gown, jingling bells announced the arrival of a short, stout woman dressed in sensible polyester slacks and a scooped-neck top. She removed her sunglasses and unwrapped a colorful scarf from her head. "Lawdy! Can y'all believe this humidity today?" She patted down her tight black curls before using the scarf to dab at her décolletage.

Hattie's face lit up. "Mrs. Busby, thanks so much for coming in early."

The woman waved off the thanks with, "So how many girls spied that early delivery truck?"

"Just a few, but if you could pin them up, it'd save having to make extra appointments."

"Sure enough. Just send them back to my station."

In the back corner of the shop, Hattie had utilized a lovely folding screen with an inlaid floral motif to partition an area for alterations. Behind the partition, a large corner table held an industrial sewing machine, racks of thread spools, a myriad of scissors and a divided box of pins, buttons and clasps. To the side of the workstation, a carpeted platform rested in front of an antique white cheval mirror.

Hattie disappeared behind the counter again, where she continued opening boxes and checking order slips while the rest of the girls waited impatiently. The first girls were coming out of the dressing room, proud mamas trailing after them, holding up their gowns as they made their way to Mrs. Busby for alterations. After a couple more girls disappeared to the dressing rooms with their gowns, the Peach Queen's mother heaved a sigh and glanced disgustedly at her watch. "How much longer is this going to take? I have an appointment at the salon in about ten minutes."

Hattie was still behind the counter, tearing through packing material, her expression panicked. "Of course, Mrs. Crenshaw. I'll be right with you," she answered with a strained voice.

Next to me, Ginny shifted and rolled her eyes, quietly mimicking the woman under her breath. "Can you believe how demanding that woman is?"

Ginny's usually good-natured demeanor was being stretched thin by the overbearing woman. At the moment, she reminded me of a spark getting ready to ignite and explode. I patted her hand and mumbled under my breath, "Remember why you're here. To show your daughter the importance of social grace, right?" I shot her a sly grin and stood. "I think I'll just go over and see if Hattie needs a hand." Hattie had seemed cool and controlled before, but she looked like maybe she could use a bit of help now.

Just as I reached the counter, the bells above the door jingled again. This time it was a model-thin woman wearing crisp linen pants and a matching jacket. Her silky silver hair was cut at a precise angle to accentuate her strong jawline and graceful neck. Upon seeing her, Hattie stopped her work, straightened her shoulders and plastered on a huge smile. So did everyone else in the room. It was as if they were all marionettes and the puppet master had just pulled their strings.

"Mrs. Wheeler! Uh . . . you must be here to pick up your alterations." Hattie's voice was thinning even more, and her eyes darted nervously between her waiting customers and a rack of clothing lining her back wall. She took a little shuffle step as if she wasn't sure which way to go first.

Mrs. Wheeler glanced over the crowded waiting area and, sensing Hattie's stress, put on a gracious smile and said, "I didn't realize you were so busy. Please don't bother with my order right this minute. I've got business at the flower shop down the street. How about I stop by when I'm done there? Perhaps things will have settled down by then."

Hattie let out her breath and nodded gratefully, promising to have her order ready when she returned. But as soon as the woman exited, Hattie turned to me with an even more panicked expression, her back to the impatient mothers still on the couch. "There's a problem."

"A problem? What?"

She nodded toward the box on the floor. "There's only one dress left."

I shrugged.

"You're not getting it," she hissed, discreetly pointing across the room. "One dress, but two girls."

I could feel my eyes popping as I sucked in my breath. "Oh."

Joining her behind the counter, I squatted down and started ripping through the mounds of packing paper. "Are you sure?" She slid down next to me. My mind flashed back to a competitive game of hide-and-seek we once played as kids. Hattie and I crouched together behind the peach crates in my daddy's barn, suppressing giggles as her big brother, Cade, searched and searched in vain. Only this situation wasn't fun and games at all.

She chewed her lip and nodded. "I'm sure."

"Well, whose dress is it?"

"Any chance you can hurry things up a bit?" Vivien Crenshaw called out from across the room. "Like I said, I'm on a tight schedule."

Hattie raised up and peered over the counter. "Be right with ya!" Then, popping back down, she started to fall apart. "I just don't know what's happened. . . . Neither of the numbers on the order forms matches the one on the dress, but I think it's Emily's. It's just been so crazy here. . . . Maybe I messed up when I placed the order. What am I going to do? Of all the dresses to be missing."

"Relax. Just tell Mrs. Crenshaw there was a mistake. The cotillion is still a couple weeks away. There's plenty of time to get Tara's dress shipped and altered. Mistakes happen, right?"

She nodded, drew in a deep breath and stood up. "Mrs. Crenshaw, would you mind coming over here, please?"

I busied myself behind the counter, folding up the packing materials, revealing more of the dress that was left in the box. I couldn't help but smooth my hand over the shimmery satin of the gown. Actually, it gave me a little thrill to finally see the dress Emily had been talking about for so long. It was gorgeous! Viewing it up close gave me a slight prickle of regret. Due to a tragic, youthful mistake I didn't really want to think about at that moment, I'd missed my own cotillion, something my mother had never quite forgiven me for. Actually, thinking back on it, I was always a bit of a tomboy and never put much stock in the debutante craze anyway. Charm classes, dance lessons . . . all that was never really my thing. Of course, being raised by a mother who prided herself on her Southern heritage, I understood the reasoning behind such formalities. Like many things Southern, it was a ritual passed down since the days before Mr. Lincoln's war. And, we Southerners lived and died by our traditions, whether it was sweet tea, SEC football or fancy cotillions.

I ran my hand over the fine lace accents on the bodice of Emily's dress. Still, it would have been fun to wear something so elegant. . . .

"What do you mean her dress isn't in yet? That's it right there."

My head snapped up. Vivien Crenshaw was pointing at the dress I was caressing. Her daughter Tara stood next to her, nodding enthusiastically as they both peered over the counter.

"Oh no. I don't think so. I believe this is Emily Wiggins's dress," Hattie responded.

At the mention of her name, Emily started for the counter. Ginny was right behind her. Guessing by the wild look in Ginny's eye and the slight flush of her cheeks, her hackles were up. I sucked in my breath.

"Let me see that," Ginny demanded. I stood and held it upright. She took a quick look and turned to Vivien. "I'm sorry, Vivien, but you're mistaken. That's the dress Emily ordered. I'd know it anywhere." And she would, too. She and Ginny had spent days scouring over the catalogs at Hattie's, searching for Emily's dream cotillion dress—special ordered all the way from Atlanta—which I'd heard described a thousand times as an off-shoulder satin sheath that would look so beautiful on Emily's slim figure. Why, she was going to look just like a princess in it!

"No, you're the one who's mistaken," Vivien countered. She reached across the counter and snatched the dress from my hands. "Go try it on, Tara. And hurry. We're pressed for time."

"Now wait just a minute." Ginny intercepted her, placing a hand on Vivien's arm. "That's my daughter's dress and—"

"Ladies, please!" Hattie interrupted. "There's an easier way to resolve this. Just give me a few minutes and I'll call the dress company and get this straightened out." She already had the phone in her hand and was dialing the number as she walked toward the back room for privacy.

In the meantime, a crowd was gathering. Mrs. Busby, pincushion in hand, came over to see about the ruckus. Right behind her shuffled one of the debs, dragging the hem of her too-long gown. Then, out of one of the dressing rooms came Belle Jones and her mother, Maggie, their eyes gleaming with anticipation. Even the dark-haired window-washing girl stopped working and came inside to gawk. I swear, the whole scene reminded me of schoolkids gathering on the playground to witness a smackdown.

Emily spoke up, her eyes full of concern. "That's my dress, Mrs. Crenshaw. I'm sure of it."

Vivien's eyes shifted from Ginny and homed in on Emily. "This isn't your dress, young lady, and you know it."

Ginny recoiled and then sprang forward, her eyes full of venom. "Are you calling my girl a liar?"

"Just calm down, Ginny," I pleaded, dashing out from behind the counter and grabbing ahold of my friend. "We'll get this figured out."

Under my grip, I could feel Ginny's muscles tensing. She was ready to fight for this dress. Thank goodness, Hattie finally came out of the back room. She was carrying a large binder, her hands trembling as she flipped through the pages. "I'm afraid I've made a horrible mistake," she started to confess.

Vivien raised a brow. "A mistake?"

Hattie nodded. "Yes, you see, I would never order two of the same style dress for a cotillion. Y'all know how embarrassing it would be for two girls have the same one." She choked out a nervous little laugh before continuing, "But it seems both Tara and Emily picked the same dress from the catalog, but I somehow got the numbers on one of them mixed up, so I didn't know there were two of the same. So when I ordered it, the company called for clarification on a number, and . . . well, the right catalog number was already ordered, even in the right size . . . so I thought I had everyone covered. . . ." She swallowed hard, unable to dredge up her usual shopkeeper's smile.

Ginny lifted her chin. "Well, it's simple enough. Which one of us placed the order first?"

Hattie turned back a couple pages in the binder. "It looks like Emily did."

Vivien clutched the dress tighter. "Why does it matter who ordered first? We picked it up first. Besides, I'm sure Emily can find something else to suit her."

Two bright crimson circles suddenly appeared on Ginny's cheeks. "No way! You heard Hattie. That's our dress."

"I don't think so," Vivien countered.

Ginny reached for the gown, but Emily stopped her. "Don't, Mama. Please. It's all right. I'll pick out another." Tears welled in her eyes, and her cheeks flushed with embarrassment as she scanned the room and took in the reactions of the other girls.

Ginny wheeled and glared at her daughter. "Why should you? They're just trying to bully us."

Emily didn't respond. Instead, she pleaded silently with the most heartbreaking expression I'd ever witnessed. I knew exactly what she was feeling. If Tara Crenshaw was the most popular girl in school, crossing her would mean social suicide. The same thing must have dawned on Ginny, too, because instantly her expression softened and she backed away from Vivien and the coveted dress.

Taking the change in Ginny's demeanor as a sign of surrender, Vivien triumphantly handed the dress over to Tara and pointed to the dressing rooms. "Hurry now, sweetie. We don't have much time to spare." Then Vivien turned a sugary sweet smile toward Mrs. Busby. "Like I said, Tara and I are on a tight schedule, so if you wouldn't mind quickly pinning the dress. It probably won't need much, just a little tuck here and there. . . ." She eyed Ginny out of the corner of her eye. "After all, we've known all along that it would be the perfect fit for Tara's figure."

Ginny clenched her fists and let out a long harrumph.

"We should go," I suggested.

Ginny bristled, her eyes darting across the room to where Emily was now hunched over the dress catalog with a friend. "Let's give Emily a few minutes, okay?"

I sighed and shook my head, remaining close by just in case quick intervention was needed. After a few minutes, Tara came back out of the dressing room, prancing in front of her friends, who serenaded her with a round of oohs and aahs.

Vivien lifted her head proudly and helped her daughter onto the carpeted block. "Just like I thought," she said. "Almost a perfect fit." She pinched a bit of fabric in the back. "Maybe take in just a little here, and the hem of course. And if you could work quickly, Mrs. Busby, so we can be on our way. We'll come back in this evening for a second fitting. Let's say around six thirty."

Mrs. Busby looked shell-shocked. "Six thirty?"

Hattie piped up. "I'm afraid we close at six tonight, Mrs. Crenshaw. You'll have to—"

Mrs. Busby held up her hand. "It's all right. I don't mind staying a little longer."

"But, Mama!" Vivien's daughter cut in. "I'm supposed to meet my friends at the library. We won't be done by six thirty."

Vivien didn't bat a lash at her daughter's outburst. Instead, to my astonishment, she said, "Of course, sweetheart. You go ahead and hang out with your friends. I'll stop back and pick it up, and you can try it on at home. You probably won't need a second fitting anyway." Then she turned back to Mrs. Busby and demanded, "But have it ready tonight, so I can make sure the alterations are done correctly. If we do happen to need another fitting, I'll want to set it up right away. Our schedule is impossibly full these days."

"*Impossibly* full," Ginny mimicked under her breath. I cringed and looked around, hoping no one else had heard her. Across the room, I saw that Emily and her friend were still poring over the dress catalog. "Hey, we should go have another look at that catalog," I told Ginny. "Bet we can still find the perfect dress for Emily."

But my friend didn't budge. She was rooted in place, a scowl on her face as she watched Tara gloatingly parade back to the dressing room, carefully holding the pinned hem away from her ankles. "We already found Emily's perfect dress," Ginny bit out. "And that little snip is wearing it."

Unfortunately, that comment was heard loud and clear. Once again, everyone's attention focused on Ginny, including Emily's. She quickly abandoned the dress catalog and sidled up to her mother. "I'm ready to go, if you are, Mama."

"Sure you don't need to look at the catalog some more?" Ginny asked tightly.

Emily shook her head. "We can do that anytime." She tugged on her mother's arm, but to no avail. Ginny and Vivien seemed to be locked in a menacing stare down. Seconds passed without a single blink from either of them. Emily tugged some more and shot a pleading look my way.

I leaned in and whispered into Ginny's ear, "We really should be going. I need to get back to the shop, and I'm sure you've—"

I was interrupted by Tara's reemergence from the dressing room. Vivien ended the stare down with a smug little smirk, taking the dress from her daughter and handing it back over to Mrs. Busby. "It's all settled, then. I'll see you this evening," she said, heading for the door, Tara following on her heels.

The second the door shut behind them, Ginny's hands shot to her hips. Her chest heaved as she drew in a deep breath and let go with, "Well, I never . . . !" and continued on describing Vivien Crenshaw with a list of colorful adjectives that would threaten anyone's good standing with the local Baptists, finally finishing the tirade with something like, ". . . I sure hope that nasty, dress-stealing, backstabbing snob gets hers one day!"

A collective gasp sounded around the room, followed by a moment of stunned silence. Emily looked like she wanted to crawl under a rock. This was definitely not social grace. "It's okay, everyone!" I assured the ladies, while trying to pull Ginny aside for a little chill time. "She's just been under a lot of pressure, that's all."

But Ginny shook me off and stomped toward the door, turning back at the last minute. "I meant what I said," she spat. Then she lifted her chin at the entire room of staring eyes. "That witch stole my girl's cotillion dress. And don't y'all think for one second that I'm going to stand for it, neither. You mark my words. I'll make sure that woman gets her due!"

Chapter 2

🍑

Debutante Rule #016: Debutantes cling together through thick and thin; we'd rather perish than forsake a friend . . . unless she's after our boyfriend.

I swear, Reverend Jones was citing enough Bible passages to please a dozen Sunday school teachers and then some. It was all I could do to sit still through the last minutes of his sermon. When we finally wrapped up the final hymn, featuring a solo part by big-haired Laney Burns, local manicure professional and wannabe gospel diva, I made a beeline for the back door.

"I've invited Cade and Hattie over for some chicken," Mama said, catching up to me in the parking lot. She'd been doing that a lot: inviting Cade over for supper. Either she thought he was too skinny, or she was conspiring, as much as I, to kick our relationship up a notch on the romance scale. "I thought it'd be nice to do a little something extra for Cade since he's been working so hard getting your new store ready and all. You don't mind, do you?"

"Mind? No, not at all." A grin twitched at the corner of my lips. I couldn't think of a better way to spend a Sunday afternoon. Cade McKenna, Hattie's brother, and I had been friends since childhood. We'd grown apart over the years, but since my return to Cays Mill, he'd obviously been interested in making up for lost time. At first, I wasn't sure about getting involved in any sort of relationship. After quitting my longtime job at Helping Hands International and throwing all my efforts into trying to save my family's business, it seemed I had enough to worry about without throwing a man into the mix. However, as things started to settle, I began to rethink that decision. Then, just when I started to come around to the idea of Cade McKenna and me as a couple, he took a construction job up in Macon. Too good of a deal to pass up, he'd said. He was gone for most of the winter, proving true that old saying about absence and the heart growing fonder. Because, by the time he returned, my heart was more than willing. Only thing was, something had shifted between us again. I'm not sure what happened in Macon, but Cade came back a different man. But I figured winter, and whatever happened during it, was over and he was back. I didn't want to push him, maybe just nudge a bit. Since hiring him to help renovate my shop, we'd been spending more time together than ever, not that this was (exactly) why I'd hired him—he was great at his work. He'd come back around in his feelings eventually. I was sure of it.

"Here they come now," Mama said. She hastened over to meet them halfway, looping her arm in Hattie's as she chatted. Despite her three-inch heels—her Sunday best—my mama still looked petite next to Hattie, who was blessed with the perfect height and a figure suited for modeling swimsuits.

"No, no need to bring anything but yourselves," Mama was saying. "I've fixed enough chicken to feed an army." That was true. I woke first thing that morning to the smell of chicken frying. Mama had been at the stove in her robe and slippers, turning chicken in a large cast-iron skillet. And that was after she'd already deviled a couple dozen eggs.

I greeted my friends with a hug, letting my arm linger on Cade's while I asked Mama, "Will Daddy and the hands be joining us?" Much to her disgust, when peaches were on, Daddy didn't break for anything. Not even church.

"Well, they have to eat, don't they?" she answered, pursing her lips and craning her neck to check out the line of church-goers still shaking the preacher's hand. "Did I see Pete Sanchez in church this morning?" she asked Hattie with mischievous gleam in her eye. "Because we could invite him, too." Hattie flinched at the mention of Pete's name, but before she could muster an answer, Mama flitted on to something else. "Oh, there's Ida and the kids. I'll just go over and remind them about lunch." She handed me the car keys. "Be right back. Get the air going, will you?"

As soon as she was out of earshot, I turned to Hattie. "What's going on?"

"What do you mean?"

Next to me, Cade tensed and shot me a warning look. I ignored him and pressed on. "The way you reacted when Mama mentioned Pete. What's up?"

Bristling, she raised her fingertips to her temples and shook her head. "I'd rather not go into all that right now. Actually, you'd be doing me a favor if you never mentioned that man's name again." Hattie was quickly working herself into a frenzy.

Cade blew out a long breath and took a step backward.

"I thought things were going so well. What happened?" I was shocked. Hattie adored Pete. They were perfect for each other. Things were getting serious between them, or at least so I thought.

"I'll tell you what happened . . ." she started, but from

somewhere within the depths of her shoulder bag, Tim McGraw started crooning a sexy tune. "Oh, shoot! This sure the heck better not be Pete calling me again." She dug around in her bag, extracting her cell and checking the display. Her brows furrowed as she raised the phone to her ear. "Mrs. Busby? . . . What?" Mrs. Busby's voice sounded frantic over the other end. Hattie gasped. "Oh, sweet Je— Did you call the police? . . . I'm on my way." She disconnected and stared at us with round eyes, the color draining from her face.

"What is it, sis?" Cade asked. But Hattie only shook her head in response before turning and darting through the lot toward her shop down the street. Without even taking time to think, we dashed after her, weaving our way between parked cars before crossing the street and running past a couple storefronts. Once inside her shop, we came to a screeching halt. There, sprawled on the floor by the counter, was Vivien Crenshaw—a wicked-looking pair of scissors protruding from the base of her throat. My eyes followed the line of her outstretched arm. Clutched in her now lifeless hand was a debutante gown, its blood-soaked satin transformed from pure white to murderous crimson.

It seemed like an eternity before the authorities arrived. In reality, it was probably only a few minutes, but something about being up close to a corpse made time slow to a crawl. It wasn't until Sheriff Maudy Payne and her deputy sauntered through the door that I was able to breathe a little easier.

"What do we have here?" the sheriff asked, removing her Stetson and running a hand over an unruly crop of mousy brown hair before bringing it to rest on her gun belt. She stood there a few seconds, shoulders back, chest puffed out and dark eyes roaming the room. Unfortunately, they turned even darker when they landed on me. Ever since last August, when I got myself tangled up in one of her murder cases, she'd been cold toward me. Of course, I don't think she cared for me much before then, either. Something to do with a long rivalry between her and my sister, Ida. Guilt by association, I guess.

"It's Vivien Crenshaw," Mrs. Busby said. The poor woman was standing off to the side with her arms clenched around her midsection as if she was trying to hold herself together. "I found her when I opened the door."

"What time was that?" the deputy asked. Deputy Travis Hanes was homegrown, although I'd never really met him until after I returned to Cays Mill last summer. I'd heard he studied criminal justice at Central Georgia Tech up in Macon and had just taken the job with the Cays Mill Sheriff's Department a few months before our last murder occurred. Now this. Guess he was learning the ropes the hard way.

Mrs. Busby continued, "Just right before I called you. Maybe a little after eleven. I'd come in to get some extra work done. When I saw what'd happened, I called you right away." Mrs. Busby started trembling. I crossed over and wrapped my arm around her shoulders.

"You came through the front door?"

Mrs. Busby nodded.

"And it was locked?"

Another nod.

Maudy motioned for Travis to check out the back room. In the meantime, she started pacing the scene, circling the body slowly, bending down here and there to get a closer look. "And the rest of you? Why are you here?"

I assumed she meant Cade and me, since it would make sense for Hattie to be in her own shop. "Cade and I were with Hattie when Mrs. Busby called. We just came along to help."

"Aw . . . I see." Maudy removed a ballpoint pen from her front shirt pocket and started poking at the dress in Mrs. Crenshaw's hand. "What time did you close up shop yesterday, Ms. McKenna?"

"I left early, I guess. Maybe around four thirty. I'd had a bad day."

"Did you lock up the place?"

Hattie glanced over to where I was standing with Mrs. Busby. "No, Mrs. Busby was staying late. Keeping an eye on things for me."

A pointed look from the sheriff prompted Mrs. Busby to explain. "That's true. I had to wait for Mrs. Crenshaw anyway. She was supposed to be coming in to pick up a dress at six thirty, but she called and canceled. Said she had something come up and that she'd call me today to reschedule."

That seemed strange. If Vivien had canceled then why did she show up at all?

"About what time did you get the call?" the sheriff asked.

Mrs. Busby pressed her lips together, tucked her chin and rolled her eyes to the ceiling. A few seconds later she finally responded, "It must have been a little before six. I only say that because I left right afterward, and when I got home the six o'clock news was still on. Channel thirteen. The weather girl was predicting rain, which would make it about six twenty," she babbled. "Wish it would rain. We could use a little relief."

"Looks like the back door was jimmied," Travis announced, coming back into the room. "Nothing else seems to be disturbed." He looked at Hattie. "You'll need to replace the lock, though."

"Don't worry. I'll see to it," Cade told the deputy.

"Travis, put in a call to the crime scene guys. We've got some work to do here."

"Yes, ma'am. Funeral home, too?"

Maudy sighed. "Yeah, give JB a call. We'll need a transport. But call Doc Harris, first. Tell him to get over here. I need him to pinpoint the time of . . . Well, lookie here."

We all took a half step forward as Maudy squinted with interest at Vivien's diamond-studded watch. She turned to Travis. "Got some gloves on ya?"

He opened a pouch on his utility belt and produced a pair of latex gloves. Maudy stretched them over her big hands and carefully turned Vivien's arm, just a fraction, so she could see the whole face of the watch. "It's busted," Maudy said. "Must have broken during a struggle. Or maybe when she fell after bein' stabbed. And it looks like time stopped a little after six thirty." She pointed at the scissors. "These yours?" she asked Hattie.

Hattie hesitated, sliding her eyes toward Mrs. Busby, who hemmed and hawed a bit before answering, "Afraid those are my fabric scissors, Sheriff. They're as sharp as a thistle."

The sheriff nodded and moved to the other side of the body, where she used her pen to lift part of the dress. She studied it for a long time. Finally, she asked, "What is this? A wedding gown?"

Hattie and I exchanged a look, but neither of us dared go down that path. The last thing we wanted to do was identify the garment as the debutante gown our friend Ginny and the very dead Vivien Crenshaw had been fighting over. Mrs. Busby, on the other hand, didn't feel the same need for discreetness. "That's a girl's debutante gown, Sheriff. Just yesterday, Mrs. Crenshaw and that red-haired woman who runs the diner were fighting over that gown." I closed my eyes and cringed as she went on, "They practically came to blows over it. But Mrs. Crenshaw won out. Made that other gal real mad, too. Why, she was fit to be tied. Should have heard the way she was talking about Mrs. Crenshaw."

The sheriff was all ears. "You don't say?"

Mrs. Busby was on a roll. "Yes, I think she even said something about stabbing the poor woman."

"No, she didn't!" I couldn't help blurting out.

Maudy gave me a cold stare then the cold shoulder as she glanced at her deputy, who'd finished up his phone calls and was busy scribbling in his notepad. "Did ya get that, Travis?"

"Yes, ma'am. Suspect threatened to kill the victim."

Suspect?

Hattie stepped forward. "Now, that's not quite what she said, Mrs. Busby. I think you're a little confused. Must be the shock and all." She turned to Maudy. "She just called her a backstabbing snob, that's all. That's not the same as threatening to stab someone."

"Oh, you're right," Mrs. Busby conceded with a nod. Tugging at her close-cropped curls, she screwed up her face and asked, "What all did she say, exactly? She said more, I know. I'm afraid I just can't recall."

The room grew silent as the sheriff looked back and forth between Hattie and me, waiting for one of us to crack, I supposed. Hattie fixated on the floor and clamped her lips tight, which left me as the bad guy. I wavered for a few seconds, finally figuring I might as well spill. The sheriff would get what she needed from one of the other ladies anyway, and who knew what "recollection" they might have of the exact wording. "They were simply arguing over the dress, that's all."

"This dress?" Maudy pointed at the blood-soaked gown.

"Uh-huh. A silly thing, really. In the end, things got a little heated between them. All Ginny said was that she wasn't going to stand for Vivien stealing her daughter's dress. Who could blame her, really?" I didn't add about Ginny stating she'd be sure Vivien got "her due." Because of course, she didn't mean *this*.

But I hadn't needed to add anything else. Maudy stood a little straighter, an unmistakable grin tugging at the corner of her mouth. She raised her chin toward Travis, arched her brows and inhaled deeply, as if she'd just caught a whiff of something very satisfying. I recognized the look in her eyes. It was the same dogged determination I'd seen the summer before, when she went after my own brother-in-law for murder.

Ginny was in big trouble.

Chapter 3

🍑

Debutante Rule #026: When in doubt, just ask
yourself, "What would Scarlett do?"

The deafening din of the after-church crowd was in full swing
when we arrived at the diner: people murmuring, dishes clinking, food sizzling, someone's baby crying . . . Hattie, Cade and
I lingered by the chalkboard menu for a second, trying to
collect our wits as we scanned the place for Ginny. She wasn't
anywhere to be found, but Emily was there. She looked up
from taking an order and tossed us a friendly but frazzled
wave. To my surprise, I also saw the same dark-haired girl I'd
seen in the dress shop the day before. Only today, she was
busing tables, not washing windows.

"Maybe Ginny's in the kitchen helping Sam," Hattie suggested. As soon as the sheriff had finished her questions,
we'd rushed right over to the diner to warn Ginny. We were
hoping to give her a heads-up before Maudy showed up to
interrogate her.

"There she is." Cade pointed to where Ginny popped

through the swinging kitchen door, a tray of juice glasses in hand, and headed for the far end of the counter, where she used her open hand to retrieve a cinnamon roll from under a glass dome. Despite everything, my mouth watered. I happened to know that Ginny and Sam purchased a couple dozen pastries every weekend from Ezra Sugar, owner of Sugar's Bakery. Cinnamon rolls, along with peach scones, were his specialty.

"Hey, all!" she called out as we approached. "Don't think there's a spot open right now." She slid the roll in front of a guy seated at the bar and handed him a glass of orange juice. "Could I get Sam to fix y'all something to go?" she called over her shoulder, heading back around the counter toward the pass-through window that separated the kitchen and diner. Several plates were sitting under the warmer, stacked high with eggs, flapjacks and grits awaiting delivery.

"We need to talk to you," Cade said. "It's important."

Ginny shrugged and double-checked one of her tickets before grabbing a couple plates. "Sure. What's up?"

"In private," Hattie added.

She shot us a flinty stare and pushed around us, plates balanced on her arms. "Are you serious? It's a nuthouse in here. It'll have to wait until later."

Cade started to protest, but I grabbed his arm and pulled him close to my face. "Watch what you say." I dipped my chin toward the far end of the bar where Frances was turned our way, staring suspiciously. "Let's not alert the press." So far, word hadn't gotten out about Vivien. I wanted to keep it that way for at least a little while. But, Frances's uncanny senses must have alerted her that something was awry. She started glancing about, homing in on various individuals before finally turning her focus out the window. I followed her gaze, dismayed to find that even though Hattie's Boutique was located across the square on the other side of the old courthouse, it was still partially visible from the diner. Even from where I was standing, I could see the sheriff's cruiser parked on the curb outside the shop.

Uh-oh. "We've just run out of time," I told Hattie and Cade, watching Frances hop off her stool and make her way closer to the front window. "We need to find a way to get Ginny alone, now."

"But be discreet about it," Hattie warned her brother.

Ginny was on her way to one of the booths with coffeepot in hand when he finally flagged her down. "Think we will get something to go, after all."

She ambled back, setting the coffeepot by the cash register and pulling the pen from behind ear. "Okay, then. What can I get y'all?"

I held my breath as Frances neared our group, but she pushed right past us with a determined gait, slapped a few dollars on the bar and passed us again as she headed out the door. I leaned forward. "Vivien Crenshaw's been murdered."

"What?"

"And you may be a suspect," Cade added.

"Me?"

Hattie touched her arm. "You had that terrible argument with her yesterday."

Ginny frantically shook her head. "I argue with people all the time, but I don't kill them!"

"Shhh," I warned, glancing around the crowded diner. "We need to go somewhere private and discuss this. Maudy is probably on her way over here right now."

Ginny glanced around, her eyes finally settling on Emily, who was standing at another table, pen poised over her order pad, addressing a group of well-dressed matrons. "Let's go back into the kitchen," she told us, then she signaled to Emily and mouthed, "Cover me?" Emily nodded and quickly turned her focus back to one of the ladies who was pointing out an item on the menu.

"What are you doing back here? There must be another dozen orders waiting," Sam said, glancing up from the grill as we entered the kitchen. He was tending a line of at least twenty pancakes, flipping each one to golden perfection. I watched in amazement as he reached over with his other hand, grabbed an egg and cracked it single-handedly, then lifted a heavy iron off a row of frying bacon. Sam defied the stereotype about men and multitasking.

Ginny started to explain, "Remember me telling you about Vivien Crenshaw last night?"

"Remember? How could I forget? You were fit to be tied." He chuckled over his eggs, then sobered. "Poor Emily, though. Went straight to her room and cried half the night. 'Bout never got her settled down." He grabbed four plates from a nearby stack, setting them up on the counter next to the grill. Removing pancakes in sets of three, he began making a neat stack on each plate.

"She was murdered last night," Ginny told him.

Sam stopped and gave us his full attention. "Murdered?"

Hattie chimed in, "It's true. They found her this morning at my shop."

"And the sheriff knows all about the argument we had over that dress."

Cade shifted his feet. "And, she's probably on her way over here right now."

Sam began nervously wiping his hands down the front of his apron. Behind him, bacon and eggs continued to sizzle. "To question Ginny?"

I nodded. "In the heat of the moment, she might have said a couple things that sounded a little threatening."

Ginny threw up her hands. "Like I told y'all, it was just talk. You know how I am when I'm angry."

Sam rubbed at his stubbly face, a day's growth shadowing his jaw. "Oh no."

"Don't panic," Cade said, stepping forward and taking control of the spatula. He started removing shriveled bacon from the grill and scraping away at burnt eggs. "We all know Ginny didn't do this, Sam. It just might be a little hard to convince the sheriff. You know how Maudy Payne can be."

Next to me, Ginny started breathing heavily. I took hold of her trembling hands. "Don't worry. All you have to do is tell the sheriff where you were around six thirty yesterday evening." I quickly explained the sheriff's theory about Vivien's broken watch. Then, I followed her worried gaze as she turned toward Sam, her mouth slack and eyes blinking double time. Sam turned a sickly shade of gray.

"Mama," Emily's voice cut through the tension. She was peering through the pass-through at us. "Sheriff Payne's here. Says she wants to talk to you." She looked down at the empty grill and Cade standing by with spatula in hand. "Uh . . . Daddy? You okay? Table four's waiting on their food."

Ginny sucked up her breath and straightened her shoulders. "Sam, throw a couple of those pancakes on a plate, and that bacon, too. Got any grits made up? Sheriff likes her grits buttered." She turned toward us with a brave smile. "Maudy's always easier to deal with when her stomach's full."

After Sam handed her a loaded plate, she started for the kitchen door, shoulders back and chin held high. Cade stopped her along the way. "Maybe you shouldn't answer her questions until we can get you a lawyer."

She shriveled. "A lawyer?" A nervous little laugh escaped

her lips as she glanced Sam's way again. "We can't afford a lawyer." Her chin jutted back out as she turned back toward the door. "Besides, I don't need one. I'm innocent."

As soon as she was out of the kitchen, Cade turned to me and whispered, "Maybe you should call Ray anyway. Just in case things get out of hand." My brother, Ray, was an attorney. His firm was in Perry, a town not too far from Cays Mill, and he'd been instrumental in helping my brother-in-law, Hollis, avoid a lifelong prison sentence last summer. I knew he'd be willing to help Ginny, too.

Hattie leaned forward and added her two cents' worth. "Please do call him, Nola. It'd be good to at least get his take on this whole thing. Get him up to speed, just in case . . . well, like Cade said, just in case things get out of hand. Our sheriff's not known to be the most judicious person."

I glanced over to where Sam paced back and forth, wringing his hands on his apron. "Sam? Want me to give Ray a call? Just to let him know what's going on? He might be able to suggest something."

Sam stopped and turned toward me, his face twisted with concern. "I think maybe you'd better do that, Nola. 'Cause Ginny was out most of the evening yesterday, and I have no idea where she went."

"No one could ever convince me, not in a million years, that Ginny Wiggins could kill someone," Mama stated. We were in the dining room Monday morning sitting across from each other, sipping coffee and eating breakfast. "I've known that girl since she was just an itty-bitty thing. She was just a few years ahead of Ida in school, you know. Both her and Sam were."

I took a gulp of coffee and nodded. Ginny was almost ten years older than me, so I never really knew her growing up. Surprisingly enough, though, ever since my return to Cays Mill, we'd struck up a friendship. Over the past few months, I'd grown to care about Ginny and her family. That's why, right after leaving the diner yesterday, I immediately placed a call to Ray. Much to my relief, he promised to break away later this afternoon and come to Cays Mill to see what he could do to help.

"She's got a fierce temper, though, that one does," Mama was saying. She paused for a second and took a tentative sip of her coffee before reaching for the sugar bowl. "Always did say redheads are unpredictable. But, if you ask me, Vivien Crenshaw probably had a lot of enemies."

"Oh yeah? Why do you say that?"

She pushed a plate of leftover bacon my way. Mama always rose early during harvest to make a big breakfast for Daddy, who, by the crack of dawn, was already out in the orchards, supervising the picking. Around eleven, she'd start putting together a light lunch of sandwiches and snacks for him and the hands. She'd developed this habit over the years, never missing a single day. Sundays were different, though. On Sundays, the laborers would come to the house for their noon meal. Mama insisted. Of course, if she really had her way in the matter, there wouldn't be any work at all on Sundays. But, as with most things involving our family business, Daddy had the final say.

"Oh, I don't know. Lots of reasons, really." Picking up a piece of bacon, she took a dainty bite off the end, chewing while she deliberated her next words. "Ever since Vivien took over as the organist at church—"

"Vivien was the organist?" That was news to me.

Mama tucked her chin and pursed her lips. "Yes, it happened about a month ago. You'd realize that if you paid better attention in church."

I squirmed in my chair. How *did* I miss that? Ever since I was a kid, Betty Lou Nix had been playing the church's magnificent pipe organ. Oh, the many glorious hymns she'd accompanied! Over the years, she'd practically become an icon of the church, poor lady. Her talents would be missed. "What a shame! When did Betty Lou pass?"

"Pass?" Mama blinked a couple times. "Oh . . . no! Betty Lou's just fine. Well, as fine as she can be considerin' Vivien practically stole the organ bench right out from under her bottom."

Mama nibbled a bit more on her bacon, while I sat back and contemplated what she was saying. Unbelievable. I'd always figured Betty Lou would be playing the organ until the day she was called up to accompany the angels' heavenly hymns. She was just that good. Guess I really was out of touch with the church, not to mention the local gossip vine, if I'd missed something as substantial as Betty Lou getting knocked off the organ bench by Vivien Crenshaw. Of course, I'd been sort of busy the past few months. "I can't imagine how Vivien got that position over Betty Lou. Was Vivien a talented organist or something?"

Mama set half the uneaten bacon slice on her plate and wiped her fingers on a napkin. "Not in my opinion. Especially not compared to Betty Lou." After a long sip of coffee, she waved her hand through the air. "Oh, there were plenty of rumors goin' 'round at the time about why Betty Lou was replaced. Nothing anyone could really put a finger on, though." Her face lit up as if she'd suddenly remembered something important. "Speaking of rumors. There were quite a few going around about the Peach Queen Pageant last year. If you remember, Vivien's daughter won the crown."

My ears perked up.

"Your Daddy and I were on our second honeymoon at the time, but when we got back, there was all sorts of talk about wrongdoings at the pageant."

"Wrongdoings?" Last year's Peach Harvest Festival, as always, culminated in the Peach Queen crowning just before the festival dance. I'd missed that high point of the festival while sitting with my neighbor, Joe, in the hospital after a day of gunfire drama. But it sounded now like there were other dramas going on that I'd missed.

Mama nodded slowly, her eyes slipping into a half-hooded gaze. "I got this information secondhand, mind you, so don't go quotin' me. But I heard something went wrong at the pageant. Something that caused one of the girls to drop out at the last minute." She paused, trying to remember, then shook her head. "Afraid I can't remember what exactly happened. Maybe you could ask around. I just remember it all sounded fishy. Especially since just a couple of the girls made it to the talent portion."

"So, you're saying Vivien might have been a little competitive."

"Competitive would be a nice way to put it. Cutthroat was more like it."

Her choice of words startled me, my mind flashing back to the scissors protruding from Vivien's throat. I flinched, causing my last gulp of coffee to go down the wrong way and send me into a coughing fit.

She handed me her napkin. "You okay, sweetie?"

I hacked a few more times and blew my nose before commenting, "I wonder if the sheriff knows about all this?"

"Don't bet on it, sugar." Mama stood and started clearing our dishes. "You know how single-minded that woman can be." She started toward the kitchen, turning back at the last minute, gasping with a hand to her chest. "Oh my Lawd!"

I stood so quickly, my chair almost toppled. "What is it, Mama?"

"The cotillion dinner. Red's Diner is catering the cotillion dinner! Oh my. What if Ginny ends up in jail, heaven forbid? Why, she's in charge of planning the meal." I rolled my eyes and sat back down. Speaking of single-mindedness. Here I'd thought she was having a heart attack or something. And it was just more stuff about the cotillion. Ever since she and Ida became members of the cotillion's Board of Governesses—a highly sought-after position, held in the highest regard in our community—they'd talked of nothing but cotillion plans.

She placed the plates back on the table with a thud and paced in front of me. "We need a backup plan."

"What do you mean a backup plan?" I didn't like where this conversation was going. "I don't really think there'll be a problem. Ginny's innocent. There's no way she'll end up in jail for murder."

Still pacing, Mama turned her head my way and raised her already well-arched brows. "Oh, really? You have a short memory, Nola Mae. It was just last summer that Hollis ended up in jail for a crime he didn't commit. What's to say the same thing couldn't happen to Ginny?"

She was right, although Hollis and Ginny were as different as night and day. Hollis was my heavy-drinking, conniving brother-in-law who lived life for the next big deal, and not always an ethical one at that. I thought back to Hollis's brief incarceration. It was such a dark time for my sister, Ida. Her husband in jail while she was expecting their third child. And my twin nieces, Charlotte and Savannah, not really old enough to understand everything going on, but bearing heavily the weight of their father's absence. I shook my head; those two were so lost without their daddy. Even the short amount of time he was locked up took its toll on Ida and the girls . . . the whole family, actually. I shuddered to think the same thing could happen to Ginny.

Looking over at Mama, I could see the wheels turning in her mind. Something must have clicked, too, because she suddenly stopped pacing, placed her hands on her hips and tilted her head to one side. Evident by the resolute expression on her face, she'd reached some sort of conclusion. That was the thing about my mama; she never admitted defeat. She'd even likened herself to Scarlett O'Hara many a time—that is, the strong-willed, determined Scarlett who persevered through Sherman's torch, not the immature, spoiled Scarlett at the beginning of the book.

She slid her eyes my way, the room practically pulsing with her determination. "Nola, I just thought of something."

I waited, dreading what was coming.

"I don't know why it didn't dawn on me before. This whole cotillion dinner, why, it's the perfect opportunity for you to showcase a few of Harper's Peach Products. Draw attention to our new line of merchandise. And the timing couldn't be better with the shop opening and all."

My head bobbled a bit. "The shop? Ah, but there's still so much to do before it will open, and I don't see—" I started, but Mama was on a roll.

"This is just the answer we've been looking for all along! A committee. Not just one person responsible for the entire meal, but a group of people. We knew Ginny couldn't do it

all anyway, her daughter's a debutante this year and she'll
be tied up for most of the evening. We'd already asked Hattie
to help out with the actual cooking, but this is even better—a
bunch of people with food experience to both plan and prepare the dishes. You, Ginny . . . who else?"

Food experience? Me?! I was the one who fumbled
through batches of runny preserves before producing anything salable last summer—and that was only because Ginny,
bless her heart, stepped in to save my bacon, or peaches, as
was the case. But pointing any of that out would be a waste
of breath. Once Mama was onto something, there was no
deterring her. So, I simply watched helplessly as she placed
her forefinger to her chin and slid her eyes upward while she
ran through a mental list of possibilities.

"Ezra Sugar!" she finally said. "Of course. He could work
on the dessert end, Ginny on the main meal, and you with
all the peachy accents. It is a Peach Cotillion, after all! We
should have a peach-themed dinner. Ginny would probably
be relieved not to have the responsibility of planning the
whole menu. And, I'm sure it's not too late to make that sort
of change." She waved her hand through the air, dismissing
all the dirty little details as inconsequential. "This way, if
something does happen, you're all up to speed on the menu
and. . . ."

Her voice trailed off as she regarded what must have been
the terror-stricken look on my face. She came over and patted my shoulder. "Oh, don't worry, sweetie. This is just a
precaution. I'm sure all this will get straightened out and
things will be just fine. Still, I'm going to mention it to the
other board members at our meeting today. It never hurts to
be prepared."

I managed a tentative nod, thinking it was a good thing
Hattie was already on board. Because if Ginny did end up

in jail for a while, heaven forbid, there was no way in heck I could ever pull off planning a dinner of that magnitude. Even coming up with Mama's idea of "peachy accents" while finishing up my storefront would be enough of a challenge. Thank goodness Ray was coming home later that day. He'd certainly be able to get all this straightened out and head off any trouble coming Ginny's way.

Chapter 4

Debutante Rule #079: Your best friend is someone who always watches your backside . . . and helps you shop for the perfect pair of jeans to cover it.

"You really think I'm the type to just sit around and let someone come in and rescue me? You know me better than that, Nola Mae. No offense to your brother, but I'm capable of straightening out my own messes. I stayed up half the night thinking about my predicament and decided the best approach is to be proactive."

It was a little after four that afternoon when I'd finally caught up with Ginny again. We were in the kitchen of Red's Diner, working on a couple large batches of Mama's peach chutney recipe. The smell of spicy cloves and sweet peaches hung in the air. "Proactive? What do you mean?"

Ginny looked up from her stirring. "I mean, I plan to figure out the real killer so I can get Maudy Payne off my back. And that pesky Frances Simms. She's been nosing around asking all sorts of questions. Even tried to corner Emily."

Uh-oh. Today was Monday, meaning Frances was hot on the trail of a sensational headline for tomorrow's edition of the *Cays Mill Reporter.* "How did it go with the sheriff yesterday?"

She put down her spoon and turned toward me. "As well as could be expected, I suppose. I'm not sure she's convinced I didn't do it. Guess the facts are stacked against me. But you believe me, right?"

"Of course! I just don't think you should get involved. It sounds dangerous," I said, remembering that the last time I got involved in police business, I ended up face-to-face with a crazed killer.

"What else am I supposed to do? Everyone's trying to blame this on me."

Well, actually, it had been Ginny's own angry outburst that triggered Maudy Payne's focus on her. But I decided not to bring it up. Why add fuel to the fire? "Weren't you able to provide the sheriff with an alibi?" I prodded. It'd stuck in my mind what Sam said about not knowing where Ginny was that evening. Something about that didn't sit right with me.

Ginny shifted. "As a matter of fact, I did. The sheriff's checking into it."

Her tone was clipped, giving me the impression that the topic was off-limits, so I moved on. "Okay. Well, did Maudy mention any other suspects?"

"She didn't say. But I got to thinking later, whoever the killer is, they had to have been in the shop to hear Vivien making plans to pick up the dress at six thirty."

I saw where she was going with this. "One of the gals who was at the shop?"

Ginny moved across the kitchen and removed a piece of

scratch paper from her bag. "That's right. Let's see. . . . Who all was there? You—"

"Me?"

Ginny held up her hand. "Bear with me. You, Hattie, Mrs. Busby . . ." She dipped her chin and raised her brows. "Debra Bearden, Maggie Jones and that's it, except for the girls, but you don't think one of them . . ."

"No, of course not."

"So, crossing off you and Hattie, we're left with Mrs. Busby, Debra Bearden and Maggie Jones. But I don't think sweet ol' Mrs. Busby could hurt a fly, do you?"

I shook my head, my mind wandering back to what Mama told me about the "wrongdoings" at the Peach Queen Pageant last year. I wondered . . . "Do you remember if Belle Jones was in the Peach Queen Pageant last year?"

"Sure was. She was in the final three but didn't participate in the last round. If I recall, there was something wrong with her costume and she had to drop out."

"So the final round came down to . . . ?"

"Tara Crenshaw and Sophie Bearden."

"And Tara won?"

"Yeah. But it wasn't much of a contest," Ginny replied. "The final round was the talent competition, and Sophie blew it. She had this great act, too—baton twirling. But she just couldn't hang on to the baton that night. Must have been nerves. Although, I'd seen her do that act at least a hundred times before, and she'd never messed up like that."

"So one competitor dropped out for some reason and the other couldn't manage an act she'd performed numerous times before?"

Ginny nodded. "That does seem a bit suspicious, doesn't it?"

"Sure does," I agreed. "And it could be a motive for

someone. Even Maggie Jones, considering that her daughter was one of the girls knocked out of the competition. But I hate to think of Maggie Jones as a murderer. She is married to a preacher, after all."

A skeptical expression flashed across Ginny's face. "I understand, but we can't rule anyone out."

She was right, of course. I recalled what Mama had told me earlier that morning, so I informed Ginny about Betty Lou Nix suddenly being replaced by Vivien as the church organist. "Strange, don't you think? Betty Lou's held that position for years."

Ginny shrugged. "Not really. Could be something as simple as arthritis setting in. And how would Betty Lou know when Vivien was going to be at the shop? I really think it has to be someone who was there that afternoon and overheard our argument."

"Oh, speaking of which, we forgot Mrs. Wheeler. What's her first name?"

"Stephanie. But she was only there for a little while, remember? She'd left before my argument with Vivien started."

I furrowed my brow. "True. Still, this is Cays Mill. Gossip spreads like wildfire here. Any one of those women could have talked about your argument with half a dozen people, including Betty Lou Nix. Heck, probably most of the county knew about it the minute it happened."

Her shoulders sagged. "I hadn't thought of that. I can see people talking about what I said, especially since I was so dramatic and all." A blush crept over her face. "But mentioning that Vivien was going to return to the shop at six thirty to pick up a dress—that part doesn't seem quite newsworthy. Whoever did this knew she was coming back at six thirty."

I sort of agreed, but there was no underestimating the things people found newsworthy around here. Suddenly, something came to mind. "Didn't Tara wonder where her mama was?" I know I'd have been worried sick if Mama went missing for an entire night.

The corners of Ginny's mouth drooped a bit. "Guess she talked to Vivien around six o'clock, asking permission to go to a sleepover at her friend's house. And that was the last time . . ." She choked back her final words, her hand flying to her face to wipe away a stray tear. "I'm sorry. This is just so hard for me. Not that I was especially fond of Vivien, even before all the cotillion dress drama, but still . . . well, I just feel so awful for that girl. And I can't help but to think of my own Emily, the same age and . . ." Ginny cleared her throat and reached for a nearby napkin, using it to dab under her eyes.

I patted her shoulder and softly asked, "Where'd you hear all this anyway?"

"The diner. Next to the Clip and Curl, it's the leading source of gossip around here."

"You forgot the *Cays Mill Reporter.*"

She sighed. "Yeah, I'm dreading tomorrow's issue. Can't even imagine what headline Frances will come up with. Just hoping my name's not mentioned."

Hated to break it to her, but Frances wasn't one to let a good smear go unused, especially if it meant a boost in sales. Poor Ginny. But I decided not to dwell on all that at the moment and got back to the topic at hand. "What about Vivien's husband? Didn't he wonder what happened to his wife? Why she didn't come home that night?"

"Out of town. He owns that quick oil change station out past the Honky Tonk. You know the one I'm talking about?"

She waited for me to nod before continuing. "Well, he has a couple more, actually. One up in Macon and one over in Buckley. Spends a lot of time on the road." Ginny's voice began to thin again. "That's why I'm so worried about Tara. Being that her father is gone so much, she was extra close to her mama. Now with her gone . . ."

Gone. Tara Crenshaw's mama was gone forever. Something Hattie once told me popped back to mind. One day, when we were talking about her own mama's passing, she'd said that there's just nothing better in the world than a mama who's always there for you. I know I'd hate to face this world without my own mother, and the idea of Tara Crenshaw having to do so, and at such a young age, was unimaginably sad.

There didn't seem to be more to say on the subject, and we fell silent.

After a little nervous fidgeting, Ginny finally abandoned her list of suspects and got busy dicing onions for our next batch of chutney. I wasn't sure, but I was guessing that her watering eyes had less to do with the onions and more to do with the idea of a young girl left motherless. I went back to stirring, my mind wandering over our conversation. If Ginny was right, the list of suspects was quite narrow indeed. That was good news. It meant there were less people for the sheriff to investigate. Of course, it also meant that Ginny was probably her top suspect.

The family pickup truck sounded like it was rattling apart as I drove Ray to the orchard the next morning. When I gave up my job at Helping Hands International, I also gave up use of the company-leased vehicles, a huge perk and one that I sorely missed. Especially now that I needed to drive the orchard rows on a daily basis to pick up crates of peaches to use for my recipes.

Over the past few weeks, my life had slipped into a regular work routine: breakfast with Mama then out to the orchard to pick up a load of peaches for my recipes, after which I'd head into town, unload the peaches at the diner, then head over to work on the shop remodel until the diner closed, when I could use its kitchen to whip up more inventory. The days were long, but I'd grown used to the predictability and steady cadence of my work. There was a certain comfort in knowing what each day would bring— something I really hadn't experienced over the fifteen years or so that I worked as a humanitarian. Then, each day was different. One day spent reuniting a family torn apart by a devastating natural disaster, the next perhaps teaching schoolchildren the importance of personal hygiene. Always something new.

Of course, during my years of traveling as an aid worker, I'd return home periodically, finding comfort in the stability of my family's farm life. Through the eyes of an occasional visitor, it seemed not much ever changed in the peach orchards. However, after returning home for a few weeks last summer, then deciding to stay on permanently, I discovered just how inaccurate I'd been. Things constantly changed in the peach farming world. New markets, new technologies and an ever-changing economy toppled the old ways of thinking and pulled farmers along—some of them reluctantly, like my daddy—to a new way of life. Innovation was the key to success. That's why my little peach product business venture was so important to my family. So far, I'd made enough money to cover expenses and then some, but I hoped the addition of the shop would boost our profit line.

"I'm anxious to see how renovations are coming along," Ray said, grabbing the dashboard to steady himself as the tire hit a crevice in the ground. Ray had come home the day before to talk to Ginny about the case. He'd have to head back to Perry sometime midmorning, though. Something about a deposition, or . . . I couldn't remember. Half the time, his legal talk went in one ear and right out the other.

I briefly smiled his way, then refocused on the road. "Afraid things are going a lot slower than I'd planned, but I'm getting there. I really want to open in time and get a couple months under my belt before the Peach Harvest Festival this summer. Plus, I've announced the grand opening on my website and printed up flyers. Nothing big, just refreshments and live music. I was hoping to draw some interest."

"Music?"

"Wade Marshall and the Peach Pickers."

"The mayor's band?"

"Thought he could play a couple tunes and cut the ribbon. Sort of killing two birds with one stone."

He grinned. "That's efficient. How's the online business going?"

I shrugged. "Okay. I think I'll see an uptick as we head into the holidays this year. But I've got a good base of steady customers locally and throughout the surrounding area. Red's Diner and Sunny Side Up Bed & Breakfast have standing orders." We were heading down to the southern portion of our farm, the part that bordered our small offshoot of the Ocmulgee. That's where most of our early producing trees were located. I slowed down even more as the path became more rugged. "Speaking of the diner, how'd it go last night with Ginny? It must have been late when you came in. I was already in bed."

"Yeah, we had a lot to talk through."

"You could have just called her, you know." Only that's not how Ray operated when it came to people he cared about. Ray thought the world of Ginny and Sam. So, in this case, his taking time from his own firm and coming to Cays Mill was more a show of support than anything else. That's the way my brother was: generous to a fault. With both his time and his heart.

"Could have," he agreed with a shrug. "But it's good to come back and see y'all." He rubbed his stomach. "And have a little of Mama's cooking."

We laughed. "Seriously, though. How'd it go?" I wanted to get the scoop before we reached Daddy and the hands.

"I have to admit, after talking to Ginny, I was a little confused."

"How so?"

"Well, although she said she was appreciative that I'd come by, she was tight-lipped, as if I was interrogating her instead of trying to help. For example, she's elusive about where she was at the time of the murder. I'm not sure Sam even knows. Which seems strange to me. There was a certain tension when I brought it up."

"I sensed that, too. Wonder what she was up to? But, I guess it's none of our business. She said she gave the sheriff an alibi." None of my business or not, I was starting to become darn curious about where my friend was that evening. Of course, one possibility popped to mind, but I quickly dismissed it. Ginny would never.

Ray continued, "And, she kept going on about suspects and such. As if she fancied herself as some sort of private investigator."

I chuckled. "I got the same impression. We actually sat down and made a suspect list yesterday." Thinking back to the list, I added, "Actually, she made some valid points about the case. Did she tell you?"

He shot me a warning look. "She did. And I told her she'd better leave the investigating up to the professionals. I'm telling you the same thing, Nola. Don't get involved in this mess. It's none of your concern, really. Besides, I'd have thought you would have learned your lesson last time."

I recalled all too well my narrow escape from death. To this day, even the slightest whiff of hair spray gave me the willies. I shuddered and brought the truck to a stop alongside a row of trees where a few workers were pulling peaches from the branches. I spied Daddy among them and shot him a cheerful wave before turning back to Ray. "Oh, don't worry, there's no way I'm getting involved. I definitely learned my lesson last time."

After grabbing a few crates of peaches, I took Ray into town so he could see Peachy Keen. I was anxious to show off my plans for the shop, and, as usual, Ray was supportive of my renovation efforts. He lauded my plans for Shaker-styled cabinetry, framed shelving with simple-line moldings, exposed brick walls and freshly finished pinewood floors topped with a scattering of braided rugs. However, I could see a hint of skepticism in his expression as his gaze fell on my unfinished shelves, still-marred flooring and crumbling mortar. Then, when his eyes wandered upward to the water-stained plaster on the ceiling, I quickly explained my idea for a dropped tin ceiling painted in off-white, which I thought would add charm and reflect the abundance of light afforded by the shop's large, deep-set transom windows and a glass-paneled double door. The ceiling tiles were on order and should arrive any day, I assured him. But the hint of incredulity that shone through his façade of well-intentioned compliments brought to the surface the doubts in my own mind about how I was going to finish this project in time. Not to mention the fact that Mama had added my peachy products as an adjunct for the cotillion dinner. And I didn't even want to think of her concept of me as her "backup plan" for the dinner itself. So, by the time I'd finished showing Ray around, I was convinced I needed to rethink my opening day. Still, I'd announced my plans, printed flyers and even posted the date on my website. No, there was no turning back. Come hell or high water, I had to finish renovations in the next three weeks.

Thankfully, Cade arrived about a half hour after Ray left. I'd just finished vacuuming the mortar dust produced from my brick scrubbing when I looked up to see him standing in the doorway wearing stained but well-fitting blue jeans and a T-shirt that clung to his muscular torso. "Sorry I'm running late. My other project took longer than I thought this morning."

Cade and I had struck a deal. Since I wasn't a full-paying customer, he was helping me in his spare time, fitting me in around his full-paying projects.

"But, I should be wrapping it up tomorrow," he continued. "That'll free up a little more time for me to devote to your shop."

I looked around, doubts still lingering. "Do you really think we'll actually be able to get all this done in time?"

He was assembling the tools he needed to start sealing the wall. "Sure. We'll easily get this done in three weeks. No worries."

Only I *was* worried. Because, in addition to the renovations, it looked like I was getting dragged into this cotillion thing. Especially if Ginny was unable to take care of her catering responsibilities, heaven forbid, and I had to step in to pull off the cotillion dinner. I sighed. Worrying about it all wasn't going to get my work done, so I moved on to painting one of the plaster walls as Cade got busy with sealing the bricks. While we worked, I stole glances his way, my mind wandering now and then to romantic notions. I wondered what it would take to rekindle the spark that developed between us last summer, or, more precisely, what had caused it to extinguish in the first place. I knew he'd been under an enormous amount of stress, struggling to keep his business going and care for his elderly father, who was in a convalescent home east of town. Still, if he needed a friend to lean on, I was more than willing to provide the support, something he probably would have taken me up on six months ago. Now, I wasn't so sure.

After a period of steady work, I caught the whiff of fried chicken from the diner next door. We'd worked straight through lunch and my stomach was grumbling. "What do you say we take a quick break and grab a bite for lunch," I suggested to Cade.

"Go ahead. I want to finish this wall and start staining the shelving." He glanced over my efforts. "Looks good where you've painted."

That's how it'd been playing between us lately—casual and distant and always polite. It was the politeness that was really ticking me off. Before he left for the job in Macon, we'd had all sorts of playful flirting going on, even a few fiery disagreements. Now, nothing. Just the darn politeness.

"Cade," I started, not really knowing how to approach the topic, "is everything okay with you?"

He stopped rolling on the sealer and turned toward me. "Sure. Why? Everything okay with you?"

I bit my cheek. "Yes, I'm fine. But you've seemed . . . oh, I don't know . . . distant. Preoccupied. Not quite yourself. Is it your father's illness? Your business, maybe?" Or me, I wanted to add but didn't have the nerve. He shrugged. "Huh? I don't really know what you mean. Nothing's wrong."

I gritted my teeth. But just as I was about to push it further, the door rattled open. Ginny came bursting in, face red, the newspaper in hand. "Can y'all believe this malarkey? Look at what Frances Simms put about me in the paper."

She unfolded the newspaper and held it up. Even from where I was standing, the headline was as plain as day: "Vivien Crenshaw Murdered after Blowout over Debutante Gown."

"Oh no!" I crossed the room and snatched the paper from her hands. "What lies did she print this time?" Ginny stood next to me and seethed while I started skimming the article. Certain phrases jumped out at me, like: "Several eyewitnesses claim the murder victim and Ginny Wiggins, proprietor of Red's Diner, argued over a debutante gown prior . . ." and "Mrs. Wiggins made threatening remarks toward Mrs. Crenshaw . . ." and then the article wrapped up with a statement from the sheriff claiming she had a strong suspect in the case.

"The problem is, none of what she printed is really a lie. I *did* do all that." She started shaking her head and babbling. "Mama always did say my temper was going to get the best of me, and now it has. Oh, mercy! All this in the paper. What's it going to do to Emily? My poor little girl. And it's all my fault." Her usual fire had been doused, and tears threatened at the corners of her eyes.

"Did you ever talk to Ray?" Cade asked.

"Yeah, he came by last night and we discussed it all."
She turned and offered me a meek and grateful smile. "I'm
just so grateful you called your brother, Nola. I was being
so pigheaded about the whole lawyer thing, but it looks like
I may need Ray after all."

"Let's hope not. Has the sheriff been over to question
you again?"

"No."

"She give you any indication that you were her prime
suspect, like telling you not to leave town?"

"No, but everyone knows I haven't traveled much farther
than Macon for the last twenty years."

I tapped the paper. "Point being, this article said the
sheriff has a suspect in the case, but it didn't necessarily say
you, did it? Maybe Maudy Payne has another suspect. Or
maybe there's something she knows that's not in the paper.
Some sort of evidence that points the finger at someone
else."

Ginny nodded, wiping at her eyes with the bottom of her
apron. "Still, poor Emily. She's going to be mortified when
she reads this paper. And, the kids at school? You know how
cruel they can be. Once they get ahold of this . . . why, it's
going to be awful for Emily. Me and my hot temper!"

"You're underestimating Emily. She's stronger than you
think, and so are you. You two will get through this just
fine."

A tear ran down her cheek. "But she's been dreaming
about her cotillion ever since she was a little girl. This is all
so unfair. First the dress and now all this." Suddenly her
eyes grew wide. "Oh no. The etiquette class is tomorrow
evening!"

"Etiquette class?" This was the first I'd heard about any

sort of etiquette class. Then again, there'd been so much debutante talk lately, I'd pretty much tuned it all out. And honestly, the idea of anyone being interested in a class on etiquette at the moment didn't fit my lingering vision of Vivien's scissor-skewered neck one bit.

Ginny's head bobbed up and down frantically as she began wringing her hands. "Yes! At the diner tomorrow evening. It's sort of a practice run for the girls to work on their table manners before the big dinner. They'll be bringing their marshals, too."

I scrunched my brows and blinked a few times until Cade spoke up from across the room. "Their dates, Nola. Marshals escort the debutantes to the dinner and dance." I did a double take. Why would Cade know something about marshals when I didn't recall it at all? Had he been one once? I racked my brain trying to remember who he would have escorted to the cotillion dance way back when. Then I shrugged it off. What did that really matter anyway?

"How am I going to face down all those people after this?" Ginny was pointing at the paper. "Everyone's probably talking about me right this instant. Saying things like, 'Emily's mom is a murderer' . . . and, oh Lawd!" She glanced at her watch. "I got to get back to the diner. Emily will be out of school soon."

Placing my hands on her shoulders, I leaned in and looked directly into her eyes. "Simmer down, Ginny. You need to hold it together for Emily, okay? Now tell me, who's helping you with the etiquette class tomorrow?"

She sucked in a jagged breath. "Well, Ida is in charge of instruction, of course—she's a master of etiquette." I rolled my eyes and nodded as she continued. "And a few of the other mothers. We're acting as servers. It's all set up like role play. Like a real dinner, minus the food. That's why the committee asked if it could be at the diner, so we could use the tables and chairs."

"Okay. No biggie. I'll come and help, too. That way you know you'll have some support in case some of those mothers come with gossip on their minds. I'll talk to Hattie, see if she can also help."

"Y'all would do that?"

"Of course. What are friends for?"

Ginny seemed to breathe easier. "Sure. That'd be fine. Maybe I'll even wear those new blue jeans Hattie helped me pick out."

"That's the spirit," I said. "Now, you better get back to the diner and take care of Emily. Remember what I said, though. She's a strong girl, just like her mama."

As soon as she left, I trotted across the room and handed Cade the paper. "Ginny's never going to live this down. Take a look at this! This is a hot mess. I'm so sick of Frances Simms and her antics. I swear, that woman is the bane of my existence. She's always causing trouble. Remember those articles she printed about Hollis last summer?"

Cade nodded and reached for the paper, glimpsing over the article with a creased forehead. "Yes, but a scandal like this sells copies. Problem is that Ginny's right: Frances really hasn't printed anything that can't be substantiated. She's just put it together in a way that makes Ginny look bad. 'Course, Ginny has done a pretty good job of making herself look bad, going off on Vivien like she did. Hattie told me all about it. Said Ginny pretty much lost it."

I thought back to the argument, the murderous look on Ginny's face as she spewed threats and hurled insults. "You're right. Still, Emily doesn't deserve the inevitable backlash this article is going to generate. I feel sorry for her.

I can still remember how hard it was to navigate high school under the best of circumstances. And this is supposed to be such a special time and all." I shook my head, wondering what could be done, if anything, to help the situation. I hated to just stand by and watch people I cared about suffering. Maybe Ginny's suspect list deserved a little more consideration. It couldn't hurt to just ask around a bit, could it?

Chapter 5

Debutante Rule #095: Even if a debutante has nothing else, she still has her manners . . . and a monogrammed handkerchief.

"Don't worry, Ginny," Hattie said as we worked on folding a stack of cloth napkins. "We've got your back. Just think of us as your posse. No one's going to dare say anything nasty with us around." After explaining the whole situation to Hattie the day before, she'd instantly rallied to Ginny's defense. So there we were at the diner Wednesday evening helping Ginny set up for etiquette class and acting as her posse—ready and willing to run interference if any mother coming to help became gossipy about Ginny being a murderer.

"I do feel much better with you girls here," Ginny replied. "And you know, Nola, you were right. My Emily *is* a strong girl. After reading that article yesterday, she just gave me a big ol' hug and told me not to worry, that it would all be okay. Can y'all believe that? I'd be crying or breaking down or something."

I shot a glance at Ginny. That "or something" no doubt had

me visualizing how our redheaded friend would have likely issued threats aimed at Frances if put in poor Emily's situation. Thankfully, Ginny was right about one thing: Emily was one strong—and smart—girl.

Ginny went on, "But, I'm telling you, these girls in town can be nasty. The best thing I can do for Emily is clear my name." She reached into the pocket of her blue jeans and pulled out the list we'd made the day before.

Hattie glanced over her shoulder. "What's that?"

"It's my list of suspects. You see, the way I figure it, I've been framed."

Framed? I knew she suspected the killer heard Vivien say she was returning to the shop at six thirty, but how had that translated into someone framing her? Of course, it *was* convenient that the murder happened right after Ginny's big blowout with Vivien. Maybe there was something to this new theory of hers.

"This is a list of all the ladies who were in your shop and heard my little tirade," she was saying. "Like I was telling Nola yesterday, I'm thinking it had to be one of these gals. They all heard me say those things, and they heard Vivien make plans to come back to your shop at six thirty, right?"

Hattie moved in closer to study the list, bobbing her head enthusiastically and agreeing with Ginny's assessment. She was being sucked right into Ginny's plan. Not a good thing. Not a good thing at all.

"Don't you think this should be left to the authorities?" I said, trying to intervene before this got out of hand.

Hattie turned a cynical eye my way. "By 'authorities' you mean Maudy Payne?"

Ginny sniggered. "Yeah, we all saw how well that went when Hollis was suspected of murder. Besides, it's all easy for you to suggest I leave it up to the sheriff when it's not you in the hot seat for murder. This is my life. And just think what Emily is going through with me being a suspect and all."

She was right. Still, I didn't want to encourage this behavior. I gave a noncommittal nod, grabbed a stack of white tablecloths and started shaking and smoothing them, one at a time, over the tables. Hattie did the same, working her way down the row of tables next to me.

Ginny paced around us, list in hand. "Anyway, I'm thinking all we need to do is figure out everyone's alibi for the time of the murder. We can start with Debra Bearden. She's one of the helpers tonight."

"And how do you plan to do that?" I asked, giving the tablecloth an extra-hard snap. "Are you just going to walk up to her and ask where she was at the time of the murder?" I chuckled. "Like that's going to work."

Ginny hesitated, raising a finger to twirl one of her curls. "I haven't figured that part out yet."

"Leave it to me," Hattie suggested. "I'm good at finessing information from people. Besides, she's a customer of mine, comes in the shop all the time. She trusts me."

The gleam in Hattie's eye worried me. She was way too gung ho about all this. Doing my best to steer the conversation in a different direction, I asked, "By the way, how's business been at the dress shop since . . . since the murder?" Grotesque images filled my mind: Vivien, the scissors, the bloodied dress . . . I shivered. It might be a while before I'd be able to go back into the shop.

Hattie paused, a troubled look crossing her face. "I hate to say it, but sadly enough, business has never been better. All of a sudden ladies I haven't seen for months are coming into the shop. Of course, they have all sorts of morbid questions. I swear, I don't know what compels people to be interested in such horrible things."

I knew how she felt. I'd often witnessed that magnetic pull toward catastrophic events during my days as an aid worker—people drawn to the horrid scenes left behind after earthquakes and tsunamis. But I'd come to realize that it wasn't necessarily voyeurism or morbid curiosity that drew them, but a strong, inherent instinct for survival. The idea of such a horrible event, especially so close to home, upsets the balance of our psyche, and some of us need to face it down in order to reassure, or fool, ourselves into thinking we're immune to such atrocities. At least I'd like to think that was the case with the curious ladies Hattie had mentioned and not that they were simply vicious gossipers who derived their entertainment from the tragic death of one of their own. I shook off the thought and changed the topic. "Emily's coming tonight, isn't she?" I asked Ginny.

"Yep. When I left home she was still fussin' over her hair. Nash is bringing her by soon."

That name sounded familiar. "Nash Jones?" I recalled the handsome young man who helped me with my booth at the Peach Harvest Festival last summer.

Ginny nodded and starting working her way around the tables smoothing out wrinkles in the tablecloths. "That's right. Belle is his twin sister. The Reverend Jones and Maggie just have the two."

"Oh, I see." That made sense. I wondered why I hadn't put that together before now. Mama was right. I needed to pay more attention at church. "He seems like a nice boy," I added.

"Sure is," Hattie said, gathering a few extra chairs from around the room to place at one of the tables. "I used to hire him all the time for odd jobs around the shop. Now he's working at the Tasty Freeze, though. With that and school, he's been too busy."

Which reminded me of the dark-haired girl I'd seen at

both Hattie's and the diner. "Who's the girl helping you now? The one with all the piercings?"

"That's Carla Fini," Ginny answered for Hattie. "She's been working for me, too. Just busing tables and washing dishes. She's a good worker." She passed me a tray of silverware and went to the counter for a stack of plates, which she started placing on the table. I walked behind her, setting out the silverware. Hattie followed both of us, placing a neatly folded napkin atop each plate.

"She's moved here from up north somewhere," Hattie added. "Living with her aunt for a while. I've hired her on for some odd jobs. Nice girl, but seems a little troubled. . . ." She paused for a second then belted out, "For Pete's sake, Nola. Who taught you to set a table like this?"

My head snapped up. She was glaring down at one of my place settings, which looked perfectly fine to me. "What's wrong with it?"

Ginny clucked her tongue, scurried around the table and started rearranging the forks and spoons. "Here, the salad fork goes first then the dinner fork, both on this side. Then over here, put the dinner knife closest to the plate, then the teaspoon and soup spoon." She finished with a flourish. "See, just like that."

I backed up and started over. "Sorry." I knew better than to mention that I had been happy to have any utensil when I worked in Indonesia where the natives preferred to eat with their hands or that I became expert with chopsticks in the autonomous mountain villages of Vietnam or found a sharp knife the only implement considered necessary in some remote parts of Africa. I had certainly been indoctrinated in my early years with table-setting protocol by Mama; I just hadn't used it often enough in the years since for it to be second nature anymore. Probably wouldn't have much opportunity in the future, considering the way things were going between Cade and me. Of course, from the way Hattie acted the other day after church, things weren't going well with her and Pete, either. I was about to ask if they'd made up yet when the door popped open and then slammed shut with a bang. It was Emily, and she looked upset.

Ginny rushed right over. "Emily! What is it?"

Emily's emotions seemed to hover somewhere between despair and rage. Hattie and I maintained our distance, busying ourselves with the rest of the place settings but still keeping one ear on the conversation unfolding between Ginny and Emily.

"Nash canceled our date for tonight."

"He did? Why?"

Emily bit her lip and swallowed hard. "He wouldn't say, but he barely talked to me at school today. I expected it from all the other kids, but not from Nash. I thought he . . ."

She didn't finish the sentence, but it wasn't hard to fill in the blank. She thought Nash really cared for her. Maybe loved her. The poor thing. Her first heartbreak. Little did she know, it probably wouldn't be her last. Hattie went to the counter and fished a handkerchief out of her purse, crossing over to where Ginny and Emily were. "Here, sweetie. Looks like you need this."

Emily drew the pretty pink lace handkerchief to her face and began sobbing.

"Oh, honey, I'm so sorry." Ginny pulled her daughter close and patted her back.

Then the door opened again. This time, it was Ida carrying a couple small boxes and dressed in an elegant cream-colored pantsuit, which even to me, Ms. Fashion Challenged, recognized would benefit from a splash of color. Perhaps a brightly colored silk scarf? I shook my head; Ida hadn't worn one of those since . . . well, never mind. I sighed. Would I ever be able to move past the horrid events of last summer? But I didn't have much time to dwell on it, because right behind Ida was a pack of giggling girls, all of them looking pretty in their spring dresses and finely styled hair. Upon seeing them, Emily pulled away from Ginny and turned for a quick throat-clearing, handkerchief-wiping propping up of her debutante self. Then she quickly turned around again, with a brave smile, and hurried over to join the group.

Next through the door strode an aftershave-infused wave of young men who strutted nonchalantly in their crisply ironed khakis and freshly trimmed hair. They immediately mixed with the girls, separating into couples. I almost cried as I noticed Emily standing off to the side, her eyes scanning the crowd, probably holding out hope for Nash.

Quickly finishing the last of the place settings, I marched over to say hello to Ida, who'd joined Ginny and Hattie in the back of the restaurant. "Thank you so much for letting us use the diner," she was saying, "and for putting all this together." She handed Ginny the boxes. "I brought a little something for the kids to eat afterward."

"How thoughtful! They look simply scrumptious," Ginny replied warmly.

A hint of pink tinged my sister's cheeks. "It's just a quick little recipe I have for peach cobbler cupcakes; there's really not much to making them. Wish I could have done more, but Junior's been so fussy. I think he's cutting a tooth." Her gaze swept over the tables. "It all looks so lovely." She dipped her chin toward the group of kids, who were getting rowdier by the second. "Looks like we'd better get busy, don't y'all think? What do you say we try to impart some manners on this motley crew?" She moved toward the tables, clapping her hands several times in an attempt to draw their attention. "Ladies and gentlemen, if you'll pair up, debutantes with your marshals, please, and approach the tables, we'll start with the proper way for a gentleman to assist a lady into her chair."

Her statement brought about an undercurrent of groans from the crowd, which she effectively thwarted with a single sharp look. I knew that expression. Ida inherited it from our mama. And speaking of expressions, I also recognized the type of look on the faces of the trio of women who, at that moment, entered the diner. I'd seen it before when my work took me once to the remote grasslands surrounding a sub-Saharan African village. En route—from the safety of my guide's jeep, thank goodness—I'd witnessed a female lion take down and ravage its prey. I shuddered. These ladies had that same bloodthirsty look, and they were eying Ginny as their quarry.

With an exchange of a knowing glance and an unspoken agreement, Hattie and I scrambled to intercept the women. "Thank you so much for volunteering tonight, ladies," Hattie greeted them.

I immediately recognized Debra Bearden—actually, she was hard to miss with her perfectly highlighted locks and rhinestone-studded jeans—but I had no idea who her two toadies were. There wasn't much time for introductions, however, because from across the room, I could hear Ida moving things right along. "At the cotillion dinner, we adhere to long-established decorum such as knowing the proper utensils for each course of the meal. For example . . ." Blah, blah, blah . . . I tuned her out and refocused on the lionesses. "We're supposed to be acting as servers tonight. The pitchers and trays are on the counter. There's no food or drinks, as we're just pretending, but please make sure to serve from the right side."

"Left," Hattie interjected. "At this cotillion dinner, we always serve from the left, remove from the right."

"Oh. The left. Sorry. Anyway, the debs and their marshals are supposed to practice receiving food and acting cordially to the waitstaff." I shrugged my shoulders and added with a giggle, "It sounds a little silly, I know, but—"

"Silly?" Debra cocked an unamused brow. "There's nothing silly about good manners."

"No, of course not," I backtracked. "I was just talking about the role play part."

Only Debra ignored the intent of my comment. Apparently she'd been waiting for a spot to sneak in a snide remark and didn't want to lose her opportunity. "No, the only thing silly here tonight is the fact that Ginny Wiggins isn't behind bars. I mean, you read the paper, right?" Next to her, the other gals nodded in snarky unison.

I bristled, ready to fight, but Hattie came to the rescue. Sucking in her breath and plastering on a smile, she stepped forward, looping her arm into Debra's. "Let's not bring up such unpleasantness now. Remember, it's all about our girls tonight, right? Come with me, Debra. We'll act as the water pourers." She headed off with Debra toward the counter, where she handed her a pitcher and motioned toward the tables with a sweet smile. I had to admit, Hattie *was* good at finessing people. Not me so much. Because as I turned my focus back to the other two ladies, I noticed they'd started whispering between themselves. I could feel my cool slipping away as I stood there listening in on their conversation, watching their eyes gleam as they took delight in my friend's troubles. "Heard Nash stood her up this evening," one of them was saying. "Can you blame him? I certainly wouldn't want to be associated with a girl whose mother. . . ."

"Excuse me, ladies," I interrupted. Clearing my throat, I

tried my best to inject some sweetness, although I'm afraid I didn't have as much of a knack as Hattie for diplomacy. "Guess it looks like we'll be acting as waitresses this evening." I indicated toward the trays stacked on the bar and smiled craftily. "Bet you two never imagined you'd be waiting tables at Red's Diner, huh?"

Despite everything, the rest of the evening went off without a hitch. The kids learned their table etiquette, or at least most did, and the lionesses kept in their claws and adequately played their roles as servers. After the place cleared out, Hattie and I stayed behind to help Ginny put things back in order.

Hattie looked around. "Did Emily go home already?"

"Yes," Ginny replied, loading plates into an industrial-sized dishwasher. "She's got a Civil War paper she's trying to finish up. It's a huge part of her final grade in U.S. History. Not that she's going to be able to focus, with all that's going on right now." She looked toward Hattie. "Any luck with Debra?"

Hattie's eyes crinkled. "Yes, and wait 'til y'all hear where she was."

"Where?" Ginny and I asked in unison. Hattie had our undivided attention.

"The Honky Tonk. That's where. From six to eleven, she said."

Ginny whistled. "Whew. Five hours. That's some sort of drinking binge." A little smile formed along the edges of her mouth. "I never knew she had a problem."

"She doesn't have a problem, Ginny," Hattie admonished. "She was working there."

"Working there?" Ginny and I echoed.

I was shocked. "Debra Bearden works at the Honky

Tonk?" Although, what would I know? I avoided the place at all costs. An aversion I'd developed after enduring many a bad experience at the riotous roadhouse, from an unwanted sexual advance to witnessing several injurious brawls and even a few perilous adventures on the back of Bodacious, the place's back-busting mechanical bull. Not to mention it was one of the places where I'd tried to track down leads to help keep Hollis's backside out of the legal fryer last year only to end up—yet again—sidetracked.

"Yeah, that seems weird. I can't imagine her enjoying that job." Ginny abandoned the dishes and went to the fridge, pulling out a couple cans of Coke and passing them to us. We bellied up to the stainless steel counter where she smoothed out her list again. Popping the top on her can, she flipped the paper over. With a pen she retrieved from one of the kitchen drawers, she began drawing a chart with columns. "Good work, Hattie. Now here's what we've got." She proceeded to label each column: one each for suspects, motives and alibis. When she was done, the paper looked a little like one of those checklists that come with the game Clue. *If only life was really that easy*, I thought.

Sipping at my Coke, I watched as she checked Debra off the list first. "Wait a minute," I interrupted. "You can't just take her word for it. Maybe she was at work all night and maybe she wasn't. And do we really know the time of death? We're assuming six thirty, because of the broken watch, but do we know that for sure? Has anyone heard what Doc Harris said? And, what if Mrs. Busby was lying about the phone call she received canceling the appointment? Maybe she made the whole thing up about the call. Because, really, why would Vivien be there at all if she'd really canceled?"

Hattie let out a noise that sounded something like the air letting out of a tire. "You really think Mrs. Busby, sweet ol'

Mrs. Busby, lied about the call and went to the store, waiting for Vivien to arrive, so she could plunge a pair of scissors through her neck? Are you out of your mind?"

Obviously I was. Of the three of us, I certainly knew darn well just how dangerous it could be to get involved in police business. Yet there I was, arguing over facts that were really best left to the authorities to investigate. Facts that could be misleading, confusing and end up with one of us—like me last year—in danger of losing our life. "I'm just saying, we need to verify a few things before we can start marking people off your list." And an acutely incomplete list at that. Ginny refused to take into account that the Cays Mill gossip mill, running at full speed, spread news faster than greased lightning. Half the people in town probably knew about that argument five minutes after it occurred, and any one of them could easily be suspects. I could think of a couple of others right off the bat: Betty Lou Nix, the jilted organ player. Or Vivien's own husband. The cops always put the spouse at the top of their suspect list, didn't they? Plus, it was certainly feasible that Vivien would have told her husband about the argument. Of course, Debra and Maggie may have told their spouses about the argument, too. Could one of their husbands have a motive? Certainly not Reverend Jones, but what did I, or any of us, really know about . . . I stopped pondering suspects and eyed Ginny as she began placing an initial next to each suspect on her list. "What are you doing?" I asked, seeing an *N* by Maggie Jones's name.

"Handing out assignments. What do you think?" She pointed the pen my way. "You're on Maggie Jones. Spend the next couple days finding out everything you can about her possible motive and her alibi. Hattie, you've got Mrs. Busby, since you work with her anyway, and I'll take Debra; Nola's right—her alibi might not hold water. So I may need one of you to go to the Honky Tonk with me so I can check around with some of the regulars or maybe talk with her boss. Or you know what?" Her eyes lit up like a bulb. "Laney Burns would be a good one to check with. I hear she's out there practically every night. She'd know for sure if Debra was there the whole evening." She glanced at our nails. "Either one of you in need of a manicure?"

All eyes settled on my hands. I quickly placed them on my lap, but Ginny and Hattie kept staring at me, their pointed gazes making me squirm. "Okay. Fine. I'll stop by the salon tomorrow."

"Good." Ginny paused for a second, chewing on the end of the pen. "Perhaps I'll take a casserole over to the Crenshaws. Offer my condolences and see—"

"You'll do no such thing!" I blurted. "You can't go over there. Your name's all over the newspaper as a possible suspect."

"She's got a point, Ginny," Hattie agreed. "That'd be downright tacky."

Ginny's shoulders slumped. "You're right. What was I thinking?"

Hattie reached over to pat Ginny's shoulder. "You were just being your sweet self, that's all. Of course you'd make a casserole. That's what we always do 'round here. Tell you what. You make one of your casseroles, and Nola and I will pop it by their house. It's the decent thing to do, after all. Make sure you tell us what's in it, though, just in case he asks. If all goes well, maybe we'll even get a chance to ask a few discreet questions, you know . . . like if Vivien had any enemies, that sort of thing. By the way, I haven't heard anything about the funeral."

Ginny piped up. "It's tomorrow. A private ceremony. Just family. But the visitation is at the funeral home tomorrow morning. Emily told me that Nate is sending Tara up to Atlanta soon afterward. He's going to have her stay with his sister for a while. She's got kids Tara's age, and he thinks it would be good for her. I don't know this for sure, but maybe he's a little afraid for her safety. Lawd knows I would be after what happened to Vivien."

We all nodded. "But what about the rest of the school year?"

Ginny shrugged. "Guess they've worked something out with the school." She tapped the paper with the pen. "So we've all got our assignments, right? Let's get right on it and maybe we can find out something before the Mother-Daughter Tea this weekend."

"The Mother-Daughter Tea?"

Hattie chuckled. "Yes, Nola. It's always been the tradition to have a Mother-Daughter Tea the weekend before the Peach Cotillion. But this year, it's extra special because the Wheelers are hosting a garden party. Lots of little local specialties to taste and—"

I gasped. "Oh, Ginny. I forgot. I'm supposed to talk to you about the menu for the cotillion dinner. Mama suggested to the committee that I add a few of my peach specialties to your menu. . . ." And so we carried on for another hour or so, discussing menus and teas and all things cotillion.

Chapter 6

Debutante Rule #021: A debutante understands discreetness. What goes on behind closed doors stays behind closed doors . . . so always make sure you double-check the locks.

"Got a busy day today, darlin'?" Daddy asked, helping me lift my daily load of peaches into the truck Thursday morning.

Busy wasn't the half of it. Working on the shop floors, making peach recipes and all the while trying to fit in a manicure appointment with Laney Burns . . . oh, and I almost forgot my newly assigned job to find out more about Maggie Jones. I grumbled under my breath. How was I ever going to get this all done?

"Honey?" Daddy's voice interrupted my thoughts. "Everything okay? You seem a thousand miles away."

I shook off my worries. "Everything's fine, Daddy. How are things coming along with the harvesting?" Looking around, I saw several workers picking peaches and placing them into soft-sided baskets attached to the front of their bodies.

"Going just fine," Daddy was saying. "I think we're going to be blessed with a good harvest this year."

I smiled. "Well, we sure could use it." I continued chatting with him as he made his way to a flatbed trailer and emptied his basket into a large bin. Once all the bins were filled, we'd use the tractor to pull the trailer up to the barn, where we'd load the bins into a hauling truck bound for the local packing plant. From there, they'd be washed, sorted, packed and shipped throughout the country.

"Hey, missy!"

I glanced up to see Joe Puckett shuffling toward me, wearing his usual faded overalls and wide-brimmed straw hat. A few of the workers paused and greeted him as he passed by. I wasn't surprised to see the fellows were well acquainted with Joe. After all, picking peaches was thirsty work, and Joe stilled the best moonshine in all the county.

"Joe!" I hurried over to meet him halfway. "How are you feeling?" I glanced down at his arm. He still hadn't regained full motion of it since he was accidently wounded from shotgun blast last summer. "Still doing those exercises the doctor recommended?"

He slowly curled his bicep, attempting to clench his fist a few times. "Yup. Every day. Gittin' better, too." He looked over at my truck. "Mind if I hitch a ride with you into town?"

"Sure thing. Hop in."

He got himself settled into the truck, while I helped Daddy finish loading a few more crates into the back. Once we were out on the main road and riding smoothly along, I struck up a conversation. "So, do you have some business in town today?"

He patted a well-worn knapsack he'd brought with him. "Yup. Got to get these books back to the library."

I smiled to myself. Because of the injury, Joe had been out of commission this last year. Since he wasn't the type to be idle and he was unable to read to fill the hours, he'd quickly become depressed. Worried about his well-being, I began visiting him from time to time. I always brought a book to read to him. I'd started with *Hatchet* by Gary Paulsen, a book I thought would appeal to Joe's strong connection to nature. After that, I introduced him to some of the classics like *The Adventures of Huckleberry Finn* and *The Red Badge of Courage*. Then, about midway through *My Side of the Mountain*, he started complaining that I wasn't reading fast enough. I told him he ought to learn to read for himself. And he did. With a lot of help, of course. We spent hours working on getting the basic phonics down, but once Joe caught on, there was no stopping him. "So, what are you reading these days?"

"Just finished up *The Call of the Wild*. Ms. Purvis suggested it."

"Henrietta Purvis? Is she still working at the library?" It had been a while since I'd been to the Cays Mill Library.

"Why wouldn't she be?" Joe snapped.

I did a double take. "I was just thinking she's been there for a long time, that's all. Thought she would have retired by now."

"You're thinkin' she's gettin' old, that's what. If you're askin' me, Ms. Purvis could do that job for another twenty years or so." I opened my mouth to defend myself, but he kept going. "The problem with you youngin's is you don't understand that us old folk still have a lot to give. Y'all think anyone over seventy has one foot in the grave. Well, it simply ain't true."

He punctuated his little rant with a grunt and a firm nod of his head. I shut my mouth and focused on the road. No need to get him any more riled up. Although, I couldn't figure out what I'd said wrong in the first place.

We rode for a while in silence until Joe broke in with, "Heard there was another murder in town." He shuffled a foot, and neither of us commented on the best-forgotten traumas of last summer's crimes. Then he rubbed at the whiskers on his face. "I feel right sorry for the woman. She might have been as mean as a spring bear, but she didn't deserve to die like she did."

"You knew Vivien Crenshaw?" I'd just turned onto Cresthaven and was pulling in front of the library.

"Yup. Mrs. Crenshaw was here most afternoons. Workin' on some sort of important project, I reckon." Joe hopped out, obviously eager to be on his way. "Don't worry none, missy," he said, turning back. "I'll get a ride back home from someone." He gave me a quick wave as he shut the truck door and headed for the entrance with a little extra bounce in his step.

Looking over my shoulder, I started to put the truck into reverse when someone tapped on the window. It was Maggie Jones, dressed in her usual just-below-the-knee skirt and plain crew neck shirt, which she'd accentuated today with a loosely knit hand-crocheted vest and dangling cross earrings.

Motioning for her to wait a second, I put the truck in park and hopped out onto the pavement. "Hello, Mrs. Jones." She was carrying a pile of books, and as the truck door swung open, she stepped back a bit, the books slipping. As I reached to save them from falling, I noticed a bodice-ripping romance slide out from among the collection of crafting and how-to-garden books. Two pink circles formed on her thin cheeks as she maneuvered to hide it back in the pile.

"Nola Mae, I know you're busy, but I just wanted to say how glad we all are that you've been coming to church regularly. Been praying for you to come back into the fold. And I know your mama feels so much peace now that your soul's back on track."

Oh my . . . but a little piety does hide a whole lot of sin, I thought. "Thank you, Mrs. Jones."

"Maggie, please."

I nodded. "Isn't it horrible about Vivien Crenshaw?"

"Yes, it is. So terrible." She glanced at her watch. "That reminds me, I should be going. The visitation is scheduled for later this morning, and—"

"At least the sheriff has some good leads on the killer."

Maggie's eyes popped. "Oh, has Ginny been arrested?"

"Ginny? No! The sheriff's been interrogating all sorts of folks who might have had motive to kill Vivien. She's been asking everyone in town about their whereabouts the evening of the murder. I thought you knew. Well, maybe asking everyone *but* you." I chuckled as if the very idea of the sheriff questioning the minister's wife for any reason—let alone murder—was preposterous.

She chuckled right along with me. "Well, I was at the church the entire evening working on coordinating details for the bazaar, with some parishioners, so if she did inquire, I could verify their whereabouts for her." She hesitated for a minute and then asked, "Why is Maudy still questioning suspects? I thought . . . I mean, the article in the newspaper made it seem like the case was solved."

"Oh, don't go believing everything you read in the *Cays Mill Reporter*. You recall last year, I'm sure." Maggie gave a little nod at that. Everyone had believed they knew the killer of a local businessman based on the innuendos and strategic wording of our very own ace reporter Frances Simms. That is, right up to the edition when the real killer was discovered and Frances took all the credit for it. I went on, "Did Vivien have any enemies that you knew of? I mean, you probably knew her well, with her being the new organist at church and all."

She slowly shook her head and shuffled her Mary Janes against the pavement. "True. Vivien has been playing the organ for a few weeks, but now that she's . . . well, thank goodness Betty Lou has offered to come back and play." I noticed

Maggie's grip tighten around her books. "Vivien was also volunteering her time to help the church get ready for next month's bazaar. Been coming in here and there to process donations and such. As a matter of fact, she stumbled across a real treasure a while back."

"A treasure?"

"Yes, she did!" Her head bobbed excitedly, a lock of mousy brown hair slipping from her tightly woven bun and her gaze snapping up to it briefly. I could tell she was itching to fix it, but didn't dare loosen her death grip on the books. "A field desk from the Civil War. Definitely from our side. It was quite the find. And the timing was perfect. My Belle's been working hard on her Civil War report for school. Finding this desk was just like bringing a little bit of history alive for her."

This conversations wasn't going at all like I'd hoped, but I was intrigued now. "How'd Vivien find something like that in the first place?"

"Well, we're not quite sure. It was just dropped off with some other donations. There's been so many showing up, it's hard to keep track of who's dropping off what. Anyway, it didn't look like anything but an old piece of junk to me. I probably would have slapped a price of a few dollars on the thing and called it good."

"Me, too. Wonder how Vivien knew what it was?"

Maggie paused, her brow furrowing. "That's a good question. Didn't ask. Guess I was just so excited with the prospect of finding such a valuable piece of history. But I do know she called Professor Scott. You know him, don't you? Just lives out that way." She nodded off in some random direction. "He used to teach history up at Mercer University, retired now. Anyway, Vivien said he came right over and authenticated it.

Said that's exactly what it was, a Civil War field desk. It should bring a pretty penny at the sale. A real boon, wouldn't you agree?"

"Uh-huh," I mumbled, searching my brain for a way to steer the conversation back to something pertinent to Ginny's case. I didn't have my heart in interrogating her—or anyone, for that matter—but if I went back to Ginny empty-handed, I'd hear no end of it. I cleared my throat and tried getting things back on track. "I wanted to tell you that Belle did so well in the etiquette class last night. Isn't this cotillion going to be a grand affair? Why, it's as big an event as, say, the Peach Queen Pageant." I paused and squinted for effect. "Oh yes, I seem to remember Belle was in the pageant last year. She's such a natural beauty, I'm surprised she didn't win."

Maggie suddenly stood straighter, her gaze slipping away from me for a beat or two before she met my eyes again, this time with a bitter expression. "She *should* have won," she spat. "If it weren't for that . . ." Her voice trailed off as she caught herself.

"That what?" I prodded.

"You'll have to excuse me, Nola. I really must remember myself. After all, pride goeth before destruction."

And murder, perhaps?

She continued in a demure voice, "Just that it seemed suspicious to me, and most people, that Belle's dress for the talent competition suddenly had a tear in it. It happened at the last minute, and there wasn't anything we could do but drop out. That's why she didn't win."

"That's too bad." I shuffled around a bit before asking, "So are you saying that you think it was done on purpose?"

Her lips pressed into a tight line. "I really couldn't say for sure. But we were careful with her costume, and it was just fine during the dress rehearsal. Sure seemed like sabotage to me. Couldn't prove it, of course. And with Belle out of the competition, it left just Tara and Sophie in the final round."

"Tara is . . . or was Vivien's daughter, right? And Sophie? Her mom's Debra? Debra Bearden?"

She nodded. "That's right."

I let out a little whistle and shook my head. "What a terrible thing for someone to do—if it's true, that is. I mean, all the time and money that must go into getting ready for a pageant."

Maggie's eyes suddenly turned as dark as two pits of tar. "Like I said, no one could prove anything at the time. But if someone really did do such a horrible thing . . . why, it'd be unforgiveable."

I raised a brow. *Unforgiveable.* Strange word choice for a preacher's wife.

Chapter 7

Debutante Fact #038: A debutante knows, when all else fails, good food is the balm of the body and the elixir of the soul . . . so make sure y'all have a good casserole recipe.

On the way to the Peachy Keen, I fought to keep my focus on the road as worries swirled through my head: Vivien's murder and Ginny's possible implication in the crime, as well as my love life problems and overtaxed schedule. Why did trouble always seem to hit in spurts? Any one of these things was enough to handle, but all these things together might just send me over the edge.

Pulling into a spot in front of the diner, I thrust the gear into park and remained in the truck for few seconds to collect myself. That's when I realized just how self-centered I'd been. Because as bad as things were for me, at least I wasn't the main suspect in a murder case. No wonder Ginny was so intent on playing detective. How scared she must be! And for good reason. Half the town had turned against her, choosing to believe what they read in Frances Simms's libelous publication.

Still, regardless of the troubles weighing down my mind, I had work to do. So I hopped out of the truck and went to unload the peaches, but as I reached for the first crate, a loud rumbling startled me. I flinched, and the crate slipped from my hand, embedding a sliver of wood in my palm. *Ouch!* Shaking my hand, I glanced about, finally locating the source of the startling noise. What I saw made me nearly forget the pain: Dane Hawkins, parking his motorcycle in front of the Clip & Curl Salon.

Much to my annoyance, my heart kicked up a notch as I watched him dismount his motorcycle, remove his helmet and run his strong hands through that thick black hair of his. Even from where I was standing, his brooding good looks had an unwelcomed effect on me, conjuring up past memories I'd rather forget. Was I ever going to be able to move past all that? I looked down at my palm; he was a lot like a festering splinter I couldn't dig out from under my skin. Of course, it didn't help that Dane kept reappearing in my life. First in the previous summer when my brother hired him to investigate Hollis's case. Then several times since he'd popped back into town to see his new heartthrob, Laney Burns, of all people. Still, every time I saw him, it took me back to the wild days of my youth, when those smoldering looks of his seduced me into making a poor decision. That decision, and the resulting pregnancy, changed the course of my life forever. I sighed, shook off the terrible memory of it all and turned my frustration to my palm.

I carefully pinched my ragged fingernails on the tiny end of the sliver but only succeeded in pushing the culprit in deeper. How irritating! I glanced back over at the salon. Speaking of irritation, why *was* Dane in town anyway? Just to see Laney? I knew he was still working as an investigator. Had Ray hired him to help out with Ginny's case? Ray hadn't mentioned it to me, but then again, he didn't always clue me in on the details of his work. What a relief it would be to know someone official was working on Ginny's case—someone other than Maudy Payne, that is. I hated not knowing for sure. I wished I could just ask Dane. Remembering I promised Ginny I'd speak with Laney anyway, I left the peach crates for later, squared my shoulders and hightailed it across the street to the beauty salon. Besides, maybe they'd let me use a pair of tweezers. Might as well dispose of two irritants at the same time.

Inside I found Doris Whortlebe, the owner, busy wrapping a woman's hair in what looked like little squares of tinfoil. Poor gal; she looked miserable. Fingering my no-fuss cropped hair and feeling grateful I didn't have to endure such torture, I looked about the room for Laney and Dane. They were nowhere to be found.

"Hey there, Nola Mae," Doris called from across the room. "What can I do for ya? A little colorin', maybe, or . . ." She gave my short hair a hopeful once-over, her expression a bit doubtful, her dangly silver earrings swishing back and forth under her jet-black shag-cut hair. "Or extensions. You'd look real pretty with a little length. Wouldn't she, girls?" she asked around the room.

"Real pretty," the tinfoil woman agreed. "Doris is right, hon. You could use a little length. Why don't you let her fix you up with some of those extension thingies? They'd look real nice."

I shook my head. "No, thanks. Maybe some other time." *Like never.* "I was just looking for Laney."

Sighing, Doris pursed her lips and pointed a comb toward the back door of the salon. "Out back. She asked that boyfriend of hers to carry a stack of empty supply boxes out to recyclin'."

"Well, he's got the muscles to do it, doesn't he?" A woman sitting nearby with a plastic bag on her curl-laden head snatched up a magazine and began fanning herself. "Whew! That Laney's one lucky woman."

"I'd say," the older woman next to her agreed. "Why, if my Henry looked like him, I'd never leave the house."

The other woman snorted. "The house? Heck, Marlene, if Henry looked like that you'd never leave the bed."

As the room burst in raucous laughter, I excused myself with a waggle of my fingers and left them to contemplate Dane's good looks, while I made my way through the salon and out the back door. I stopped in my tracks. "Oh, pardon me," I said, clearing my throat and diverting my eyes from their brazenly passionate embrace. Guess they'd really missed each other.

Laney reluctantly pulled herself from Dane, giggled nervously and reached over to swipe a lipstick smudge from his chin. "Uh . . . hi, there, Nola Mae. What brings you out here?" She managed a polite smile while furiously chomping on the chewing gum she must have stashed in her cheek during their kiss. As she patted her well-teased pouf of hair back into place, I noticed her nails weren't painted her usual signature red, but a subdued shade of pink. Probably something called Flushed Pink, whereas later on that evening she'd certainly be changing it out for something more along the lines of Burning Red Hot.

"Sorry to interrupt," I muttered, offering what I hoped was an apologetic smile but probably seemed more like a scowl. Despite my intentions of putting the past to rest, seeing them this lovey-dovey up close was making my stomach turn. "But I saw Dane and—"

"It's Hawk. Remember?" He shuffled away from Laney and shoved his hands into his jean pockets. He regarded me with a perturbed look—due to the fact that I messed up his name, or because I'd interrupted his ardent reunion with Laney, I couldn't be sure. "I'm just using my professional name now."

"Hawk, right. That's what I came over for, actually. I'm wondering if you're back in town on official business." Sometime between high school and now, Hawk did a brief stint in the army and then joined the police force up in Atlanta. More of the free-agent type, though, he'd quit that job to open his own investigative business. The work seemed to suit him.

He nodded. "That's right. I'm here on a job."

"So Ray *did* call you?"

His dark brows furrowed. "Your brother? No. I'm working a security job. It's not my usual gig, but the pay's good. And"—he threw a wink Laney's way—"it allows me to be closer to my girl."

I tried hard not to cringe. "Security?"

"Isn't it wonderful?" Laney sighed, wrapping her hands around his midsection and laying her head against his shoulder. "Hawk's going to be working right here in Cays Mill for Congressman Wheeler."

"That's right," Hawk went on. "Seems he's beefing up his security team. There's rumor he might run for president one day."

My eyes widened. "Really?" I knew Jeb Wheeler's congressional seat was up for reelection the next year, but I had no idea he had such high political ambitions. "Sounds like a great opportunity for you, Hawk."

"For both of us," Laney emphasized, pressing closer to him.

"Why'd you think Ray called me?" Hawk asked.

"You remember Ginny Wiggins? She owns the diner with her husband, Sam."

He nodded. "Yeah. Guess so. Why?"

"She's a suspect in a murder. A local woman, stabbed to death in Hattie's Boutique just a few days ago. Ginny's my friend, Ray's, too, so I was thinking maybe he called you in to help."

"No, afraid not, darlin'." His chest puffed out, full of smugness. "But, if she needs my help, all she's got to do is call."

Oh brother.

Laney's lashes fluttered. "Isn't he just something."

Yeah, he was something, that's for sure. "That's good of you, Hawk. But hopefully she'll be cleared from the sheriff's list soon. But, I *was* wondering about something." I leveled my gaze on Laney. "You're out at the Honky Tonk quite a bit, aren't you?"

She popped her gum and glanced nervously at Hawk. "I wouldn't say *a lot*. Here and there, maybe."

"Do you know Debra Bearden? I heard she works there."

"Debra? Oh, sure. She used to tend bar."

"Used to?"

"Yeah, she quit."

"She did? When?"

Laney chomped a few times on her gum before replying. "Just last night as a matter of fact. Came in right before her shift, plopped her apron up on the bar and told her boss that she didn't need that stinkin' job no more."

"Really?" That seemed strange. She must've gone straight over there after helping with etiquette class. "Had she been working there long?"

Laney looked upward and shrugged. "Oh, since last summer, I guess. Just a few nights a week, usually the closing shift and sometimes weekends, too. Hated it, though. Wasn't much good at it, neither. Always wondered why she was workin' there in the first place. Her husband's got a good job at the mill."

"The mill?" I hadn't kept track of the mill over the winter, assuming it shut down after all the trouble it had over the past year.

"Yup." She pulled the wad of gum out of her mouth and tossed it down the alley. "He's the new foreman. You knew some company from up north bought out the mill, right? It's doing much better, too. Couldn't have been easy to turn it around, either, considerin' Ben Wakefield 'bout run it to the ground."

I rubbed down the goose bumps on my arms. "Let's *not* go there, okay?"

Laney nodded her head and gave me a knowing look.

Pausing a second, I regrouped my thoughts and asked, "Did you happen to see Debra working last Saturday evening?"

"Yup. She was there. She was working happy hour that night." She paused a second, then shook a manicured nail my way. "Come to think of it, I saw her later on just as the band was kickin' into gear."

Hawk's jaw jutted out. "So, you were there last night and Saturday night, too?"

Laney sidled closer and rubbed his arm, staring up at him with doe eyes. "Oh, baby. Don't go getting all upset. Saturday night at the Honky Tonk is live-band night. And you know how I love to dance." Then she turned to me and said, "Sounds like you're onto something, Nola. Are you thinkin' Debra had something to do with the murder? 'Cuz I've known Ginny Wiggins all my life, and she doesn't seem like the murderin' type to me."

Finally, someone on our side. Even if it was Laney. "I don't really know what to think at this point, Laney. All I know is Ginny's innocent."

"Well, I'll keep my ears peeled. You know half the ladies who come into the salon could tell you what you've done before you do it. If I hear anything, I'll let y'all know."

Gee, that was easy. Not only was Laney an abundance of information, I didn't even have to fork out money for a manicure. I thanked her and said good-bye, letting them get back to their steamy reunion. Only I'd just made it back across Peach Tree Boulevard when I heard Hawk calling my name. "Hey, Nola. Wait up!" He caught up to me outside the diner just as I'd reached my truck. "I forgot to tell you about Roscoe."

Roscoe! The most adorable basset hound pup in the world. Last summer, Roscoe spent some time with me out at the farm and I'd fallen hopelessly in love with the little fellow's solemn brown eyes, soft fur and impossibly long ears. "Is he okay?"

"He's fine. Just that I'm staying at Sunny Side Up again, and you know how Margie feels about dogs messing up the place." I nodded. Who could blame her? Margie Price, owner of the Sunny Side Up Bed & Breakfast, bought the neglected, dilapidated property a few years ago and painstakingly restored every inch of the three-story antebellum home to its original glory. I could understand why she made a "no pet" rule. "So, he's staying with Laney then?"

Hawk shook his head. "Oh no, Laney's allergic. So he's out at your place. Didn't think you'd mind, being that y'all got along so well last time."

"At the farm?" Of all the nerve! Part of me wanted to tell this imposing egotist where to go, but sadly, another part of me melted at the thought of that sweet little dog in my arms again. I loved the idea of having Roscoe around, but. . . .

"Yup. Stopped by there on my way into town. Had the nicest visit with your mama." He patted his taut stomach. "She makes darn good biscuits."

Now my jaw dropped. Hawk and my mother? Chatting it up over biscuits and coffee? All these years I'd avoided telling Mama about Hawk's very existence, practically denied it myself in an attempt to bury all those awful memories, and here he goes and just pops in to have coffee with her. I forced a tight smile. "And how did Mama take to the idea of watching Roscoe?"

Hawk grinned. "She loves the little fellow. I could tell."

"Hmm. Well, thanks for letting me know." I still couldn't believe he'd impose like that without asking first. Typical Hawk. I turned back toward the truck. Unlatching the tailgate, I grabbed one of the peach crates and let out a yelp. "Ouch!" I cried, looking down at the sliver in my palm. I'd forgotten all about that splinter, until now.

"Hurt yourself?"

I looked over my shoulder to see Hawk still hovering nearby. "It's nothing. Just a little splinter." But before I could react, he stepped forward and grabbed my hand. I tried to pull back, but he held firm. "It's okay, Hawk. Really."

He gripped my hand tighter and pulled it close to his face. "Would ya hold still, darlin'? I bet I can fix this."

I rolled my eyes and groaned. This whole thing was stupid: me standing there on the curb with Hawk removing a splinter from my hand. What was it with men like him? Always reacting to every situation with macho fervor, playing the part of man who rescues the damsel in distress.

"Got it," he announced triumphantly, dropping my hand and wiping his own on the back of his jeans. "Better?"

I nodded slowly, backing up a step or two and examining my now splinter-free hand. "Hey, thanks. That does feel better."

"Glad I could be of service," he replied with a wink, his attention suddenly wandering over my shoulder. "I'd offer to help with those crates, darlin', but it looks like your boy-friend's here." He nodded toward the walk. There was Cade, leaning up against the entrance to my shop, his arms folded across his chest and an irritated look on his face.

I swallowed hard and shot him a little wave.

He didn't reciprocate. Instead, he turned his back and walked away.

A few hours later, Cade finally showed up to help me finish sanding the rest of the pine floors, a job that required a lot of loud machinery and not much opportunity for conversation. A good thing, too. That distant politeness of his had suddenly changed to dark broodiness. He hardly said more than two words to me while we worked. By the time I wandered into the kitchen at Red's Diner later that day, my emotions were spent. All I wanted to do was test out a few recipes and head home for a hot bath and early bedtime.

Ginny had something else in mind, though. She greeted me just inside the diner's door, Hattie next to her. "Glad you're finally here. I called Hattie earlier and asked her to help us with our recipes tonight. That way we can discuss the case, too."

I begrudgingly followed my friends back to the kitchen, wishing we could skip the detective talk and just get on with our work. We were supposed to be testing recipes for appetizers. Since the cotillion committee had decided they wanted a peachy twist on the menu, we'd brainstormed a list of simple ideas to add just the right amount of peach to Ginny's already selected menu. Tonight we'd planned to make crostini topped with peach salsa and melted Brie. Since I already had been making peach salsa for the shop, it seemed to be an easy solution. Plus, if the appetizer was a hit, maybe it would pique interest in some of my other products.

Ginny started by washing the peaches in the back sink, while I gathered the peppers and other spices from a large pantry. Hattie washed her hands and began cutting stems out of several tomatoes. As we worked together, my mood started to improve. With three pairs of hands to help with washing, peeling and dicing, the work was moving along quickly. It wasn't until we had all the ingredients in the industrial-sized food processor that Ginny pulled out her list again. "Okay, girls." She pointed her pen our way. "What do y'all have for me?"

Hattie blanched. "Uh . . . actually, I haven't had a chance to find out much. I've been so busy at the shop and all."

Ginny raised her palms upward and shook her head. "Didn't you talk to Mrs. Busby?"

"A little. But she didn't really have anything new to say. And when I asked her if she remembered anything else about finding the body, she got all worked up. This whole thing has been such a shock to her. She's so upset, she can hardly get her work done. Just this morning, she had to rip out and redo the hems on two debutante gowns because she'd sewn them unevenly. That's not a bit like Mrs. Busby. I say we mark her off the list. It's obvious to me she's not capable of murder. Besides"—she pointed at the blank spot under the motive column—"she doesn't have any motive."

"That we know of, anyway," Ginny amended. "No, we'll leave her up for a little longer. Just until we're sure."

Hattie started muttering something, but thankfully Ginny looked down at her list at that moment and I quickly hit the button on the processor, drowning Hattie's words with the loud hum of the pulsating machine. As soon as the ingredients were combined, I flipped the switch again and said, "I may have something." I dumped the combined ingredients into a large stainless bowl and thumbed over my shoulder toward the pantry. "Hey, Hattie, would you get some French bread and cut it into slices?"

"Make them somewhat thin," Ginny added, pen still hovering over her list. "So? What'd you find out?" she prodded, her eyes sparkling with hope.

"Well, I talked to Maggie Jones today and was able to steer the conversation to last year's Peach Queen Pageant. I think we were right about the pageant, Ginny. Maggie seemed to think a little sabotage was used to narrow the field of competition. But there's no concrete proof, just her feeling." *A bitter, vengeful feeling*, I thought, remembering the way Maggie described the incident as "unforgivable." "And she did seem upset about the whole thing." I went on to tell them about the tear in Belle's dress and how she had to drop out, leaving only Tara Crenshaw and Sophie Bearden in the final round. "Doesn't that seem suspicious?" I glanced between the two.

Hattie nodded, arranging thin slices of baguette onto a large baking sheet. "So, you're thinking that Vivien sabotaged the dress to eliminate Belle from the competition?"

I nodded. "Maybe she saw Belle as her daughter's biggest rival for the crown."

Hattie shrugged. "That makes sense, I guess. But even if Vivien did sabotage the dress that belonged to Maggie's daughter, I don't really think Maggie would exact revenge by killing her. I mean, who kills someone over something as petty as the Peach Queen Pageant?"

"Pageant mothers, that's who," Ginny stated. "You underestimate just how competitive those things are." She pointed at the chart. "So, I'm marking the Peach Queen Pageant down as a motive in Maggie Jones's column. Especially if she still seems bitter about the whole thing. Maybe she's been building up steam all this time and she just snapped." She slid her pen across the paper and peered at me. "Did you find out where she was at the time of the murder?"

"Maggie claims she was at the church most of the evening, getting ready for their upcoming bazaar." I crossed to the fridge and pulled out a block of Brie. I'd suggested this cheese for the appetizer because I knew the buttery, creamy texture with just a hint of salty snap would pair well with the heat in my salsa. I hoped that, along with perfectly crisped French bread, it would prove to be a tiny bite of peachy heaven.

"Alone?"

I carefully ran a sharp knife around the edge of the rind, peeling it away from the cheese. "Don't know for sure. I didn't quite know how to ask that. . . . Oh, she did mention other parishioners being there." I shrugged. "Sorry, I don't know who."

Ginny let out an exasperated sigh, tossed the pen aside and began rubbing her temples.

"But I did get a chance to talk to Laney," I quickly added, trying to inject some hope into the situation. "Asked her about Debra Bearden, and she told me that she remembered seeing Debra working the Honky Tonk last Saturday night. Couldn't swear she was there the whole time, but she remembers seeing her there during happy hour and then later that evening when the band started playing. That would have been around eight."

"Happy hour runs from about five thirty to seven," Hattie explained, doling spoonfuls of salsa onto each piece of bread. "So there's no way Debra could have made it to my shop and back to the Honky Tonk during that time."

"Right." Ginny picked up her pen again.

"There's something else, though," I continued. "According to Laney, Debra marched into the bar last night and quit. She'd apparently had enough and didn't need the job anymore.

Laney thinks Debra was an odd fit for bartending in the first place. Guess she hated the work."

"Weird. Then why work there at all?" Hattie asked.

Ginny moved to place an *X* by Debra's name. "Doesn't really matter," she said. "She has an alibi, so I'm marking her off the list. That leaves Mrs. Busby and Maggie Jones." She glanced up with a smile, the first I'd seen on her face in a while. "We're narrowing it down, girls."

My heart sank. Ginny was so anxious to get to the bottom of things she was overlooking—or perhaps denying—the obvious fact that news travels so fast in this town that practically anyone, at this point, could be a viable suspect. I also wouldn't have marked Debra off the list so soon. Something about Debra quitting her job so abruptly seemed strange to me. Still, Ginny seemed to feel better with the progress we'd made on the case, even if that left only the minister's wife and the shaken, elderly Mrs. Busby as prime suspects. Why bring all that up and dash her hopes? Instead, I busied myself placing thin pieces of cheese on top of each mound of salsa. I could hardly wait to taste them. "If this recipe works," I started telling the girls, "I'm going to print up some recipe cards as an example of one of the ways to use my salsa. I think customers would like that, don't you?"

"They sure would," Ginny agreed. "And speaking of recipes, I made one of my best chicken casserole recipes today. You remember, don't ya, Nola? I made it for you when you were having all that trouble last summer. The one with white wine in the sauce?"

How could I forget? It was delicious: creamy white wine sauce with robust chunks of chicken and a tender medley of vegetables all topped off with a flaky, buttery crust. My mouth watered just thinking about it.

She continued, "It'll be just the thing to help soothe

Vivien's poor widower, don't you think? Thought you two could take it over there tonight. Just say y'all made it. Nate won't know the difference."

"Tonight?" both Hattie and I chimed in unison.

"Sure. Why not? While you're there, see what you can find out. Maybe he knows something about his wife that will help us get to the bottom of all this. Unless"—she shot us a pointed look—"you two have something better to do tonight than making sure your best friend doesn't spend the rest of her life in prison?"

Well, when she put it that way . . .

Chapter 8

Debutante rule #067: A debutante is like a tea bag. Ya never know how strong she is until she's sittin' in hot water.

"This must be it," Hattie said, pulling in front of a two-story brick colonial later Thursday evening. She glanced at the address Ginny jotted down for us and back at house number on the mailbox. "Yup. This is the place," she affirmed. "It's already after eight. Do you think it's too late to stop by?"

"Maybe. But, I'm not going back to tell Ginny we didn't get this delivered. Are you?" I gripped the casserole and climbed out of the compact car. On the way up the walk, I paused for a second to take in the expanse of the lawn with its precisely cut grass, punctuated by two live oaks and exquisitely designed flower borders. As we ascended the steps to the front door, I stole a glance at the sun, which was just starting to dip low on the horizon. I always loved this time of the evening, when the sun was setting. More than anything, I wanted to be home at the farm, sitting on the front porch, watching the changing sky with a slice of Mama's peach pie and Roscoe playing at my feet. Actually, I wished to be just about anywhere rather than on a mission for Ginny, ferreting information from a newly bereaved widower.

Hattie must have felt the same way. "I just hate this," I heard her mumble under her breath as she reached out to knock on the door. But before her knuckles connected, it swung open, revealing a startled Maggie Jones. Nate Crenshaw was right behind her. I noticed a slight twitch along his strong jawline as his dark eyes settled on us.

"Oh, Hattie!" Maggie exclaimed. Then peering over Hattie's shoulder at me she added, "And Nola. How nice to see you girls." Only the wide-eyed look on her face along with the pink flush of her skin indicated otherwise. Furtively, she glanced back at Nate and said, "Thanks for looking, Nate. I'll check back again with you tomorrow to see if it's turned up." Then she anxiously pressed past us and continued down the walk, her long hair falling across her face as she kept her gaze lowered.

I stared after her. In all the years I'd known Maggie Jones, I'd never seen her wear her hair anyway except in a severe bun. Not that I didn't like her look; I did. I'd never been one for long hair myself, preferring short, blunt cuts. But it certainly softened Maggie's appearance.

Hattie must have noticed Maggie's change of appearance, too; she was staring after her with a squint-eyed look. Then, clearing her throat, she took the casserole dish from my hands and held it out to Nate. "We just wanted to bring this by. You have our deepest sympathies," she said, her voice sounding a little flat.

"That's kind of you. Thank you," Nate said, taking the dish and setting it on a small table just inside the door. "Several ladies have brought things by this afternoon. I'm touched by everyone's outpouring of concern." He looked down at the dish on the table, then back up at Hattie and me,

swiping a hand over his closely cut salt-and-pepper hair.
"I'm sorry. I don't quite recognize . . . Were y'all friends of
Vivien's?"

Hattie nodded and tugged me forward. "This is Nola Mae
Harper. And I'm Hattie McKenna. I've known Vivien for a
long time. She was one of my first customers."

"Customers?"

"I own Hattie's Boutique."

"Oh, that's where . . ." His features clouded over as his
gaze fell to his shoes. He shuffled a bit, absently running the
toe of his black loafer over the threshold. I cringed at the
thought that Hattie's store was the scene of his wife's murder
and here we were intruding on him like this. I glanced at
Hattie to see her reaction. But Hattie had cocked her head and
was giving Nate a squint-eyed look as well.

"Everyone is sick over Vivien's death," I quickly said,
nudging Hattie. What was up with her?

Nate's head snapped up. "Apparently not everyone," he
shot back, the sudden vehement tone of his voice surprising
me. "That woman who owns the diner, for one. The paper
made it sound like she killed Vivien over some stupid dress.
If that's true, then I hope she rots in jail."

Hattie shifted and replied bitingly, "I don't think the sheriff
has made an arrest yet. I'm sure she has other suspects in
mind."

"But we hope, for your sake, that everything is resolved
soon," I added, trying to smooth over Hattie's statement.
"So you and Tara can feel some closure, I mean. It's just that
I can't imagine Vivien having any enemies. She seemed like
such a wonderful person."

Nate shook his head. "Enemies? No, of course not. Everyone
loved Vivien. She spent so much of her time helping others."

"Yes, she did," I agreed. "All the time she volunteered at

the school, not to mention her work at the church." I looked
to Hattie for help, but she was glaring at Nate with tightly
clamped lips, so I rambled on, reaching for anything to keep
the conversation going. "I know the ladies at the church
appreciated her help with the bazaar."

"The bazaar," Nate reiterated with a furrow of his brow.
"That's right. She'd been talking about the bazaar recently.
She was excited about her work there. Afraid I don't even know
what exactly she was doing. She was always going on about
her committees and causes. I'm sorry to admit, I often tuned
her out." His lowered his gaze, his shoulders noticeably droop-
ing. "I've had so much stress with the business and everything,
I'm afraid I've been a little self-absorbed. I regret that now."

My thoughts wandered briefly to Cade. I'd been neglecting
him, tuning out his affection too often over the past year.
What if something happened . . . ? I swallowed back a
despairing pang of guilt, trying to refocus my thoughts.
"She'd been helping sort donation items for the bazaar," I
offered, hoping to give a little insight that might be comfort-
ing. "Actually, I heard she was instrumental in discovering
a valuable Civil War relic. All the church ladies were so
pleased. They seem to think it would bring a lot of money
for the church."

Nate's face seemed to sink even further. I blinked a few
times, replaying my last statement in my mind, wondering
if I'd said something to make him feel worse. Finally, he let
out a jagged breath and admitted, "I didn't even know Vivien
cared about such things. I should have listened to her more.
Now she's gone, and it's too late."

Since Hattie obviously wasn't going to say anything and
I had no idea how to respond to Nate's anguish without
making him feel even worse, the conversation died, and an

uncomfortable silence enveloped the porch. I shuffled about, muttering a few more condolences, and said good night.

"What is wrong with you?" I asked, turning to Hattie as soon as the door shut.

"Oh, come on!" Hattie snorted as she wheeled and started back down the steps. "He's a good actor, that's for sure."

I did a double take. What had her so agitated?

"Seriously, Nola?" she said after noting what must have been a confused look on my face. "Didn't you think it was weird that Maggie Jones was here?" She blew out her breath and raised a brow. "Well, it's obvious to me. I mean, the way she was all dolled up and everything."

"All dolled up?" I asked as we climbed into the car. "She just had her hair down, that's all."

"And rouge!"

Well, maybe, though I'd thought she was just blushing. . . . "Wait! What are you implying, anyway?"

"That they're having an affair!" Hattie's face twisted into an angry scowl as she jammed the keys into the ignition and flipped the air on high.

The cold blast hit me directly in the face as I reached to adjust my vent. "What's wrong with you, Hattie?" I asked, wondering why so much anger. And why was she so ready to assume Nate and Maggie were having an affair? "I think you may be jumping to conclusions."

Hattie turned to me, tears threatening the corners of her angry eyes. "I swear, all men are dogs. Isn't there a single decent man left in the world?" She started fiddling with the air again, her hands trembling as she adjusted the knob.

Reaching over, I placed my hand over hers and squeezed. "Tell me what's going on, Hattie. It's you and Pete, isn't it?"

She stiffened at my words, then nodded, pulling her hand

back for a quick swipe at her face before rooting in her bag for a hankie. "He's been . . ." Her breath caught as she buried her face in her hands. "Cheatttting on me," she wailed.

"Cheating?" I shook my head. "That doesn't seem like Pete." The Pete I knew, or at least had come to know over the past several months, adored my beautiful friend. More than adored, actually. He practically worshiped her—something I'd admittedly been envious of from time to time. That and the fact that dating the flower shop owner afforded her certain perks like a constant stream of fresh-cut flowers and even long-stemmed roses on a regular basis. I swiveled in my seat to face her head-on, pausing for a second while she finished blowing her nose. "This is crazy, Hattie," I said, hoping to talk some sense into her. "Why do you think he's cheating? Is it just some rumor going around? Because you know how this town loves its gossip."

"No," she said, dabbing at her eyes. "I have proof." She took a long cleansing breath and started explaining the whole ordeal. Apparently, the day the debutante dress shipment came in, after the whole fiasco between Ginny and Vivien had receded and the shop cleared out, she'd left Mrs. Busby in charge to lock up while she made a mad dash down the street to see Pete. "I was just so upset. It'd been a horrible day."

"I understand," I said. "The mixed-up dress order, then Ginny exploding like that. I bet you were emotionally drained."

"Exactly. I just needed to see him," she replied with a drawn-out sigh, before going on to explain that while at Pete's she stumbled upon a mysterious note, written in a distinctly feminine scroll. "I didn't mean to be nosy, I really didn't. It's just that it was there. Right out in the open."

"What did it say?"

"Something like . . ." Her voice caught as she struggled to maintain composure. "Like . . . 'Meet me at the usual spot tonight after work.'" She shook her head. "I can't remember exactly. But I knew what it meant."

That was it? "That could be anything, Hattie."

"Oh yeah? Like what? I mean, who has a 'usual spot' with someone other than his girlfriend?"

I searched my brain for a plausible explanation. The fact that I couldn't come up with one quickly enough really agitated her. "See what I mean," she lamented. I bucked up, preparing for another onslaught of tears, but instead her expression tightened and she began angrily wringing her handkerchief. "Just ticks me off that I didn't know what he was up to all this time. I mean, how stupid am I? But don't go telling anyone about this, you understand?"

I nodded.

"Especially not Ginny. She's got too much to worry about right now with all this murder stuff going on. And knowing Ginny, she'd take it personally. Especially since she was the one that introduced us in the first place."

"She was? I didn't know that."

Hattie quickly swiped the hankie under her eye and nodded. "Yeah. It was so sweet of her." She let out a long sigh. "You know what she did?" I shrugged, and she continued with a melancholy voice, "She mixed up our to-go orders on purpose one afternoon, then called me and asked if I wouldn't mind running down to the flower shop to make a quick switch. Of course, it was love at first sight. Well, lust, at least." Another long sigh, this one punctuated with a little sob as her shoulders drooped with the memory. "I'm telling ya, Nola, he was the sexiest man I'd ever seen."

"Well, not to worry," I interjected, before she got herself all worked up again. "I won't mention anything to Ginny."

The Crenshaws' porch light suddenly switched off, and the front curtain parted slightly. Hattie, still caught up in her walk down memory lane, didn't seem to notice, but I imagined Nate was peering through a window and wondering what in the world we were doing still parked in front of his house. "Let's go someplace and talk about this," I suggested.

She sucked in a shaky breath. "I don't know. I could sure use a drink, but I'm not in the mood for the Honky Tonk."

Boy, could I relate. I was never in the mood for the Honky Tonk. "How about coming out to the house. Daddy's always got plenty of Peach Jack around."

She tossed the handkerchief aside with a firm nod and gripped the steering wheel. "Sounds perfect. Let's go."

I stood on the porch Friday morning, coffee mug in hand and Roscoe wallowing at my feet, as I watched the sun break over the top of the orchard. The air was heavy, tiny droplets of dew clinging to the grass like little silver beads that would soon dissipate with the first of the sun's hot rays. Lifting my coffee mug, I inhaled its rich, nutty aroma along with the clean freshness of morning and the unmistakable sweetness of ripening peaches before taking a desperate drink, hoping the caffeine would assuage the pounding between my ears. Too much Peach Jack the night before had left me feeling like something scraped off the bottom of a shoe. I still wasn't sure how one glass turned into several, but the longer Hattie and I talked, the more we drank, until we'd nearly finished off the bottle.

The screen door screeched open, and Mama shuffled out, her yellow flowered robe cinched at the waist and sleep lines running down the side of her face. She was carrying her own mug of coffee. "Mornin', hon." Roscoe left my side and trotted to her.

"How's my baby doin'?" Mama asked.

I started to answer but glanced over and saw her scratching Roscoe behind the ears and realized she was speaking to the dog, not me. *Baby?* Guess Mama and Roscoe had bonded.

She moved toward one of the wicker rockers, settled in and set the mug aside before tapping her hands against her thighs. He jumped right up and nestled in like a regular lapdog. Mama grinned and rubbed her cheek along the top of his head. "Isn't he a good boy?" she asked.

"He sure is," I replied fondly, reaching over to rub the soft spot on the tip of his muzzle. His eyes practically rolled with the pleasure of all the attention.

"By the way," Mama inserted. "Why is Hattie McKenna sleeping on our davenport?"

"Sorry, Mama. We were up sort of late last night. We didn't wake you, did we?"

"Lawd no! If I can sleep through your Daddy's snoring, I can sleep through 'bout anything." She stretched out a slippered foot and nudged an empty Peach Jack bottle lying next to the chair. "Looks like you two threw back a bit of alcohol. Were y'all just exceptionally thirsty or was there some sort of trouble you were tryin' to drown?"

Leave it to Mama. She'd never really beat around the bush about anything.

"Trouble," I finally responded, and I took a long drag from my coffee. I knew I'd just opened a can of worms. Mama couldn't stand to see anyone she loved having trouble. I was in for a long heart-to-heart now. I took another gulp of coffee; these talks with Mama weren't easy for me under any circumstance, but with a fuzzy brain, it'd be downright dreadful. "I'm having a little trouble with Cade—nothing to worry about, though—and Hattie's having trouble with Pete. And we're both troubled over Vivien Crenshaw's murder and the fact that Ginny's the top suspect."

Mama pressed her tiptoes to the ground, sending the chair into motion, her head nodding in unison with the rhythm of the rocker as she stroked Roscoe's back and mulled over my troubles. "Problems with Cade, you say?"

"Nothing I can't fix," I said, backtracking and wishing I hadn't brought it up in the first place. "Just a little communication problem."

"I see," she said with a pointed look.

I knew if I didn't change the topic quickly, she'd get stuck on the Cade thing. "Really, Mama. I'll get it figured out. Besides, my man problems pale in comparison to what's going on between Hattie and Pete right now."

She adopted an all-knowing expression. "Aw . . . What'd he do?"

It didn't surprise me that she blamed him for whatever the problem was. In Mama's eyes, men had an inherent bent toward misbehaving, their mischievous nature only held in check by a strong woman. "She seems to think he's cheating on her," I reported.

Mama stopped rocking and blurted, "Cheatin'? Pete Sanchez? He doesn't seem like the type."

"Shh!" I thumbed toward the house and motioned for her to be quiet. I didn't want Hattie to wake up and hear us talking about her.

She lowered her voice and leaned toward me. "What makes her think he's two-timin' her?" Roscoe lifted his head and nudged her arm, begging for more attention, but she was too wrapped up in the conversation to notice. Disgruntled, he jumped down and started sniffing around the porch.

"Some note she found in his shop," I replied. "She thinks it was from another woman."

Mama busied herself picking at the dog fur that'd attached itself to the front of her robe. "You know," she finally said, "I pride myself on being a good judge of character, and I'm just not sensing that young man is the cheatin' type. There's got to be some other explanation. That's all there is to it."

I nodded. "I agree with you, Mama. I'm not seeing it, either. She just jumped to conclusions," I muttered into my cup, taking a sip, "like she did about Maggie Jones."

Mama shot me a look. "What about Maggie?"

"Oh, nothing. really." But Mama gave me one of her determined-to-know-more looks. I explained that Maggie was one of the gals on Ginny's list of suspects for Vivien's murder.

"Murder?" Her eyes grew wide. "The preacher's wife? Why, I never . . ." She visibly shook off the preposterous assumption, but then a slight curl of her lips betrayed another thought.

"Mama? Do you know something about the murder?"

"Oh heavens, Nola Mae, of course not." She shook her head, ending that possibility. But then her eyes twinkled just a mite, like she had another little tidbit to share. "I was just thinking how people are not quite what they seem sometimes."

I was game. "Like . . . ?" I smiled back.

She drew in her breath and started rocking again. "Well, don't go repeating this, you hear?"

I promised.

"I was at the library the other day lookin' for some recipe books. . . . You know the fair's right around the corner and I'm thinking about entering the baking—"

"And you saw Maggie there?" I prompted to keep her on track.

"That's right." Mama's lips strained as she tried to suppress a smile. "She was using one of the library's computers, you see. And she must not have seen me comin', because she didn't bother to hide what she was looking at on the screen."

Mama covered her mouth as a few raspy laughs escaped her throat.

"Tell me," I pleaded.

She began fanning her eyes as they watered with laughter. "A man. And my Lawd, he took up practically the whole screen."

"A man?"

Mama clutched her midsection as she laughed some more. "A big, brawny, long-haired Scotsman wearing one of those thingies they wear. . . ."

"A kilt."

"Call it what you want, but it was obvious from the picture that he didn't have anything on under it." She took a swipe at her red-tinged cheeks and continued giggling.

My brow shot up. "Nothing on under . . . ? Oh, never mind," I said, holding up my hand. "What did Maggie do?"

"She 'bout died of embarrassment. Poor thing." Mama chuckled some more, then with a shake of her head, she turned serious. "Only, there was something strange about the whole thing."

Stranger than the preacher's wife staring at naked men on the library's computer?

Mama continued, "She had a notebook with her, and it seemed she was taking notes."

"Taking notes? On the Scotsman?"

Mama shrugged. "Or on his . . . well, you know."

"Mama!" I laughed right along with her. Then, I thought back to the romance novel I saw slip out of Maggie's stack of reading material. Not a big deal to me; I liked a hot romance every once in a while. And brawny Scotsmen in kilts were nice, too, for that matter. But I recalled how Maggie blushed and scrambled to hide the risqué cover. She was sure working hard to keep that side of herself hidden. Not that I could blame her, being a preacher's wife and all. Still, I wondered what else she was keeping secret: an affair with Nate Crenshaw? Maybe Hattie was right after all. Or was there something more sinister going on? Preacher's wife or not, there was more to Maggie Jones than met the eye— much more than hair tightly wound in a bun and high-buttoned blouses. . . .

The sound of the screen door pushing open interrupted my train of thought. Looking up, I saw Hattie stumble out onto the porch with her bag slung over her shoulder. She cringed and moved her hands over her ears as the door swung shut with a thump. "Mercy, but my head hurts. How much did I drink last night?"

Mama pointed down to the empty bottle. "Looks to me like you two put away a fair share of this stuff." She playfully clucked her tongue. "Serves y'all right if you're both feelin' like mean little men are wrestlin' behind your eyeballs." Then, as she took in Hattie's apparent misery, a look of pity crossed her face. She stood up and spread her arms for a hug. "Aw, come here, girls," she beckoned. And when we did, she pulled us in close, one of us on each side. "I realize you both are going through some difficult times, but just remember that we Southern gals come from strong stock; what doesn't kill us only makes us stronger, right? Besides, all these problems will pass. You'll see."

Over the years, I'd come to realize that Mama had a talent for spewing just the right platitude for every direful situation. Oftentimes, it was just the right twist of words to calm and soothe frazzled nerves; other times her heavily redundant clichés got on my every last nerve. Today, I just took comfort in her embrace and the fact that she truly believed a healthy dose of grit could get us Southern gals through just about anything. Only, what Mama didn't know—heck, what nobody knew at the time—was that "these problems" weren't going to pass anytime soon. In fact, they were going to get a whole lot worse before they got better.

Chapter 9

Debutante Fact #030: Sometimes there's nothing like a good cry to set the world straight. . . . That's why a debutante always wears waterproof makeup.

Later that morning, I walked through the door of Peachy Keen with the old Czar radio I'd borrowed from Mama's kitchen in my hand, prepared for a full day's work. But I was astounded by what I saw. Somewhere between when I'd left yesterday evening and this morning, Cade had made incredible progress. Not only was the shelving done, but he'd installed my checkout counter—a solid wood piece of cabinetry I'd found at a local flea market, stained dark green and accented with white beadboard and trim. It looked perfect where Cade had placed it along the side wall of the store. I could already imagine myself standing behind it, ringing up orders and gift wrapping packages for customers. But even though I felt a huge sense of relief knowing things may get done in time after all, a feeling of sadness engulfed me. Cade must have worked all night to get this much done. Was that his new plan? Work nights so he could avoid me? Or maybe get things wrapped up as soon as possible so he could be free from me once and for all? Either scenario was unacceptable. Deciding it was time to talk this through, I swiveled on my heel and marched outside, my head bent with determination as I made my way down Orchard Lane and toward Cade's house.

Only as I passed by the courthouse green, I spied something that caused me to pause: Debra Bearden and Nate Crenshaw, standing by the courthouse statue, engrossed in an animated conversation. Even from where I was watching, Debra's sweeping arm gestures suggested that she was angry about something. About what, I wondered.

My curiosity piqued, I continued down the walk, pretending to go about my own business until I was out of their line of sight. Then I doubled back across the courthouse lawn and stooped behind a row of lilac bushes that ran along the back side of the statue. Straining my ears, I could just make out part of their conversation.

"I don't know why you're being so obstinate about this, Nate." I moved closer to the shrub and peered through a bare spot in the branches so I could better see them. Debra's legs were planted wide as she leaned toward Nate with a steely expression.

"I'm not being obstinate. I simply don't know where it would be," Nate replied, taking a step backward.

"Vivien kept it tucked inside her purse."

Nate shrugged. "I'm sorry, Debra. I'd like to help you, but Vivien had so many bags. I wouldn't even know—"

"The large beige one with gold accents," she inserted, her voice tinged with despair.

Nate sighed. "Quite honestly, there's so many other things I'm trying to sort through right now, but I'll keep my eye out for it. If I find it, I'll call you." It was a brush-off, and Debra knew it.

Desperately, she reached out and clutched his arm. "I can't

imagine it would take all that much time to just look through the house for it. It's awfully important to me, Nate."

"I'm sorry. I can't look now. I'm on my way to the bank for a meeting." He gently shook off her hand. "But like I said, I'll keep an eye out for it."

I watched as Debra clenched and unclenched her fists, wrestling with the idea of ceding control over the situation. Finally, she gave up and walked away, shoulders slumped in defeat.

As I waited for Nate to move on and the coast to clear, I thought back to what I'd heard Maggie say the night before when she was leaving Nate's house. Something about checking back later to see if he'd found it. Whatever "it" was. Were both Maggie and Debra looking for the same thing, I wondered.

"Strange finding you here, Nola Mae," came a voice from behind. I turned my head and found Frances Simms hovering behind me. Her dark little eyes gleamed with smugness as she observed me stooped over in the middle of the lilac bushes. She leaned in and parted a couple branches, peering at Nate Crenshaw as he walked back across the lawn. "Eavesdropping, were you?"

"Uh, no. I was just . . . uh . . ." Frances practically smacked her lips as she watched me struggle to explain. Finally, I gave up and moved past her, mumbling something about needing to get to work.

She pursued me across the courthouse yard, nipping at my heels and spewing questions like a yappy little dog. "Was that Debra Bearden I saw walking away just a minute ago? Is that who Nate was talking to? And why were you spying on them?"

Picking up my pace, I kept my gaze forward and headed straight for the closest bit of safety: my shop. Luckily, halfway across the lawn, a man called out to Frances, waving her down, and she reluctantly gave up on me—for the moment, anyway. Relieved, I wanted to head back up Orchard Lane to Cade's house, but that would take me right past her again. I massaged my temples, trying to rub down the headache creeping up behind my eyes. I headed into the diner for another cup of coffee to give me some time to shake Frances.

Most of the morning crowd had already moved on with their days, leaving only a few stragglers who still occupied the stools along the front counter. I spied Ginny weaving between tables with a large gray tub, piling in dirty dishes to take back to the kitchen. "Hey there, Nola Mae," she said, spritzing a tabletop with green sanitizer and giving it a quick wipe before hoisting the tub to her hip and motioning for me follow her. On the way, she nodded to one of the coffeemakers behind the bar. "Grab that coffeepot, would ya? I could use another hit of caffeine."

Obliging, I followed her through the swinging door to the kitchen where she set the tub on the counter by the sink. Sam was there, rinsing dishes and placing them in a large divided tray that he would eventually slide into an industrial-sized sanitizing machine. Seeing me, he nodded and offered a quick smile before turning back to his work.

"Come over this way," Ginny said, moving toward the grill area where she could peek through the pass-through window and keep an eye on her customers while we visited. "Looks like there's somethin' on your mind. What gives, Nola Mae?" She filled a couple mugs with coffee, sliding one my way and snatching a sugar pack from her apron pocket. She tapped it a few times against her palm before tearing it open and pouring the contents into her coffee. "And it better be good news. 'Cuz I've had enough of the other to last a lifetime."

I went on to tell her about running into Maggie Jones at Nate's house the night before. Then, about the conversation I'd just overheard between Nate and Debra Bearden. I explained how I thought the two might be connected. "Both women seemed adamant about getting something from him that Vivien had. Especially Debra. She was pleading for Nate to look around for some bag of Vivien's. She said Vivien kept it—whatever "it" is—tucked in her purse."

"Can I get a refill out here?" a man yelled from the dining area.

Ginny lifted her head and peeked through the window. "Be out in just a second," she hollered, before turning her focus back to me and asking, "Something in her purse, huh? Do you think Vivien was holding something for them or owed them something?"

"Actually, I think it's much more deviant than that." Since overhearing the conversation, I'd begun putting two and two together and come up with a pretty good reason why Debra might have been so desperate. "Think about it. Even though her husband has a well-paying job, Debra took a job in a place she didn't really want to work. Then, just days after Vivien was murdered, she quit. Now we know she's desperate for whatever was inside that purse."

"Blackmail!" Ginny concluded. "Vivien was blackmailing her, and Debra needed the extra money to pay her off. And the blackmail evidence was in her purse!"

"Exactly." I took a long, satisfying drag of coffee and smiled.

Ginny whipped the list out of her apron and plucked the pen from behind her ear. She started furiously scribbling notes along the side of her chart, then paused and looked up, pen still hovering over the paper. "Wait a minute. You said Maggie was at the Crenshaws' last night and she was also looking for something."

I nodded.

"You think she was being blackmailed, too? Honestly, what would anyone have on her? She's a preacher's wife, for heaven's sake."

I didn't have an answer yet, but a mental image of a barely kilted Scotsman popped to mind along with a racy book cover. Whatever it was Maggie was hiding, Vivien had figured it out and was using it for extortion.

"For cryin' out loud, Ginny! Where's my coffee?" the customer complained again. "Do I have to get it myself?"

Ginny tossed the pen aside and slapped her hands up on the counter. Sticking her head through the window, she yelled, "Would you hold your horses, Randy! I said I'd get you some coffee and I will. Just give me a minute." Turning back to me, she lowered her voice. "Now that I'm thinking about it all, it does sort of make sense that Vivien might resort to extortion. Everyone's been saying her husband's business is in trouble. He owns a few of those quick oil change places, you know? I think he's taken a hit with the economy being the way it is right now."

My mind flashed back to something I'd just heard Nate say about a bank meeting. I made a mental note to get ahold of Hollis. As bank president of Cays Mills's only local bank, he'd more than likely know more about Nate Crenshaw's business than anyone else.

Ginny was still going on, pointing excitedly at her suspect list as she spoke. "If we're right about this, then it's just a matter of figuring out what Vivien had on these ladies."

"And which one had the most to lose," I added, tipping back the rest of my coffee and setting the empty mug on the counter. "For now, though, you'd better get back to work. I think I'll head down the street and see if the sheriff's in her office. We'd better tell her about this latest twist in events. If we're right, she needs to know."

"If we're right?" Ginny said with a set jaw. "Of course we're right. We're close to solving this thing, Nola. I can just feel it." She refolded the paper and crammed it back into her apron. "And don't worry, I'll call Ray this afternoon and fill him in on everything." She snatched up the coffeepot and started back out to the dining area with a little extra bounce in her step, bumping open the door with a swing of her hips.

Neither Maudy nor Travis was at the sheriff's office. Deciding to try to reach them later, I headed back to Peachy Keen to get some work done. Only this time, I found the door unlocked and Cade inside on the ladder, working on putting up the pressed metal ceiling.

"You're here," I said, noticing how his T-shirt stretched tautly over his torso as he reached overhead to place the ceiling panels. Unable to help myself, my eyes lingered a bit, working their way up his muscular arms to the profile of his angular face, which was covered with two-day stubble. His hair was mussed, giving him that just-woke-up look. For some reason, this scruffy look of his was incredibly attractive to me. I imagined how rough his whiskers would feel against my lips.

Flustered by my thoughts, I averted my gaze and cleared my throat. "I didn't think you'd be back today," I added.

He squinted down at me. "Don't you want me here?"

"Of course I do! It's just that it looks like you worked all night. And you got so much done. It's wonderful, thank you."

"You're welcome." He motioned toward a stack of ceiling panels, asking me to hand one to him. "Everything should be wrapped up by the first of next week. That'll give you plenty of time to stock the shelves and put on the finishing touches."

"That's amazing," I replied, stretching to hand him a panel of tiles. Only, it didn't feel all that amazing. Sure, it was good that things were progressing so quickly; just a few days ago, I was stressed we wouldn't finish in time. But the way things were going, I knew I wouldn't see Cade much after the job was finished.

We continued to work in silence, the clicking rhythm of the automatic nail gun piercing the unnerving stillness in regular intervals. Finally, I couldn't take it another minute. I put my hands on my hips, set my jaw and waited.

Finally, he glanced down the ladder. "The next tile panel?" he asked, hand outstretched.

I shook my head. "Cade, I think it's time we talked this through."

"Talked what through?"

"I don't know what. That's the problem." My voice sounded shrill, even though I was trying to stay calm. "Ever since you came back from Macon, you've been acting differently."

His expression tightened, and I noticed a little tick along the line of his jaw. He hesitated a second, then suddenly he was down the ladder and towering in front me. "Why do you care?"

I swallowed hard. Not because I was scared. Although maybe I should have been; anger was evident in his eyes, which were flashing dangerously as he gazed down at me. No, it wasn't fear I was swallowing back but the rush of desire I felt from his closeness. "I . . . I do care."

"Doesn't seem like it. Right after you came back last summer, I thought maybe something might work out with us. We had a couple fun dates, or at least I thought they were fun, then all of a sudden you were busy. Every time I asked you out, there was some new excuse."

He was right. Sort of. I'm sure it did seem that way from his point of view. Really, it was just a matter of poor timing and even poorer communication. Still, I *was* busy at the time. Busy trying to figure out my own life. I'd just made a career change, moved back home after years of independence, took on the task of trying to save my family's business and became entangled in a murder case. That was a whole lot of busy. Still, instead of being honest about my feelings, or asking him to wait, I'd simply put him off.

"I couldn't figure out what your problem was," he was saying, his tone eerily controlled. "Then, I was at this bar one night, up in Macon, and I ran into a friend of yours."

"A friend?"

He tipped his head lower, his eyes searching mine. "That detective guy, Dane Hawkins."

My heart stopped.

"We had a few beers. Yakked it up a bit. He's a nice guy actually."

I nodded, swallowing down a lump in my throat.

"We got to talking about growing up in this area, things we did as kids, people we knew and . . . and then he said something that really surprised me."

"I should have told you. I'm sorry. It's just that we were so young at the time. I just wanted to forget about him and the whole—"

"But you couldn't, could you?" he said, his tone changing from anger to resignation. "It all makes sense to me now. The strange way you started acting when he came into town last summer. The way you always seem flustered when he's around. He's the reason you've been on the run all these years, isn't he?"

I nodded. *Yes, he was the reason.* I hated the hurt it caused Cade, but at least we were getting it all out in the open now.

This was the chance I needed to tell him about my youthful indiscretion, a lost pregnancy, the guilt and shame. . . . I started to feel a huge sense of relief. It was going to be good to come clean and move past all this, finally.

"Does he know?"

"No. I've never told him. Never will."

He shook his head and let out a long sigh. "It's obvious you've been in love with him all these years."

My eyes grew wide. "In love with him? No, that's not true." *Where did he get that idea?* Nothing could be further from the truth.

He turned his shoulder away, holding up one hand. "Come on, Nola. I'm tired of the lies. I saw you two yesterday." He pointed to the front of the store, where he'd seen Hawk removing my splinter. "Right out there."

"That wasn't what it looked like," I started, but Cade shrugged away my explanation and was walking toward the door, his body moving stiffly and his gaze fixed straight ahead. That's when I realized this could be my last chance.

"No!" I reached out and grabbed his arm, turning him to face me. He stared at me, shocked by my outburst, but no more shocked than I was at finally facing him, or was it at openly facing my own past? I swallowed, tried to speak, my mouth suddenly dry . . .

He shook his head, started to turn back, but I held his arm fast and found myself now pleading: "Why doesn't anyone listen to me?"

He scowled. "Listen? To what? You don't talk to anyone, Nola! You think we can read your mind or what? You are standoffish and don't like anything about our community, turning us down or tuning us out time and again, and you expect what in return?"

"It's just . . . nothing ended up the way I meant it to."

He sighed, as if resigned or maybe defeated, and pulled his arm from me. "Yeah, you fell in love with Dane, and he didn't fall in love with you. Well, welcome to the club."

"No!" How could Cade be so wrong? Then a shiver shook me as his words penetrated. He was dead right. How could Cade—or anyone—know what I felt? I never talked, not *really* talked, to anyone. I kept my feelings locked inside a shell of guilt, tangled in years of self-condemnation for a sin I never intended, mixed with resentment that everyone would denounce me or maybe that no one cared enough to ask what was wrong. But would I have told them if they had asked? Could I tell Cade even now, on the brink of losing him forever? Losing him . . . I couldn't lose him. . . .

"I lost the baby." The words slipped out, like a frosty breath, prickling my skin. Instantly tears flooded my eyes. I squeezed them shut, stepping back, ashamed and shaking, hands clasped over my mouth to hold in the sob swelling in my chest.

I sensed Cade step closer, felt his hands take my shoulders, and at his touch the sobbing began as wave after wave of words tumbled out of my mouth in no coherent order: my indiscretion with Dane; an unplanned pregnancy; the overwhelming shame and how I prayed and prayed for the baby to just go away, and then when it did . . . the shock and guilt. Guilt that set me on a course of compensation and atonement for the next fifteen years. Guilt that still lingered and pricked at my soul every time I caught a whiff of my nephew's fresh baby scent, or heard the delight in my twin nieces' surreptitious giggles. I told him everything but never looked him in the eye, never raised my head. Finally, spent of emotions and my tear ducts empty, I looked up at him.

I saw a glisten in the corners of his eyes as he said, "I'd have been there for you," and I knew he was right. All I could do was nod. Then he pulled me close, and finally, a sense of peace that had eluded me all these years washed over me, but all I could say was, "Thank you."

Chapter 10

Debutante Rule #023: To be a successful debutante you have to always look like a lady, even if it means you have to work like a dog to do so.

"I just can't believe the nerve of that Stephanie Wheeler," Mama said in lieu of a greeting as I walked into the kitchen Saturday morning. She was facing the stove, flipping bacon in her cast-iron skillet.

"The congressman's wife? What'd she do?" I let out a sigh and made a beeline for the coffeepot. I'd hardly slept the night before. One minute I was having the most pleasant dreams about Cade's strong arms wrapped around me, and the next I was lying awake, tossing around blackmailing schemes in my mind. It's like I was trying to sleep on an emotional roller coaster, with breathtaking highs and stomach-wrenching lows.

"What didn't she do, you mean?" Mama hissed, giving the bacon strips a hard turn. Obviously Mama had been awake for a while. She was already charged up and ready to take on the world. Not me. My caffeine-depleted brain could hardly make sense of what she was saying, let alone figure out why she was so upset with the congressman's wife. So, I got busy filling my coffee mug as she continued, "We had a cotillion committee meeting yesterday afternoon at the diner. You know, just to make sure all the kinks were ironed out, since the ball is just a week away now." She turned and shook the spatula my way, little spittles of grease hitting the floor. Roscoe scrambled to lap them up.

"No, Roscoe!" I corrected him.

"Don't you dare yell at that sweet thing," Mama admonished before turning a sugary smile toward Roscoe. "You love my cookin', don't ya, boy?"

Oh brother. I opened my mouth to remind her of what happened the last time someone spoiled Roscoe with people food, but I decided against it. There was no reasoning with Mama once she set her mind on something, and she'd gone gaga over the long-eared ball of brown and white fur. Something I could completely understand, I thought, sipping my coffee and staring down at Roscoe with my own fond smile.

Mama turned back to the skillet, asking, "You did get the menu lined up with Ginny, didn't you? 'Cuz I really talked you up at the meetin' yesterday. Told the gals how wonderfully peachy everything was going to be."

"We're working on it." I took a seat at the table and focused on my coffee, avoiding her gaze. Truth was, Ginny and I had been working more on Vivien's murder than the peachy accents for the cotillion dinner, and things were falling behind schedule. I'd meant to stop in on Ezra at Sugar's Bakery to make sure everything was squared away with the cake but had been waylaid by my bittersweet but oh-so-relieving reconciliation with Cade yesterday afternoon.

"Looks like I was right, as usual," Mama said, bringing her coffee mug and a plate of bacon to the table. "You and Cade have worked out your troubles, haven't y'all?" A little raspy giggle escaped as she nibbled on a piece of toast.

My eyes connected with hers as I reached across the table for a piece of bacon. "Yes, we have. And thank you, Mama." I left a lot unsaid, but she knew what I meant. It'd suddenly struck me that I'd probably never outgrow the need for my mama's advice. She was the wisest woman I knew. I wondered if she'd have any insight to my ideas on Vivien's murder.

I was just about to ask when she started back in again. "Getting back to my story. Well, I'm supposed to be in charge of the centerpieces. So, I went in yesterday mornin', just before the meeting, to firm up my plans with Pete over at the flower shop, and guess what? He told me the centerpieces had been changed."

"Changed?"

"Yes, changed. Oh, he was all apologetic and everything. Said Stephanie Wheeler came in last weekend and changed the order. Apparently she didn't approve of my choice of light coral peonies for the centerpieces. She substituted them with peach-tipped white roses. Can you believe the nerve of her?"

I made a few sympathetic noises, but really, what was there to say? Peonies? Roses? Did it really matter all that much? It did to Mama, but to me . . . certainly not compared to murder, a friend wrongly convicted by public opinion and the possibility of blackmail in our little community. I'd been churning blackmail ideas around in my mind all night. It was just a matter of proving some of my theories and I'd be able to help clear my dear friend. I started to tell Mama about my ideas, but she was still complaining about Mrs. Wheeler.

"Right from the get-go I knew it was a mistake to let her have the Peach Cotillion at her place. I told the other gals, too, but they were all caught up in the romantic possibility of having the cotillion at the plantation. Like it's going to be *Gone With the Wind* all over again. And let me tell you what really burns my behind: Stephanie Wheeler's attitude, that's what. The woman's been on the committee for as many years as I can remember, and never once have the Wheelers offered their place for the event. It's obvious they're only doing it this year because Jeb is up for reelection." She ripped the tip of her bacon strip off and tossed it to Roscoe, who practically snatched it in midair. "It's just like tomorrow's Mother-Daughter Tea. Usually it's a simple affair at the diner. Ginny always fixes the place up real nice with tablecloths and special teacups that she keeps stored just for the occasion. But oh no! That wasn't good enough for Stephanie. She insisted that the tea be moved to her place. Can you imagine a garden party in this heat? Those poor girls are going to melt tomorrow."

"You're right about that, Mama," I quickly agreed. Actually, the thought of fancy dress clothes sticking to my body while I sipped hot tea and made polite chitchat was enough to send me running for the hills. Thank goodness I wasn't roped into planning or participating in that event, too. Next weekend's cotillion was going to be about as much "polite society" as I could stand for a while.

While she paused to sip her coffee, I took the opportunity to switch gears. "There's something important I'd like to run by you, if you don't mind."

She quit sipping and gave me her full attention. I went on, "It's about Vivien Crenshaw. You see, yesterday I overheard a conversation between Debra Bearden and Nate Crenshaw," I started, but a knock at the door interrupted me.

Mama turned toward the sound. "Well, who in the world would that be?"

"Shoot!" I glanced at the wall clock, a surge of panic kicking in as I realized I'd lost track of time. "It's Cade. He needed to be out this way on business so he said he'd stop by and pick me up this morning. We're going to work on the shop and then maybe have dinner at his place this evening."

Mama's brows lifted enthusiastically. "Well, doesn't that sound pleasant?" Another knock sounded. Louder this time. I got up to answer the door, but Mama intercepted me. "You're not going to answer the door looking like that, are you?"

I ran my tongue over my teeth and patted my hair. "Well, we can't let him just stand out there, now, can we?"

She cinched her robe tightly and started for the front of the house. "I'll stall him for a few minutes. You run on upstairs and get yourself ready," she said over her shoulder.

I did as she said. As I reached the upstairs hallway, I heard her voice down below. "Well, come on in, Cade. Nola's just upstairs fixin' up a bit so she can look her best for y'all."

Cade and I spent the rest of the morning finishing the tin ceiling panels. Overall, the installation of the embossed metal panels was much easier than I anticipated, and the final result was amazing. I'd chosen a simple hammered tin, which I intended to finish with a coat of antique white paint. Still, even without the paint, the ceiling gave the room just the vintage look I was hoping to achieve. I decided I'd live with them unpainted for the time being. I rather liked the look. Along with the knotty pine floors, simple shelving and exposed brick wall, I thought it created a warm, inviting country look.

Cade moved next to me. "It's really coming together, don't you think?"

I nodded. "Thanks to you. You do nice handiwork, Mr. McKenna."

"Nice handiwork?" He chuckled and turned toward me, moving his hands to my waist and tugging me forward. "That's just another way of saying I'm good with my hands, right?"

I slapped playfully at his arms. "Don't be getting too sure of yourself," I teased, secretly happy that Mama had talked me into putting a little extra effort into my looks that morning. "There's still a lot of work to be done."

His dark eyes gleamed mischievously as he pulled me closer. "Well, let's not waste time, then," he murmured, his lips just inches from mine. But he quickly pulled back and dropped his hands as the door flew open.

I turned just as Emily came rushing inside, stopping in her tracks as soon as she saw Cade and me embracing. "Oh!" she exclaimed, then quickly recovered. "Daddy sent me over to get you," she said, her face masked with worry. "There's something you need to come see right away."

Both Cade and I followed her next door where she led us back to the diner's kitchen. Ginny and Sam were huddled together, their gazes fixed on a purse resting on the stainless steel worktable. It was a beige purse with gold accents.

I recalled the purse that Debra Bearden had been asking Nate about. "That looks like Vivien Crenshaw's purse." My eyes darted between Ginny and Sam. "What's it doing here?"

"I just found it stashed behind those crates we have by the back door," Ginny answered.

"Back there?" I could hardly believe my ears. What would Vivien's purse be doing outside the diner's back door? I shot Ginny a questioning look.

"Don't look at me like that!" she shrieked. "I have no idea how this thing ended up out there. Someone is out to get me, that's for sure."

Sam took charge. "Calm down, honey. Getting hysterical isn't going to help this situation one bit. I'm going to call Ray and tell him what we found." He reached into his apron pocket and took out his cell, pointing it toward Emily. "Sweetie, I need you to go out there and do your best to keep the customers happy while we get to the bottom of things." Then he turned to Cade and asked, "Can you help me out, buddy? There's not much to breakfast. Just eggs, bacon and flapjacks. An occasional order of toast. The hash is already prepared; all you have to do is fry it." He pointed toward the stove. "Grits are in that big double boiler over there. We've got an extra apron hanging on the hook, if ya need it. Just holler if something comes up."

Cade readily agreed, snatching an apron and tying it on. Sam started punching a number into his cell phone. "I'm going to try to reach Ray," he explained as he waited for the call to be picked up, "but one of us needs to call the sheriff soon. Maudy would be ticked if she thought we didn't call her. . . . Ray! Glad I reached you. We've got a problem." Sam held the phone to his ear as he headed toward the office, where he could speak in private. Cade was already at the grill cracking eggs and pouring pancake batter as he squinted at the order tickets.

"This isn't good, is it?" Ginny whispered.

I shook my head. "No, it's not." Leaning in, I inspected the bag. The only thing I could tell for sure was that it was expensive. "Did you touch it a lot?" I asked, thinking of fingerprints.

"Well, yeah. I just saw it and wondered who might have lost her purse, so I opened it. I was just looking for an ID, some way to figure out who it belonged to, you know?"

I nodded. I hadn't told Ginny the specific description of Vivien's purse I'd heard from Debra—so Ginny wouldn't have known whose it was. "Did you see anything else inside?" I asked. "Like . . ." I shrugged. *Like something worth killing for?* I wondered.

Ginny shook her head. "No. Nothing. Just a billfold, lipstick, tissues . . . all the usual stuff."

"Then the killer must have already removed the blackmail

fodder." Which meant he or she would no longer be looking for it. Did that mean Maggie and Debra should be eliminated as suspects since they were looking for whatever was inside the purse? I glanced toward the kitchen's back door. Or, did one of them recently find the purse, remove the item and discard the handbag inside the stack of crates in order to make Ginny look guilty? In reality, anyone could have snuck down the back alley and left the purse there.

Sam came back into the kitchen area, a grim look on his face. "Maudy's on her way over. Ray told me to call her immediately but not to answer any of her questions until he gets here. He's leaving Perry now."

"I think that's good advice," Cade commented from the grill, where he was juggling a pile of breakfast hash, a heap of scrambled eggs and several rows of pancakes. Amazingly, he was keeping it all together.

Sam crossed over to Ginny and put his arm around her. "Don't worry, honey. We're going to get this worked out. You'll see."

Ginny wrapped her arms around his middle and buried her head in his chest. "Sure hope so. 'Cuz with this red hair of mine, I'd look just awful in one of those orange jumpsuits."

"That's not going to happen," I reassured her. "Ray will see to it."

"She's here," Cade said, peering through the pass-through window out into the diner. "And the deputy's with her."

Before he could get another word out, the kitchen door swung open and Maudy sauntered in, gun belt jingling and Stetson low on her forehead. Next to her, Travis was staring wide-eyed at the purse. Maudy inhaled, her lips forming a little sneer as she asked, "Well, what do we have here?"

"Vivien Crenshaw's purse," Ginny explained with a wobbly voice.

Maudy removed her hat, tucked her chin and raised her brows. "Is that so?" Then she looked over at her deputy with a smirk. "This, Travis," she started, "is what I call the missing key."

"Yes, ma'am," he replied, shifting his feet anxiously. "The victim's purse. Could be the purse she supposedly had with her the night she was murdered."

"Could be," Maudy replied, swiping her tongue over her bottom lip. She slid a sly glance toward Ginny. "How exactly did you get it?"

Sam kept one arm around Ginny as she answered. "I found it inside a stack of crates outside the back door."

"Ginny," Sam interrupted. "I don't think you should answer any more questions until Ray gets here."

Maudy snorted and shot Sam a dirty look before going back after Ginny. "Decided to call your lawyer, huh? Why's that? Got something to hide?"

Ginny shook her head. "No, it's just Ray advised me to call if anything else came up with the case. I'm sure this is just one more attempt to frame me. You know I'm not capable of murder, right? I mean, we've known each other practically all our lives."

Maudy scowled. "All I know is you're in possession of a crucial piece of evidence, possibly stolen from the crime scene, and you're not willin' to answer any of my questions. Seems suspicious to me." She glanced over her shoulder. "Seem suspicious to you, Travis?"

Travis removed his hat and ran a hand over his hair. He must have recently gotten a haircut; the longer strands in the back looked evenly trimmed around the collar, and his ears sported bright white walls around the tops. "Yes, ma'am. It does seem a bit suspicious."

Maudy nodded and turned back around, leveling her gaze

on Ginny. We all stood there for a second, in a silent standoff. Even Cade stopped grilling and was watching intently from the sidelines.

Maudy, I'm sure, was hoping for Ginny to break down, but Sam's grip tightened around her waist, encouraging her to hold strong. I was struggling with my own self-control, wanting more than anything to jump in and defend Ginny. I was also kicking myself for not heading over to the sheriff's office first thing this morning and reporting my suspicions about Vivien being a blackmailer. If I had, this whole fiasco might have been avoided. I was going to keep my mouth shut now, though. Better to let Ray lay out all the facts and deal with the sheriff in his lawyerly way.

Finally, Maudy broke the silence with a long, dramatic sigh. "Well, I guess I have no choice, then." She nodded at Travis. "Let's take her in. She can sit in a cell and wait for her lawyer to get here."

"You can't do that!" Ginny shrieked. "The Mother-Daughter Tea's this afternoon." She glanced at the wall clock. "In just a few hours actually!"

Sam jumped in. "Ease up, Maudy. For Pete's sake, we called you as soon as we found the purse. Doesn't that prove we're not trying to hide anything?"

Out of the corner of my eye, I caught Cade frantically motioning for me. I scurried over to the grill and glanced through the window to the dining room. Frances Simms was standing just outside the kitchen door, camera in hand, ready for any action that might come her way.

Behind me, Ginny's voice was coming in loud and clear. "I can't believe you're doing this to me. You know I'm not a killer!" Ginny said, struggling against Travis's grip as he dragged her toward the door that led out to the diner.

I started to suggest they use the back door, but it was too late. Travis burst through the door, pulling Ginny behind him. Frances's camera flashed like lightning as she clicked off several shots. At least it was probably too late to sneak them into today's edition of the *Cays Mill Reporter*. It'd be Tuesday before we'd see them.

I ran through the kitchen to catch up to them just as Emily cried out, "Mama! What's going on?" She left her customer hanging and ran to her mother's side, her face twisted with worry. The diner went dead silent. Again, several flashes from Frances's camera lit up the area, capturing Emily as she clung to one side of her mother, Travis on the other.

I stepped up and placed my hand over the camera's lens. "Take one more picture and you'll regret it," I threatened. Frances's birdlike eyes popped with surprise, but she let go of the camera, letting it dangle from the strap around her neck.

Maudy held up her hand and assumed her professional persona. "Everyone stay clear now. This is official police business."

I rolled my eyes. *Great.* That was sure to get tongues wagging.

Turning back to Ginny, I saw her shake off Travis and pull Emily close. "Don't you worry, sweetie," she said. "Ray's on his way, and he'll get to the bottom of this." She glanced over Emily's shoulder at me. "But I may be just a little late for the tea. Don't fret, though, 'cuz Nola will take you until I can get there. Won't ya, Nola Mae?"

"The tea?" I was barely able to utter the words, my jaw was so slack from the shock of the discovered purse, Ginny's arrest, Frances still skulking on the sidelines, and what is Ginny worried over? The tea! And she wanted me to take Emily? Inside my head, my mind came up with all sorts of reasons why that wasn't a good idea, but my mouth must have had a will of its own, because I heard myself mutter, "Sure, I'd be happy to." Compared to everything else going on, why not?

"But you'll be there as soon as you can, right Mama?" Emily asked, her voice sounding much younger than her seventeen years.

Sam stepped up with a brave smile. "Of course she will, sweetie. Don't worry, this will all be straightened out in no time."

Chapter 11

Debutante Rule #010: A debutante's tea isn't just sweet; it's sugar-shocked. And, that's the way we like it.

Sputtering into place in the long row of luxury sedans and decked-out SUVs, I put the truck in park and shifted in my seat, adjusting the straps of my dress and straightening my windblown hair. I started cranking up the window and motioned for Emily to do the same. The Harper Farm truck had a model 2-70 air conditioning—crank down the two windows and drive seventy.

"I wish more than anything that Mama could be here right now, but since she can't, I'm grateful you're here," Emily said. Her long auburn braid swung beneath her wide-brimmed hat with a two-toned pink bow that perfectly matched her pink and white flowered sundress.

"Sure," I replied, trying to smile through my misery while I eased my feet back into the high heels I'd kicked off en route. I sighed, preferring a clunky pair of field boots any day over these instruments of torture. Still, it was just a streak of luck that I had anything to wear at all. After learning that I'd be going to tea, I had Cade run me back out to the farm. By the time I got there, I only had an hour or so to get presentable. Not an easy feat for a gal with a limited wardrobe selection.

Emily nodded toward the walk where staff members were waiting to escort guests to the party area. "Guess we should head on in, huh?" she asked, making eye contact with a young man dressed in black pants and a white shirt. He skipped over to the truck and opened the door for her.

Another young man was making his way toward my side, but I waved him off and climbed out on my own, turning back at the last minute to grab a small-brimmed black cloche-styled hat I'd borrowed from Hattie a few frantic moments before we left town. I hadn't known hats were mandatory until I'd already picked up Emily and we were on our way. Luckily, the hat's large showpiece silk flower was the perfect complement to my all-purpose black dress.

We were escorted up the steps to the multi-columned porch and through ornate double oak doors where Stephanie Wheeler was greeting guests. Despite the heat, she looked cool and fresh in a pale yellow chiffon dress and a vintage straw hat. Several uniformed housemaids stood behind her, peeling off one by one to escort small groups of chortling women through the home and, I presumed, out to the back gardens. I watched in amazement as Stephanie greeted each guest by name, warmly grasping their hands and making pleasant comments about this and that. She was definitely charming—an indispensable asset for a politician's wife.

As we made it to the front of the line, she reached out and shook Emily's hand. "Hello, Emily and . . . ?" Her brows furrowed quizzically.

I quickly introduced myself and explained, "Something's come up and I'm standing in for Emily's mama."

"I hope nothing's wrong," Stephanie remarked with concern.

Both Emily and I hesitated, unsure what to say. Finally, I mumbled something about Ginny having another obligation, and we moved through the line where a young woman, not much older than Emily, smiled warmly and offered to escort us to the gardens.

For years, I'd admired the Wheeler Plantation from afar, always wondering what lay beyond the impressive white columns, deep porch and magnificent two-story colonnade. Unfortunately, our attendant was moving us so quickly from the foyer and through the main hall, I was getting whiplash trying to see everything. I did, however, slow my pace enough to catch a glimpse of a study with dark-paneled walls and floor-to-ceiling bookcases. Then, a few steps later, we veered off to the right and into a large sunny room with pale yellow walls and airy drapes flanking a row of doors leading to the garden.

"Oh my!" I heard Emily exclaim as she took in the expanse of the room. My own eyes were immediately drawn across the room to a painting hanging above the marble fireplace. It portrayed a formidable man with wavy black hair, a sternly set jaw, and hauntingly piercing eyes that matched the confederate gray of his officer's uniform.

"I see you've met General Aloysius Wheeler," the young woman said, noticing my interest in the painting. "Mr. and Mrs. Wheeler are so proud of that portrait."

It reminded me of a scary movie I'd once seen where the portrait's eyes moved. I couldn't catch myself before a little shiver belied my feelings about it. I glanced quickly at the housemaid, but with a little grin she leaned in and whispered, "Agreed. I for one would be happier if they hung it in the attic, or someplace where I wouldn't have to look at it all day. Gives me the creeps." She stood upright and shook her head. "But, the general is Congressman Wheeler's claim to fame. You see that framed letter next to the portrait?"

I squinted, noting a faded parchment written in fancy script. The paper itself appeared wafer thin and yellow in spots. "It looks really old," I commented.

"I'd say!" she enthused. "It's a commendation from Mr. Robert E. Lee himself. Thanking General Wheeler for his outstanding service to the Confederate cause. Why, the congressman's practically built his entire political career on the coattails of his famous ancestor."

I nodded, vaguely recalling General Wheeler from my high school history class. I couldn't quite remember the whole story, but something about the general thwarting Union forces and saving much of our area from the devastation of Sherman's torch. Though I now had to wonder if maybe he scared away those Yanks with his steely eyes.

The young housemaid beckoned us through the doors and outside. A large patio of massive flagstone slabs set under the shade of an expansive white pergola was set with a dozen cloth-covered round tables. Two massive flower-filled urns marked wide steps leading down to the lower garden where the debutantes were playing a lively game of croquet. Next to me, Emily raised up on her tiptoes a couple times and anxiously smoothed away invisible wrinkles in her dress.

As if on cue, the other mothers, dispersed about the patio in tight little groups, glanced at the steps to see the newcomers to the tea. The giggly group to my left—I didn't recognize anyone there—gave us only cursory looks, slight nods and went back to their high-pitched sniggering about who knows what. The cool-looking mothers straight ahead, with their designer dresses, glitzy jewelry and expensive hand-bags, offered Emily an approving glance then gave a quick inhale at my all-black outfit, which, I had to admit, looked like a black eye in the sea of pastel colors. Off to the right, a small group of whisperers sent darting looks our way; their covert pointing told me they had obviously been awaiting Emily's appearance, further fuel for their gossip about Ginny. I sighed; at least only that one group seemed aware of Ginny's current situation. So far.

"Go ahead," I told Emily, nodding toward the other girls.

She looked at me with a worried look. "I hate to leave you up here by yourself." She glanced at the less-than-welcoming women. "You probably don't know anyone here."

With no children of my own, I wasn't well acquainted with many of the mothers in town, but I certainly knew a few from the dinner rehearsal at the diner. Like Debra and Maggie, who would both certainly be here with their daughters. And maybe if I got lucky, I could corner the two and gauge their reactions when I mentioned that Vivien's purse had been found. "Don't be silly," I said, waving her away and snatching a glass of iced tea off the tray of a passing waiter. "I can hold my own."

Emily eagerly nodded and bounded down the steps to join her friends. I stared after her like a mother hen, until I saw her happily involved in conversation with a couple other debutantes. Then, sipping my tea, I scanned the crowd for a group of my own to join; and right in the middle of the scandalmongers stood Debra Bearden—just the person I was hoping to run into today.

"Hey all," I said, sidling up to the group and doing my best to smoothly insinuate myself. "Isn't this home just gorgeous? And the gardens." I sighed dramatically. "So lovely." I was trying to imitate what my sister, Ida, would say in such a situation. I'd watched her sweet-talk her way through numerous social soirees over the years. She was a master mingler. Unfortunately, my own sweet talk wasn't winning over this group. One of the women simply raised her chin and moved in closer to the gal next to her, squeezing me out while she bent in to whisper something to her friend. But another stepped forward, her mint green taffeta dress rustling like a snake slithering through grass. "Nola, isn't it? How nice of you to bring Emily. And at such an"—she cast a sly glance at her compatriots, who now all hung on her words—"well, an awkward time for her family."

Behind the woman, Debra's eyes twinkled with devilish delight as I opened my mouth to respond and found no words. I took a sip of tea, something I'd seen Mama do strategically when collecting her thoughts in such situations, then smiled and said brightly, "I'm just so pleased to be here." Yeah, right. I thought I'd passed their bait successfully only to see Debra now step forward as well. I braced myself.

I squinted at Debra, wondering if she knew the purse she'd so desperately been looking for had been discovered. Then again, maybe she did know. Maybe she'd somehow found the purse since her desperate conversation with Nate by the fountain, taken what she needed and ditched it behind the diner to frame Ginny. Who knew? One thing was for sure: it burned my butt to know these gals were talking about Ginny with malicious smiles. I drew in my breath, ready to set these women straight, when I noticed everyone gawking at something behind me.

Turning, I saw Stephanie had walked into the patio area, her hand resting on the suit jacket of a handsome man. I'd never met Congressman Wheeler before, but I recognized those piercing gray eyes of his immediately. They were identical to the ones I'd just seen minutes ago in the portrait of General Wheeler.

"Ladies," Stephanie called out. "If y'all would please be seated, I have a surprise announcement."

An excited murmur hummed through the crowd as everyone shuffled to find a chair. I immediately homed in on Debra, intent on sitting at the same table so I could pump her for information, but I was waylaid by Emily. "Look," she said, pointing back toward the French doors. "Belle Jones is here. Let's sit with her and her mama," she said. I readily agreed, sliding my eyes back toward Debra, who'd chosen a table with one of her cronies. They were still whispering between each other, casting furtive glances our way. By now, they probably had Ginny tried, convicted and sentenced.

Belle and Emily slipped into easy conversation as we settled at the table. Maggie, not so much. She seemed preoccupied, or maybe it was distracted, as her gaze darted about the room. I noticed her mouth was drawn tightly, lines etching her normally smooth face as she toiled nervously with the edge of the table covering. A waiter brought by two glasses of tea. Without tasting, Maggie stirred in a couple teaspoons of sugar, her spoon clinking against the glass. "Where's Ginny?" she asked, glancing around.

"Something's come up and she's running a little late. I'm just holding down the fort until she gets here. Is everything okay with you?"

Maggie set her spoon aside and sat a little straighter. "Of course. But . . . is there something going on that I should know about?" she asked, touching the brim of her pillbox hat, making sure it was securely fastened over the tightly woven bun at the nape of her neck. "Everyone keeps looking at me."

Everyone was looking at Emily and me—word about

Ginny being hauled off with the sheriff was getting around fast. The ladies who had been whispering in Debra's group had now joined other mothers at tables, and the gossip was spreading like honey on hot toast. But Maggie and Belle had joined the party at the last minute, so they hadn't been privy to the latest gossip, and I wasn't about to tell them. I made a point of looking around before answering, "If anything they're admiring your beautiful hat. Where'd you get it?"

Maggie ducked her chin modestly, but a slight smile tugged at the corners of her mouth. "Up in Atlanta. My husband and I were up there last year for Church Leadership Conference and . . . well, it caught my eye. I'm afraid I splurged a bit."

"Well, good for you. Everyone deserves a little treat now and then."

Maggie nodded and smiled politely, her eyes drifting over my shoulder to where Stephanie and the congressman had positioned themselves at the front of the patio. Stephanie cut through the low din of conversation by demurely clapping her fingers against her palm, "Ladies, if I could have your attention please. I'm delighted to announce that my husband, Congressman Wheeler, has decided to take a few minutes from his busy schedule to talk with us today. As soon as he's through speaking, refreshments will be served." She flashed a dazzling smile and made a sweeping gesture. "So, please, sit back and enjoy."

An enthusiastic applause arose from the tables as the congressman stepped forward and prepared to speak. Out of the corner of my eye, I caught a glimpse of two dark-clothed figures near one of the pergola's posts. I turned my head and squinted. One of them was Hawk. He stood out like a sore thumb, with black trousers and a black T-shirt that clung to his pumped-up muscles. His eyes met mine, and I shot him a quick wave, which he answered by widening his stance and folding his arms across his chest. I swallowed down a round of giggles that threatened to escape.

"It's an honor to open our home for this year's cotillion," the congressman was saying. "It's just one of the small ways that my beautiful wife, Stephanie, and I"—he paused and cast a loving look toward his wife, soliciting a few "awws" from the crowd—"can give back to our community. . . ." Blah, blah, blah. I sighed. Mama was right. This whole venue was nothing more than a ploy to gain votes. Tuning out his speech, I let my mind wander as I looked out over the yard, which rolled gently down to the Ocmulgee River. Off to the right, an ornately carved bench rested under the low-dipping branches of a massive live oak. For a second, I imagined lovely belles in hooped-skirted gowns frolicking about, their white-gloved hands clasping dainty parasols.

I focused back just in time to hear the congressman wrapping up his speech. He stood with his chin held high and his hands clasping his lapels as he said, "As my great grandfather, General Aloysius Wheeler, would have said, 'It's only through kind Providence and the humble spirit of graciousness that I strive to serve the people of this great state of Georgia.'"

A spirited applause erupted from the group. I clapped lightly, glancing around, wondering what all these people saw in the man. Personally, I didn't trust the guy. I shook my head, feeling guilty about my knee-jerk reaction. What was my problem? I'd never even met the man before. Nor did I disagree with his politics. So why did I distrust him so much? Cade was right when he said that I had trust issues, a habit I'd probably picked up from working as a humanitarian. The thing with emergency relief work is that it's usually conducted in situations where some sort of evil or natural disaster has broken down all pretenses of civil society. A smiling government official could be the front man for the very powers that were shooting innocent civilians. The willing hands helping to unload relief supplies could be the same hands that would transport them to a black market for easy cash. You had to know who you were dealing with and keep alert at all times. Over the years, I'd learned to be cautious, keep my guard up and trust few. Now I recognized just how much my work had changed me. But I was home now, back in the States, away from the horrors and fears of those years. It was time to change. Yup, I needed to work on that. Starting with the congressman.

I adjusted my attitude and clapped enthusiastically as the congressman tossed us one final wave before disappearing back into the house, Dane and the other security man falling in step behind him.

Then, as if on cue, several pairs of waitstaff, dressed in the same black pants and white shirts as the valets, entered the patio carrying large trays of tiered plates filled with finger sandwiches and petit fours, one for each table. Emily's eyes gleamed as she took in the fancy arrangement of food. Other waiters then stepped forward, steaming porcelain teapots in hand. They tipped delicately with their right hands, holding the spouts over the white tea towels draped on their left arms. Each filling of a cup was finished with a little lifting of the spout, a flourish and a nod. For a second, I became caught up in the formality of the experience, feeling like a pampered princess. "This sure is fancy, isn't it?" I whispered to Maggie.

"Yes, lovely," she mumbled, staring blankly into her tea.

Glancing across the table at the girls and assuring myself that they were fully engrossed in their own conversation, I shifted in my chair and leaned closer to Maggie. "Did you hear about what happened at the diner this morning?"

She looked up with dull eyes. "No. What?"

"They found Vivien Crenshaw's purse."

Her eyes darted briefly toward Belle before refocusing on me. Lowering her voice, she leaned in and asked, "Her purse? Who found it? Where?" She seemed genuinely surprised by the news.

"Ginny found it in the alley behind the diner. The sheriff has it now." I didn't bring up the fact that she took Ginny in for questioning.

Maggie's lower lip trembled slightly as she continued to stare at me for a couple beats before averting her gaze downward to her plate. She grew silent, fidgeting with her untouched food.

"Anyway," I added nonchalantly, "it may prove to be a break in the case."

"A break in the case," she echoed, her voice barely a whisper. She pushed her chair back abruptly and started to stand. "If y'all would excuse me for a second, I need to make a quick phone call." She snatched her clutch off the table and started toward the patio doors.

"Is Mama upset about something?" Belle asked, wide-eyed with concern.

"No, I'm sure everything's fine," I assured her, folding my napkin and placing it next to my plate. "But I'll go and check on her just to make sure."

I'd just stood and started after her when Ginny appeared in the doorway, wearing a black-and-white polka-dot dress and a wide-brimmed white hat that contrasted with her red hair. Emily let out a little gasp. "Mama!" she cried, jumping out of her seat and rushing toward the patio doors, grasping her mother's arm and tugging her toward the table. The patio grew silent as everyone turned Ginny's way. By the look of things, the news of Ginny being hauled away by the sheriff had run the gamut; there wasn't a single lady, including our hostess, who wasn't gawking at Ginny like she was some sort of apparition.

Oh boy, I thought, suddenly divided on whether I should take off in pursuit of Maggie or hang back and help defend my friend against the throng of loose-lipped ladies. But I needn't have worried. In her typical fashion, Ginny bucked the onslaught of caustic glares by straightening her shoulders and lifting her chin defiantly before weaving through the tables with unshakable confidence.

I stepped aside from the chair, holding it out for her as she approached the table. "Everything okay?"

"Yes, thanks to that brother of yours," she whispered back. Then, quickly glancing around the patio, she added, "I take it the word's out?"

"Yes, out and traveling fast. I haven't seen today's edition of the *Cays Mill Reporter*," I hedged.

She waved her hand through the air. "Nothing interesting. But I'm dreading Tuesday's edition. Especially after the pictures Frances must have got this morning."

I nodded discreetly toward Emily. "Well, at least she's doing fine. Especially now that you're here." I motioned for Ginny to take my chair. After she settled, I leaned down and said, "I could stick around a little longer if you want."

Ginny glanced up with a brave smile. "Thank you, Nola, but I'll be just fine. But would you mind terribly if I canceled for tonight? I'm afraid I'm just not up to working on the menu today. I'm exhausted. But tomorrow, for sure. Regular time."

I placed a hand on her shoulder. "Of course. I understand. I should probably spend some time with Ray anyway. I haven't seen much of him lately."

She shook her head. "Sorry, hon. He's already left. Said something about a dinner engagement tonight." She reached up and squeezed my hand. "Thanks for everything today.

You're a good friend, Nola. Now get going," she said, shooing me toward the door. "Certainly you've got better things to do than hang out here."

Back inside the Wheeler home, I searched the sunroom and adjacent hallway for Maggie but didn't see her anywhere. In the main hallway, waitstaff whizzed by, carrying trays of sandwiches and other treats toward the patio while I pretended to linger and admire the artwork—mostly colorful renditions of Civil War scenes. I recalled seeing a collection similar to this one hanging in Doc Harris's waiting room.

"My boss is a huge Civil War buff," came a voice from behind.

I turned to face Hawk. "Sure seems that way. Liking your new job?"

"It's a job," he said with a frown. "What are you doing in here anyway? Looking for the bathroom?"

"No, I was actually looking for someone." I described Maggie to him. "Have you seen her?"

"Yeah, she came in a few minutes ago, asked me where the restroom was. You can cut through here. There's a hall-way off the far wall that leads to the kitchen. The bathroom's on the right."

"Great," I replied, shooting him a quick wave and head-ing off in that direction.

The bathroom door was shut, so I folded my arms and leaned against the wall to wait for Maggie. From my vantage point, I could see directly into the kitchen, where several employees were bustling about, pouring tea into pots and filling plates. They were generating quite a bit of noise, but even at that, I could hear Maggie's voice inside the bathroom as she spoke on her cell to someone. I moved closer, pressing my ear against the door and catching a spurt of her conversation. "But it'll only be a matter of time before everyone finds out, and it'll ruin my husband. . . ." I stood upright as a server walked by and gave me a strange look. Then suddenly, the doorknob jostled and Maggie emerged from behind the door.

"There you are! Is everything okay?" I asked, noticing the puffiness around her eyes.

"Yes, of course," she replied, trying to move past me.

I shifted to block her way. "Are you sure? You seem upset about something?"

A perturbed look crossed her face. "Thank you for your concern, Nola. But it's personal." Again, she started past me, obviously anxious to get away.

"Did Vivien know something about you, Maggie? Something you were afraid she might tell everyone?" I asked.

She turned toward me, her face tight with tension. "That's ridiculous. Why would you say something like that?"

I took a step closer, wishing there was an easier way to approach the topic. I hated to hurt Maggie's feelings, but I needed to get to the bottom of things. "Because I think it's true. That's why you became so upset when you learned her purse had been found this morning. There was something she was keeping in her purse that would be terribly embarrassing to you, wasn't there?"

Maggie took a step backward, her eyes widening, but she quickly recovered. With an upward turn of her chin, she launched into fervent denial. "You're acting crazy, Nola."

"Am I?" I hesitated, then decided I needed to come right out with it. "Was Vivien blackmailing you?"

"Extortion! Why, maybe that's something you came across while traipsing through third-world countries, but you're back in civilization now. Things like that don't happen around these parts."

"Things like what, Maggie? Murder?"

"Are you suggesting that I . . ."

"No, I don't think you killed Vivien Crenshaw. But if you were being blackmailed, then it's more than likely someone else was, too. Someone with more to lose. Someone who decided to permanently remove the threat of exposure by murdering Vivien." I paused to let the implication sink in before continuing, "Perhaps if you went to the sheriff, told her about what you know, it might convince her to take a look at other possibilities, maybe consider other suspects." Someone other than Ginny, hopefully. "In fact, if the wrong person is convicted of this crime because you held back evidence . . ." I left the rest unsaid, allowing her to fill in the blank.

"Evidence?" Maggie echoed. Her face took on a pained expression, and she started wringing her hands. For a second I thought she was going to cave, but suddenly she pulled her shoulders back and leveled her gaze. "I don't appreciate your impertinence, Nola Mae. Your mama would be ashamed of you speaking to the preacher's wife this way." With that, she turned on her heel and stomped away.

For a second, I wondered what had caused her to flip-flop so quickly, but then I noticed Stephanie Wheeler was hovering in the entrance to the kitchen. I hoped she hadn't overheard our conversation. How embarrassing for Maggie if she had.

"Hello, Mrs. Wheeler," I said, feeling a bit awkward. "It's been a wonderful party, thank you."

"I'm so glad you've enjoyed yourself." She looked down the hall where Maggie had stormed off. "Mrs. Jones seemed upset. I hope it's not something I've done."

I waved her off. "Oh no. Nothing like that. Everything about this afternoon has been just lovely. She's just going through something personal, I think."

Stephanie's expression seemed to relax. "Is there something I can do for you?" she asked, pointing toward the kitchen. "More tea, perhaps? Or something else to eat?"

"Oh, that's okay. But thank you." Gosh, did this woman have Southern hospitality down pat, or what? "I was actually just filling in for Ginny today, and she's here now, so I'll just be on my way. Thanks again," I said, taking a step backward. Only when I turned to leave, I ran smack into Hawk. He placed his hands on my shoulders to steady me.

"There you are, Mr. Hawk," Stephanie said from behind. "Be a dear and show Ms. Harper to the door, will ya? I really should be getting back to my other guests." Then, she graciously added, "It's been lovely meeting you, Ms. Harper. Please do come back anytime."

As soon as we were outside, I took a deep cleansing breath and yanked off my hat. "Thank goodness that's over with," I said, running my fingers through my hair. I probably had the worse hat head ever, but I couldn't stand the thing one second longer. "For the life of me, I can't see why women like these types of things." I rolled my eyes and added, "So boring and stuffy."

"You think that's boring, you ought to work security for these people."

"Not liking your new job?"

He shrugged. "It's just not what I thought it would be." We'd reached my truck. I opened my purse and retrieved my keys. "I hired on for security, but I'm more like an errand boy," he continued, taking the keys and unlocking the door for me.

"Errand boy? What do you mean?"

He held the door. "Well, I act as security when the congressman goes out, but when he's here at the house, the missus finds other things for me to do. Like this morning, I had to help the kitchen staff set up for this shindig, and yesterday she had me cleaning out the attic ballroom for the dance. I even hauled a bunch of junk down to the church for her."

"Sounds more like grunt work than security," I sympathized. The front door opened, and the other security guard walked out, crossed the drive and hopped into a dark SUV with darkened windows. "How's your coworker?"

Hawk shrugged. "Franco? Better off than me, that's for sure. Haven't seen him doing any crap jobs. 'Course he's been with the congressman for a few years. Maybe it's a seniority thing."

"Maybe things will get more exciting closer to election time," I offered. I started to get into the truck, struggling to figure out a way to lift my leg high enough to climb into my seat without having to hike up my dress.

Hawk watched with amusement. "Need a boost?" He started to reach for my hips.

I slapped his hand away. "No, thanks. I can manage."

He raised his hands in mock surrender and stepped back, watching with a smirk as I turned this way and that. Finally, I gave up, lifted the hem of my dress to my thighs and clumsily worked myself into the seat. Midway, I glanced over my shoulder and caught him ogling my legs. Sliding behind the wheel, I adjusted my dress and shot him a dirty look. He answered with another smirk and a solicitous wink.

Chapter 12

Debutante Fact #064: There's one thing debutantes should know about religion: Good Baptists always recognize one another at church, but never at the bar.

Sunday morning before church, Mama loaded me down with a large coffee thermos and a bag of carefully wrapped muffins to take out to the orchard for the workers. Roscoe tagged along, his short, stubby legs propelling him forward on the grassy path between the rows as his nose hugged the ground in search of interesting scents. Every once in a while, I turned around to make sure he was still following. I'd found out the hard way that one tempting whiff could set him off on a wild goose chase.

As I walked, I basked in the feel of the warm sun on my shoulders and inhaled the familiar smell of fresh-cut grass mixed with the tanginess of ripening peaches. Every once in a while, I'd hear the hollow din of doves as they called out their morning greeting. Spring had always been my favorite season on the farm. I had such fond memories of spring morning walks with Daddy, each of us kids following him as he wandered the orchards testing peaches for readiness. We'd squeal with excitement when he picked the first ripe gems of the season, holding them out for us to taste and laughing as peach juice dribbled down our chins.

This was my first harvest since coming back home last summer, and I was too busy with other aspects of the business to help pick peaches. Not that I minded running Harper's Peach Products. In many ways it was just as satisfying to take our peaches and turn them into a product that could be enjoyed any time of year. It was like providing people with a bite of summer all year long. Still, I missed the familiar earthy connection I'd always felt after spending the day working the crop.

Suddenly, the rumbling of the bin tractor coming down the path caused Roscoe to whimper and scamper for my heels. "Fraidy cat," I teased, squatting down next to him and running my hand along his fur for comfort. Manny Rosales maneuvered the tractor alongside us and cut the engine.

"Good morning, Nola." He nodded hopefully toward my bag. "Something from your mama?"

"Sure is," I said, pulling out a muffin and holding it out to him. "Peach streusel muffins; still warm, too."

He graciously accepted my offering, biting in and rolling his eyes with pleasure. I retrieved a paper cup from the bag and poured some coffee from the thermos. "Is that your first pick of the day?" I asked, eyeing the packed bins in the back of the trailer.

"Yes, ma'am. We're on the second round in the west orchard and will probably start picking the Sunbrite peaches this afternoon."

I nodded. Peaches were picked in rounds, starting at the top of the tree where the fruit ripened first. Workers would pick only peak fruit, leaving the rest to mature until a later date. Eventually, after three or four rounds, the entire tree would be harvested. The whole process could take up to two weeks per variety, with pickers rotating through the orchards to ensure that all fruit was harvested at the height of ripeness.

"Your papa's working us hard today," he added with a grin, finishing off the last of his muffin and reaching over to shove the tractor into gear.

"How's he holding up?" I asked. Sometimes I worried about my daddy working too hard. Just last summer the doctor told him to take it easy, even recommended a vacation so he could rest up a bit.

Manny thumped his fist against his chest. "Don't worry. Mr. Harper's a strong man," he assured me. Then he cranked the engine to life and took off with a spurt and puff of blue smoke. Like many things around the farm, the old tractor had seen better days. But hadn't we all, I thought, my daddy flashing to mind. He'd hinted more than a few times that he and Mama were ready to retire. I knew they were hoping I'd take over the farm, since Ray was busy with his law firm and Ida had her own life with Hollis and the kids. Guess I was their last hope of preserving our family heritage. Not that I was feeling pressure or anything.

"Come on, boy," I beckoned to Roscoe as I continued down the row toward the work site. A few minutes later, I came upon the crew. They were busy packing peaches into front packs that were strapped to their bellies like baby carriers.

Daddy spied me as he was emptying his peaches into one of the bins. "Hey, darlin'."

"Hey, Daddy." I eyed the way he was rubbing his lower back. "You doing okay? Are you working too hard?"

"Now don't you get started on me, Nola Mae. I get enough of that from your mama. She's always fussin' at me. Says I'm too old for this, too old for that."

"Sorry, but it wouldn't hurt to take a break and sit down

for a while." I held up my wares, trying to entice him away from his work. "Mama sent coffee and muffins."

"Tempting, but I best not." He glanced up at the tree branches. "They're really coming on fast. It's the heat. If we don't get this entire parcel picked today, they'll over ripen and we'll lose money."

I nodded. "Take it you won't be coming in for the noon meal, then?"

"No, we're going to have to take our lunch out here. Let your mama know, okay?"

I didn't even try to talk him out of it. Mama would be furious that he was missing Sunday brunch, but once Daddy decided on something, there was no changing his mind. So, I left the goodies, waved good-bye to a couple of the fellows and called Roscoe. We'd barely started back to the house before he let out a high-pitched howl and took off through the trees. "Roscoe!" I called. "Come back here!" *For heaven's sake, what does he smell now?*

But I didn't have to wonder for long, because I spied Joe Puckett up ahead working over one of the trees and filling a large white bucket with peaches. Roscoe reached him first, jumping anxiously against his legs. Joe immediately took out a piece of jerky from the reserve he kept stashed away in the front pocket of his bib overalls and offered it to an eager Roscoe. "I see you have a friend visitin'," he said as I approached.

"You remember Roscoe, don't you?"

Roscoe rolled onto his back, eliciting a belly rub from Joe. "'Course I remember Roscoe. I might not be standin' here if it weren't for this little fellow." True, Roscoe—or more accurately, Roscoe's nose—saved Joe from taking a chest full of buckshot last summer. "Only he's not so little anymore. Looks 'bout full grown," Joe was saying. "Is he a good coon dog?"

"Heck if I know. You'd have to ask his owner. I'm just taking care of him for a few days." I nodded toward his bucket. "Preparing to make a batch of brew?" Joe lived in a shack in the woods that bordered our property on a piece of land his granddaddy won—"fair and square," as Joe liked to say—from my granddaddy over a hundred years ago. The Puckett family had lived a self-sufficient lifestyle on the land ever since. Somewhere along the line, my father struck a deal with Joe, allowing him to take as many peaches as he needed to continue making his special brew—a sort of peach-infused corn whiskey that people around these parts referred to as peach shine. Much like the legally distilled Peach Jack that my Daddy was so fond of, but a whole lot more potent.

"You bet," he replied, reaching up high with his good arm to squeeze a peach. Satisfied, he plucked it from the branch and placed it in his bucket. "What do y'all call this type again?"

"Sunbrites."

He rubbed at his whiskers. "Sunbrites, eh? Well, they're my favorites."

"Mine, too." The Sunbrite was a firm yellow flesh peach, great for making cobblers and pies. Apparently they made good hooch, too. I picked a few more and added them to his bucket. "Ms. Purvis suggest any good books lately?" I asked, noticing his face light up when I mentioned the librarian's name.

"As a matter of fact, I'm 'bout through with a book called *Soldier's Heart*. It's all about the Civil War. Ms. Purvis suggested it."

That reminded me of something Joe had told me earlier. "Remember when I gave you a ride into town the other day?"

"Yup. Ain't nothin' wrong with my memory."

I cringed. "Of course not. I was just thinking about

something you said. About Vivien Crenshaw being at the library working on some sort of project. Any idea what type of project?"

Joe shook his head. "Nope."

"How about Maggie Jones? Ever see her there?" Mama mentioned seeing Maggie at the library—the whole Scotsman-in-a-kilt thing. I was wondering if there might be some sort of connection.

"You mean the preacher's wife?"

I nodded.

"Yup. She's there all the time. Using the computer for somethin' or another."

"Really? Ever see her and Vivien talking?"

He pull a red hankie out of his back pocket and took a few swipes at his neck while he mulled over my question. "Not that I recall," he finally answered. "Oh, maybe a word in passin', but that's about all." His blue eyes settled on me. "Why? You fixin' on Maggie for the murder?"

I shook my head. "No. But whatever Maggie and Vivien were doing at the library might be important to the case." I realized that if Mama had spied Maggie's interest in kilts, maybe somehow Vivien had discovered it as well. Could that be connected to blackmail?

He scratched his whiskery chin. "Sorry I can't help ya. But Henrietta might know. Want me to ask her?"

"Henrietta, now, is it?" Was I imagining it, or did I notice his cheeks turning red with my chiding? I eased up on the teasing. "Thanks, Joe, but that's okay. I'll probably just pop by sometime soon. I've been meaning to pay her a visit anyway." After helping him finish filling the bucket, Roscoe and I hightailed it back to the farmhouse. Mama would pitch a fit if we were late for church.

.   .   .

A chorus of "amens" rang through the congregation as Reverend Jones finished the final blessing. "Now before we start the hymn, I have a few announcements to read," he began. I shifted uncomfortably, the back of my legs sticking to the wooden pew. Even with all the church's windows opened wide, it was hot as an oven inside. Most of the gentlemen removed their suit jackets before the opening prayer, and the ladies were fervently fanning themselves with the weekly bulletin. Red-faced babies fussed, and school-aged kids squirmed in their seats. Mama, Ray and I were seated a few rows behind Ida and Hollis. Ida had already left the pew to stand in the back with Junior, and the twins were picking at each other. Several times I spied Hollis leaning over and whispering warnings in their ears.

I tuned back in for a second and listened to Reverend Jones talk about an upcoming potluck dinner, before my eyes started wandering again. This time my gaze landed across the aisle on Cade and Hattie. Hawk was there, too, of all people. That surprised me, but to see him sitting right next to Cade irritated me to no end. Next thing I knew, they'd be going out for beers again, chumming it up and talking about goodness knew what. I sighed. I already regretted pouring my heart out to Cade the other day. What was I thinking, divulging so much of my past like that? What if word ever got back to Hawk about the baby? Not that he'd even care. Or would he? I shuddered, not wanting to think about it too much.

"You okay, hon?" Mama leaned in and asked. I nodded and slid my eyes back to the pulpit.

"Next item, the church bazaar," Reverend Jones was saying. "As you all know, this is a generous community. As of today, we have more donations that we know what to do with!"

Happy murmurs ensued from the congregation. The preacher held up his hand for silence and continued, "If any of you can spare the time, please come down to the church this week to help sort and mark items. We're in desperate need of helping hands. Just remember, you'll be doing the Lord's work." With that, he gave the signal, and Betty Lou Nix fired up the organ. Laney stepped into the choir box, and with a toss of her wildly teased hair she raised her red-tipped nails to her bosom and launched into a heartfelt rendition of "Amazing Grace." It started a bit wobbly, but by the second stanza she was belting it out like her own salvation depended on it. I noticed Hawk was hanging on her every word. I should've known. He didn't give a hoot about church; he just came by to hear Laney sing.

When she finished, everyone clapped and started filing out of the pews, a few lingering in the aisles to visit while others dashed ahead, eager to get on with their days. I spied Ezra Sugar ahead, quickly told Mama I'd meet her at the car and set out after him. I still needed to double-check the status of the cake for the Peach Cotillion.

I followed him across the lot, gaining on him as he made his way down Blossom Avenue, but I stopped short when I heard someone calling my name. Hattie and Cade came up behind me, Cade saying, "Hope you don't mind, but I told your mama not to wait for you, that I'd give you a lift home after lunch."

"Lunch?"

Hattie smiled my way, wiggling the key in her shop's lock. "I've got some things to do. See y'all later," she said, opening the door and ducking inside.

"I didn't think she was open on Sundays," I said to Cade.

"She usually isn't, but she told me she was going to meet Mrs. Busby here. Guess Mrs. Busby won't work alone in the shop anymore."

"I can't blame her." A murder in the shop would freak me out, too.

He pointed toward the diner and held out his arm. "So, will you have lunch with me?" He smiled, the lines around his eyes deepening against his tan skin. Something about his expression, or perhaps his manner, put me at ease. All the apprehension I'd felt earlier about revealing too much of my past suddenly melted away.

"Love to," I said, wrapping my hand around his arm.

Only instead of heading into the diner, we stopped at the entrance to Peachy Keen. "What's going on?" I asked.

He removed the set of keys I'd loaned him and opened the door. Stepping back, he motioned for me to go inside first.

I entered tentatively, then stopped just inside the door. A blanket, set for a picnic for two, was spread in the middle of the floor. On the corner rested a giant orange and white cooler with the McKenna Contracting logo. He'd already tuned in the old Czar radio. The slow beat of a country melody filled the room. "What's all this?" But before he could answer, my eyes drifted around the room. "Cade! You finished the shelves and . . . everything!"

He nodded, placing his hand on the small of my back and propelling me forward. "Yup. Yesterday while you were at the tea, I snuck in and wrapped things up. Looks good, doesn't it?"

I was still gawking around. "Good? It looks fabulous."

"There's still a little more to do," he said as we settled on the blanket. "I need to touch up the varnish on the shelves over there, and there's a piece missing on that trim work . . . just odds and ends. For the most part, you can start setting up, if you want." He opened the cooler and pulled out a couple bottles of beer. He removed the top off one and handed it to me.

"Beer? Isn't it a little early?"

"We're celebrating." He clinked his bottle against mine before tipping it back for a long sip.

I shrugged and lifted mine in the air. "What the heck," I said, taking a swig, swallowing it down and asking, "But what exactly are we celebrating?" I glanced about. "The store?"

"No, but we can celebrate that, too, if you want." He started pulling things out of the cooler: some paper plates, a bag of chips and some wrapped sandwiches. "Sorry. I didn't have time to put anything together, so I asked Ginny to help me out. She filled the cooler early this morning for me."

Shaking my head, I blinked back my emotions and said, "No, don't apologize. This is wonderful." Truth was, he could have been serving crackers and squirt cheese for all I cared. I was just touched he'd gone to the trouble of planning something so sweet, and that my friend had helped him. "So you never said what it is we're celebrating."

His expression became serious as he focused his eyes on mine. "New beginnings. We're celebrating new beginnings."

"You mean, between you and me?" My heart kicked up a notch.

He nodded. "I realize maybe you're not completely over that Hawk guy, but—"

"You're wrong," I started, but he held up his hand.

"I've made you something." He reached behind the cooler and pulled out a large, flat object wrapped in paper grocery bags from the local Pack-n-Carry. "Open it," he said, handing it to me.

I took it, measuring its weight in my hands and wondering what it might be. It felt like a large, square board. Was it a . . . ? "Cade! A sign! You made me a sign." It was perfect: white with a painted logo in the corner of the smiling peach my nieces had created last summer and the words "Peachy Keen" carved in large letters. Simple but classy; just what I would have picked myself. I looked up, happy tears pricking the edges of my eyes. "How did you know? I was just going to put up a banner until I had time to get one designed, but this is perfect. Absolutely perfect." I set it aside and threw my arms around his neck, planting a small kiss on his cheek. Then that small kiss grew into a bigger one, and before I knew it, we'd completely forgotten about lunch.

Chapter 13

Debutante Rule #027: Debutantes may not know what they're doing all the time. But rest assured, if you're from a small town, someone else does.

If I ever got to heaven, I hoped it would be just like Sugar's Bakery. Standing just inside the bakery door Monday morning, I took a moment to inhale the slightly burnt smell of deep brewed coffee mixed with the scent of vanilla and warm sugar and . . . ah, I could spend an eternity in Sugar's and never tire of the aroma.

"Nola Mae Harper." Ezra, the bakery's owner, popped out from the back of the store and greeted me with his usual large, toothy grin. Every time I saw him, the mere bulk of his size caught me off guard. At well over six feet and with a shoulder spread that rivaled any SEC player, but with the disposition of sweet kitten, Ezra Sugar was the embodiment of a gentle giant. "Haven't seen much of you lately."

"Been busy trying to get the shop up and going."

"Aw, that's right. You open in a couple weeks. Are you ready?"

"I will be," I told him. The evening before, Ginny, Hattie

and I had spent several hours experimenting with variations of vinaigrettes and salad greens. While we chopped, diced and mixed, we discussed the murder investigation and filled Hattie in on our theory about Vivien being a blackmailer. Although we didn't come up with any real answers to the mystery, we did end up creating the most divine peach pecan salad ever. Now, I was anxious to see if Ezra had come up with any dessert ideas. "I'm supposed to check with you to make sure things are on track for the cotillion dessert this weekend."

"As a matter of fact, I've got the design done." He glanced over my shoulder and out his front window toward the sidewalk. He shot me another toothy grin. "Things are sort of slow right now. Why don't y'all come back to my kitchen and see what I've got figured out so far."

I returned his infectious smile and maneuvered around the counter, following him through a swinging door. "Oh my, Ezra!" I enthused and then fell into immediate kitchen envy. Ezra's kitchen was a culinary masterpiece. Every appliance was state-of-the-art, with large stainless worktables alongside a marble-top pastry table. "Your kitchen is the stuff dreams are made of," I gushed, stopping myself before I actually started drooling.

He dipped his chin and nodded modestly. "Baking is my passion." He motioned for me to follow him around the counter to where he pulled out a notepad. "Here's what I have so far."

I looked down at the sheet, surprised by what I saw. I was expecting to see a sheet cake, or maybe a tiered cake, but what he'd designed instead was a bunch of individual round cakes. Each one was decorated in a cream-colored fondant with little peach polka dots and topped with the cutest miniature sugar peaches. "These are absolutely adorable!" I raved. "You're so talented, Ezra."

He tipped back his head and let out a booming laugh. "Talented, huh? Well, thank you, but let's see if I can actually pull this off." He sighed and swiped a hand across his apron. "It's been hectic here. Business has really picked up."

"That's because word's out about your baking."

He smiled again, nodding his head. "Hey, I'm not complaining. That's a good thing. I've just reached the point where I think I'll need to bring in some help."

I nodded, hoping for the day Peachy Keen reached that point.

"Yoo-hoo!" came a voice from the front of the store.

Ezra slapped the notepad shut and headed toward the front of the shop. After taking one last look around, I followed him. We found Betty Lou Nix in front of the dessert case, bending over and peering at the array of tempting sweets.

"Hello, Mrs. Nix," Ezra greeted.

The spry woman straightened up and smiled. "Hello, Ezra. And Nola Mae! What a surprise to see you here."

I moved around the counter and joined her next to the dessert case. She tapped on the glass and ordered a dozen cinnamon rolls. "I'm buying these to take over to the church. The ladies and I are working on sorting items for the bazaar."

"That's so nice of you to volunteer," I said, watching her carefully count out her bills. I held up my hand. "Let me get this," I said, fishing bills out of my bag. "Think of it as my contribution to the cause. You and the other ladies always give generously of your time to the church. This is the least I can do."

Her cheeks blushed with pleasure as she tucked her bills back into her purse. "Well, I always do say that the church feels like my second home." She chuckled. "Of course, I might just be the oldest member of the congregation, so I've had more time to settle in, if y'all know what I mean."

We laughed. I took my change and thanked Ezra. Then I dashed ahead to hold the door for Mrs. Nix. "Mind if I walk with you?"

"I'd be delighted."

Out on the walk she turned toward me and offered a roll. "No, thank you," I said, thinking there might not be enough for all the church ladies. We continued down the walk, discussing the heat before I turned the conversation back to the church. "Everyone's happy you're playing the organ again, Mrs. Nix. Not that we didn't enjoy Vivien's organ playing, but . . ." I wasn't sure how to finish without saying something that sounded ill-mannered.

No need to worry, though. Mrs. Nix jumped right in with, "If that wasn't the darndest thing!"

"What's that?"

"Vivien Crenshaw taking over the organ playing, that's what." She paused for a minute and turned to face me straight on. "Maggie Jones came to my house one evening and told me that I wouldn't be needed anymore. That they had a new organ player." She shook her head, her grip tightening on the bakery bag. "Just like that! At first I thought maybe I was slipping. You know, messing up the songs. I'm no spring chicken anymore."

"Oh no. That's not the case," I assured her. "Your organ playing is just . . . heavenly." That put a smile on her face. We started walking again, passing by Pistil Pete's and Hattie's Boutique on the way. I continued, "That's why everyone was so shocked when she replaced you with Vivien." I leaned toward her ear. "I don't want to speak ill of the dead, but she just didn't have your talent."

Mrs. Nix let out a happy little sigh. "Well, all I know is the next day after Vivien's death—awful, wasn't it?"

I nodded.

"Anyway, after it happened, Maggie came by my house and practically begged me to come back and play the organ. I had it in my mind to tell her to go fly a kite, but I remembered that we all have an obligation to use our God-given talents to serve others. Isn't that what Reverend Jones is always preaching? Why, when you look at it that way, playing the organ is my duty."

"So, what do you think the real reason was that she replaced you with Vivien in the first place? I mean, certainly it wasn't the way you were playing, because she couldn't wait to get you back."

Mrs. Nix stopped again, her bright eyes darting up and down the walk before she leaned forward and said, "If you really must know, I think that woman was bullying Maggie."

"Vivien? Bullying Maggie?"

"Yes, that's right. One Sunday, after the church cleared out, I went to the back storage room to look through some old hymnals. The storage room by the preacher's office. You know which one I'm talking about?"

I had no idea, but I nodded anyway.

"I heard the sound of voices coming from the office. It sounded like an argument at first, but then I thought I heard someone crying. I couldn't figure out what in tarnation was going on, so I peeked around the corner, and you know what I saw?"

I leaned closer.

"Well, I saw Maggie all hunched over in a chair like a child being scolded. And right there, towering over her, was that Vivien woman. She had a mighty mean look on her face, too."

"Did you hear anything they were saying?"

Mrs. Nix shook her head. "Nope. But you know, I saw something I won't ever forget. I saw Vivien walk right over to the offering basket sitting on the preacher's desk, dip her hand in and take out a fistful of bills."

"Oh my! What did Maggie do?"

"Not a blasted thing, I tell you. She just sat there like a bump on a log. I was going to go on in and say something myself, but that Vivien woman kind of scared me."

"Sounds like you weren't the only one."

"You got that right. But I did tell Reverend Jones about it."

"You told Reverend Jones?"

"Darn right I did! Felt it was my duty. That Vivien Crenshaw was a piece of work. If you ask me, she got her comeuppance." She punctuated her statement with a firm nod and held out the bag. "Sure you don't want a roll, honey? There's plenty to go around."

I reached out my hand and smiled at the spunky Mrs. Nix. "In that case, don't mind if I do."

I took my cinnamon roll, said good-bye and headed back to Peachy Keen. For the rest of the day, I mulled over this new information while I unpacked product, stocked shelves and organized display areas for items I planned to consign for local craftsmen: peach-scented soaps made by a local stay-at-home mother who'd recently started her own soap business; and jewelry crafted by a local artisan who designed Georgia-themed trinkets.

My enthusiasm grew as I worked. Things were really coming together, and I hoped that one day my shop would be as successful as Ezra's bakery or Hattie's Boutique. If I could pull it off, the income from the shop and my online order business would be enough to cover the farm's recent losses with some left over to afford my own vehicle or maybe even rent a small place of my own. Although lately I'd come to realize that Mama and Daddy had visions of me living at the farm forever, even taking over the entire operation one day. I laughed, thinking how just last year I wasn't even sure I could take care of the farm for three weeks, let alone run the operation full-time; I doubt they were sure, either. But, I was getting way ahead of myself. Counting my chickens before they hatch, as Nana used to say. Still, the possibilities excited me, and I couldn't help but think I'd made the right decision leaving my job with Helping Hands International and deciding to stay in Cays Mill permanently.

After working steadily until late afternoon, I was ready for a glass of iced tea. I also wanted to discuss the case with Ginny, so I headed next door to the diner. She was standing at the counter, rolling silverware into napkins as Carla moved about bussing and cleaning tables. "Hey there, Nola Mae."

I waved at Carla and took a seat at one of the barstools across from Ginny.

Ginny said, "I want to thank you again for standing in for me at the tea. I'm glad I was able to make at least part of it for Emily; the important thing is that Emily had a good time. Thank goodness that whole fiasco with Maudy Payne didn't make it into Saturday's edition." She tossed a roll of silverware on top of the pile she'd already done and turned around to scoop up a couple glasses of ice. "I'm dreading tomorrow's paper, though," she said over her shoulder.

"I bet." I picked up some silverware and started rolling, while Ginny filled the glasses. Then she pulled two plates out from under the counter and crossed over to the dessert case, pulling out a peach pie.

"Want some?"

"Oh yeah. Definitely." My stomach rumbled, and I realized I hadn't had anything since the cinnamon roll earlier that morning. She dished up a couple slices and settled on the stool next to me. I began quietly filling her in on everything Mrs. Nix had told me, including the fact that Reverend Jones knew about Vivien dipping into the coffers.

"Well, I certainly hoped he set her straight."

Maybe he had, I thought. But any sentiment against the preacher would be lost on Ginny. Never in a million years would she doubt a man of the cloth.

She continued, "At least now we know for sure that Vivien was a blackmailer. I mean, why else would Maggie just sit by and let her take from the offerings? But what in the world could that woman possibly have had on the preacher's wife?"

I quirked a brow, but didn't comment. "So, have you learned anything else about the case?"

"As a matter of fact, Travis came in today. I always serve the fried chicken special on Mondays. It's his favorite."

I scooped up a forkful of pie and moaned. Ginny's peach pie could bring a grown man to his knees, that's for sure. "Did he have something new to say?" I asked, my mouth still half full.

"Well, it wasn't easy, but I used my chicken to pry a little information out of him."

"Uh-huh." I just couldn't stop shoving in the pie.

"Well, he was saying that they had the lab boys working on identifying prints they'd lifted from Vivien's purse."

A sudden clinking of dishes caused both of us to turn around. "Ya okay there, Carla?" Ginny asked.

"Yes, ma'am. Sorry," Carla replied, moving the large tub to another dirty table. I watched her closely for second as she fumbled with a couple glasses and dropped a spoon.

"Anyway," Ginny went on, drawing back my attention. "They fingerprinted me the other day, just to eliminate my prints from the others on the purse, since I'd touched it and all. Ray thought it was okay. He said it was normal procedure."

"I'm sure he's right. He knows all about that type of stuff." I was trying to sound upbeat. Poor Ginny. Being fingerprinted by the police must have been upsetting to her. "Did Travis have anything else to say?"

"Yup. As a matter of fact, after he was good and full of mashed potatoes, he happened to mention a couple more things. It turns out that Doc Harris did determine that the death occurred around six thirty that night. And that the phone call Mrs. Busby received that night of the murder, the one canceling the appointment, was made from a nonregistered cell phone. Not from any of the Crenshaws' normal phones."

"Aw. Well, that answers that question. No wonder Vivien showed up—someone else canceled the appointment." I speared a piece of pie and raised my fork in mock salute. "Good work, Ginny."

"Ms. Wiggins," Carla interrupted. "I've got all the tables cleaned. Do you mind if I head on out? I've got to get to the library to research my Civil War project."

"Oh sure, honey. You go on ahead. See you Thursday."

I stared after Carla, my mind working overtime. "Does the sheriff have any idea how that purse got behind the diner?"

"I don't think she has a clue."

"But she doesn't seem to think the purse implicates you in any way, does she?"

"No. Like I said before, thanks to that brother of yours, I'm pretty much in the clear. You should have seen him on Saturday, Nola. He was like a knight in shining armor. Waltzed right into Maudy Payne's office and plopped down a signed statement that cleared my name."

"A signed statement? From whom?"

"A witness who backs up my alibi." There we were, back to the alibi. I opened my mouth to ask more, but she hastily continued, "Anyway, I'm all in the clear. No worries with Maudy Payne." Her shoulders slumped a little. "Just with everyone else in town. I swear, Nola, these women around here are ruthless. What they don't know, they just make up. I'm worried sick every day, wondering how all this is affecting Emily."

I reached over and touched her arm. "I know. I'm sorry. Hopefully the real killer will be found soon. Have you talked to Emily today? How'd it go at school for her?"

Ginny shook her head and pulled the suspect list out of her pocket. "Not yet. She's at a friend's house working on a school project. That's why Carla was here. I usually have her fill in on the days Emily can't make it." She snatched the pen from behind her ear started making a few notes. "Sure wish I could make more sense out of all this." Seeing how defeated she looked, I tried to steer things away from the case. "So, how is Carla working out for you?"

"Oh, great. She's a good worker. But Emily says she doesn't fit in at school. Too bad. I wish they'd give her a chance. I know she seems as tough as a two-dollar steak, but under that bad-girl exterior, she's really a cool kid." She paused and pointed at my empty plate. "She helped me make that pie, you know."

"Really?"

"Yup. Turns out she loves to mess around in the kitchen." She started clearing our plates. "Speaking of which, I'd better get back there and help Sam with the dishes or he's gonna pitch a fit." She turned back as she headed for the kitchen. "See y'all later?" she asked, referring to our nightly cooking session.

"You bet. Be back in a couple hours." In the meantime, I knew just where I was heading: to the library to talk to one really cool kid about a couple things, including a designer handbag.

Chapter 14

🍑

Debutante Rule #003: A smart debutante knows not to go countin' her friends until she knows which friends she can count on.

I left the diner, worked my way down Branch Street, turned at the corner and headed north past the Clip & Curl Salon. The library was located across from the high school, so I planned to cut through the church parking lot and take the alley behind it as a shortcut. But as I neared the church, the back door flew open, and Debbie Bearden came running out looking like she'd seen a ghost. She ran across the lot to her car, holding her hand over her mouth like she was ill.

What in the world? I thought, watching her speed away. Then I noticed the church door was still standing half open and there didn't seem to be any cars in the lot. I glanced next door to the parsonage, but there weren't any cars parked there, either. Although, maybe the preacher was out and about in their only car. Wondering if I should lock it or if maybe Maggie was still around, I walked into the entryway. From where I stood, I could go either upstairs to the main floor where the sanctuary was or down to the basement where I knew the church ladies had been busy sorting items for the sale. I could hear the faint sound of music coming from downstairs. Maggie was probably down there still working. "Maggie!" I yelled, heading down the steps. "Are you down here, Maggie?" No one answered, but maybe she couldn't hear me over the music.

I stopped short just inside the door of the basement, astonished by the piles of stuff crowding the room. I could see why Reverend Jones called for more volunteers. Almost every inch of the place was packed with junk. Heading toward the sound of the music, I began weaving my way through tables piled high with clothing, boxes of books and children's toys. That's when I saw Maggie on the floor.

"Maggie!" I cried, running over and kneeling down next to her. She was wearing a work apron, the pockets stuffed with scraps of paper, pens and sheets of self-adhesive price tags. A dozen or more paperback books were scattered on the floor around her.

"Maggie!" I said again, giving her a little shake, but there was no response. *What was going on?* I glanced to the table above, piled high with boxes of used books. Did a box of books fall on her? I tried to rouse her again, this time noticing a couple of reddish pills on the floor under her face. "No, no, no!" I cried, patting her cheeks. "Wake up, Maggie. Wake up!" Her skin was deathly pale and her breath so shallow, I was afraid I was too late.

I jumped up, quickly located the radio and turned off the music. Whipping out my cell, I dialed 911. My hands shook so badly, it took me three tries to get the number right. As soon as the operator answered, I blurted, "I need an ambulance at the Baptist church right away. It's the preacher's wife. It looks like she's swallowed a bunch of pills!"

· · ·

Upon hearing the sirens, I ran upstairs to meet the ambulance, recognizing one of the EMTs from Ida's premature labor with Hollis Jr. at the house last summer. "Where's the patient?" he asked, bag in hand. Two other guys popped open the back of the ambulance and extracted a stretcher.

I led the way to Maggie, praying that help had arrived in time. As they began frantically working on her, I heard another set of heavy boots thundering down the stairs. This time it was Maudy Payne. "What's going on here?" she demanded.

I told her about finding Maggie unconscious on the floor and the pills I discovered by her face. I decided not to mention seeing Debra running out the back of the church. She'd probably found Maggie and assumed she was already gone. I rubbed down the goose bumps prickling my skin. Who could blame her for panicking?

I stood by, silently watching as a paramedic frantically worked, checking her vitals, repositioning her airway and administering an oxygen mask with something that looked like a bulb attached. While one of the EMTs started squeezing the bulb, the other picked up and examined one of the red pills while he relayed information over a walkie-talkie mounted on his shoulder. I could hear bits and phrases of his conversation mentioning things like possible overdose and a faint pulse. After he finished his call, he quickly whispered something to Maudy before motioning to the others. They hoisted Maggie onto a stretcher and rushed like crazy for the stairs. As they did, a book slipped out of the pocket of Maggie's work apron and fell to the floor. Maudy picked it up and gave it a quick glance, her face flushing red as her eyes caught a glimpse of the scantily dressed Scotsman on the front cover.

She quickly tossed it aside with the other spilled books and moved in to get a closer look at the remaining pills on the floor. "The paramedic thinks these are sleeping pills," she commented. "It's probably a good thing you came along when you did." Her eyes narrowed. "Why did you come by, anyway?"

I made a point of glancing around the room, as if I was interested in the preparations for the bazaar, and said, "I was cutting through the alley and heard some music coming from down here. I just thought I'd stop by and check out how the bazaar was coming along." *Close enough*, I thought.

Maudy's gaze also took in the disarray of the rummage items. She shook her head and whispered to herself, "Why would she do something like this? And why down here?"

My heart sank as I thought about their daughter, Belle, and how she'd take the news that her mother tried something like this. Or, heaven help her, if she died. Then a horrible thought occurred to me. I clamped my hand over my mouth and shook my head. Had I driven Maggie to this? All that talk at Saturday's tea about Vivien's purse being found and how I thought whatever was in it would lead to the killer? Was it too much for Maggie? Or was she really Vivien's killer and her guilty conscience drove her over the edge?

"Are you going to be sick?" Maudy asked, taking a step backward.

I lowered my hand and swallowed hard. "No, I'm okay. But someone needs to tell her family right away."

"I'll take care of it." She took out a plastic baggie and used a ballpoint pen to scoop in the leftover pills. "I'd love to know where she got these pills. You didn't see a prescription bottle on the floor somewhere?"

I shook my head and looked around the area, thinking maybe it had rolled under something. Once again, my gaze landed on the book with the kilted hunk, then traveled down to the author's name—Sindy St. Claire. *Huh, what a strange way to spell Cindy.* Curious, I picked it up and opened to a random page, reading the first sentence that stood out to me: *I found myself pinned against the stone, the Highlander's dark eyes penetrating mine as his hand deftly moved under* . . . "Oh my!" I exclaimed out loud, snapping the book shut.

Maudy turned back and chuckled. "Pretty raunchy stuff, huh? Not really something I would have expected to find at a church sale."

"Me, either," I said. My mind flashed back to what my mother had said about catching Maggie looking at a half-naked Scotsman on the computer at the library. Then it occurred to me: *Sindy,* a clever play on words; probably a pseudonym. Certainly this was sinful stuff. At least in the eyes of a churchgoer like Maggie. Hmm . . . I gripped the book a little tighter. "Sure would be embarrassing for someone to find it here during the sale. Mind if I take it with me?"

Maudy raised a brow. "Sure, if that's your type of thing, Nola. Go ahead."

Clearly, she'd misunderstood. I briefly considered telling her my thoughts about the book, and its author, but I'd promised myself not to jump to conclusions, and this idea was certainly highly speculative. Instead, I tucked the book away in my purse thinking it was best to wait until I had some concrete proof.

We turned off the lights and locked up the church. Back out in the alley, Maudy asked a few more questions before taking off to find Maggie's family to let them know what happened. As soon as she sped away, I got on my cell phone and called Mama. Since she was close to Reverend Jones and his wife, I figured she'd want to know. And I needed to hear her voice. Finding Maggie that way had shaken me to the core.

"What?" Mama's voice shrieked over the phone. The news sent her into an immediate tizzy, and she was shocked, to say the least, about the sleeping pills. "I don't believe for a minute that Maggie Jones would take her own life," she said, but instead of dwelling on the details, she jumped into action. "I'll get ahold of the Ladies' Society and start a prayer chain right away. And then I should go to the hospital to wait with the family. Oh, this is just awful. Just awful," she lamented.

"I feel like I should head to the hospital, too," I said, quickly making my way back down the street toward where my car was parked in front of my shop. Not that I knew Maggie that well, but after finding her that way, after my confronting her, upsetting her the other day, I . . . well, I just wanted to be there. We agreed to meet there as soon as possible.

As I slipped my phone back into my bag, my hand brushed up against the romance novel that had fallen out of Maggie's apron. Could my theory possibly be correct? Was Maggie leading a double life: preacher's wife by day, erotic romance writer by night? Reading such books might be embarrassing but not enough to result in the kind of anxious call I'd overheard her make through the bathroom door the day of the tea. But *writing* such a book . . . well, that might be a different story altogether. Everyone knew she wrote the church's programs and its promotional materials—but was I making too much of a jump in my thinking? I shook my head. This was hard to believe and even harder to prove. But there was one person who might know—our town's librarian, Henrietta Purvis. I made a mental note to pay her a visit soon.

A little while later, I made my way through the County Medical Center's double sliding doors and into the emergency room waiting area. Mama was already there, huddled off to one side with Reverend Jones, Belle and her brother, Nash. Mama had her arm around Belle and was whispering something in her ear. I went to them.

Reverend Jones stood as I approached. "I'm so sorry about Maggie," I told him.

"They're still working on her, but the doctors think she'll be all right. Thank God you came along when you did. I'd hate to think what would have happened if . . ." His words trailed off as he plopped back into his chair and buried his face in his hands. Nash moved closer and tried to comfort his father. After a few seconds, Reverend Jones collected himself and looked up at me, his brows wrinkled with confusion. "I just don't understand this. I just saw her a few hours ago and she was fine."

I slid into one of the plastic molded chairs near them. "She didn't seem depressed or upset?"

"No, nothing like that. Maybe a bit frazzled. She'd been awfully busy with the church bazaar and Belle's cotillion coming up this weekend."

With the mention of the cotillion, Belle let out a little sob. "Is it something I did?"

"No, sweetie. It's nothing you did," Mama immediately assured her.

"Absolutely not," her father reiterated, reaching over to rub his daughter's shoulder. Nash remained silent, his eyes like two empty holes, his face pale. I'd first met Nash last summer at the Peach Harvest Festival. I'd known him to be a sensible young man, but there was no sense to this situation, and he, like the others, appeared at a loss to understand this tragedy.

Looking at her family, I couldn't imagine Maggie would ever do something to hurt them. Still, if she was depressed or overwrought with guilt or afraid that her secret was about to be discovered, maybe . . . "Had Maggie been acting strangely at all? Maybe distracted or going out more than usual?"

The preacher shook his head. "Going out? No, not at all. Other than the couple nights she spends researching her project, she hardly goes out."

"Her project?"

"Yes, she's working on a self-help book for women."

My eyes popped. So she *was* a writer. More proof that Sindy St. Claire and Maggie Jones were one and the same. But a self-help book? Was that what Reverend Jones really believed his wife was writing? Or, did he already know about Sindy St. Claire and was just covering for his wife?

"Isn't that just like Maggie?" Mama spoke up. "Always doing what she can to help others."

Not knowing what to add to that, I simply nodded and tightened my grip on my purse. For a while, we all sat engrossed in our own thoughts as the whir of emergency room activity continued around us. Twice the automatic front doors slid open, the first time for a man with his hand wrapped in a bloody dish towel. He was immediately admitted and taken away by wheelchair. The second time, a young mother came in carrying a bundled child. She moved around the reception counter to a small desk where a nurse was waiting to enter her information into a computer.

I offered to go look for coffee, but no one was interested. So I sat back and let my eyes wander to the show playing on a small television mounted in the corner of the room. A few minutes later I turned again to the sound of the front doors sliding open. This time it was Maudy Payne. She glanced our way briefly before leaning in to say something to the front desk nurse. Then she quickly disappeared through emergency room doors. Finally, after another ten minutes or so, both the sheriff and a man in scrubs emerged and approached our group.

"Are you Margaret Jones's family?" the man asked. His name tag identified him as a nurse.

The preacher stood and nodded. "Yes. I'm her husband."

"I'm afraid your wife has slipped into an overdose-induced coma, Mr. Jones. This sometimes happens in these cases." I jumped up to put my arm around his crumpling shoulders as the nurse continued, "But I want you to know that the doctors have done everything they can. We'll be transferring her up to the ICU soon."

"I'd like to see her," Reverend Jones said, his voice wobbly with emotion. Behind me, I could hear Belle starting to cry. Nash had stood and was pacing in front of us.

The sheriff stepped forward. "I'll need to ask you a few questions first, Reverend." She glanced toward Mama and me. "I'd appreciate it if you two ladies would stay here a minute with the children." Then she nodded at Reverend Jones. "Come with me," she stated, leaving no room for discussion about it and leading him toward a private registration room behind the reception area.

Mama and I exchanged a look but didn't express our surprise at this latest turn of events out loud. Instead, Mama continued to try to calm Belle while we waited for the sheriff to finish with the preacher. When he finally did return to our group, his face was ashen and he was noticeably trembling. Mama jumped up and placed her arm on his shoulder. "What is it, Reverend? What's going on?"

He looked at us with a dazed stare. "Maggie didn't try to kill herself," he answered, his words coming out slower than usual. "The sheriff says it was an attempted homicide."

"You mean someone tried to murder Mama?" Nash asked,

his expression turning from confusion to anger as his gaze flitted around the room. "Like they killed Tara's mother?"

I was afraid of what he might be thinking. "The two might not be connected," I started, but his icy gaze had moved across the room and landed on the sheriff. For a second he stood there, his facial muscles tense as he watched Maudy give the nurse some paperwork. Then, with an explosion of energy, he sprang forward and barreled toward her. I went after him. Reverend Jones was right behind me.

"What are you going to do about this, Sheriff?" Nash demanded, jabbing his finger at Maudy. She stepped back in a defensive position, her hand moving instinctually toward the baton on her belt.

I inserted myself between them and held up my hands. "Easy now, Nash. I'm sure Sheriff Payne is doing everything she can."

Reverend Jones stepped in and grabbed his son's shoulder. "Calm down, son. This isn't going to help anything."

Nash shook his head and backed down. I breathed a sigh of relief.

Maudy gave us all a once-over before turning to leave. "I'll be in touch," she mumbled on her way out the doors.

"Wait!" I called out, dashing back to retrieve my bag where I'd left it on my chair. "Excuse me," I said to the others before running to catch up with the sheriff.

She must not have heard me calling after her, because I was barely able to reach her before she climbed into her cruiser. "Wait!" I yelled again. "There's something I need to tell you."

She stepped back out and turned a shrewd eye my way. "What?"

Slightly out of breath, I quickly relayed seeing Debra leaving the church right before I discovered Maggie unconscious in the basement. She cocked an eyebrow at me, obviously wondering why I hadn't mentioned that earlier when I'd explained about why I went into the church in the first place, but I ignored the unspoken question. "There's something else, too," I continued and told her about what Mrs. Nix had seen in the church office that day and everything else I'd theorized about Vivien blackmailing both Maggie and Debra. "I'm not sure what she had on Debra, but this is what I think she was holding over Maggie." I pulled out the book we'd found at the church earlier and explained what I was thinking. "So you see. If Vivien was blackmailing these two ladies, it was possible she was blackmailing someone else, too. Someone with more to lose."

Maudy ran her tongue along the inside of her cheek and drew in a deep breath. "My, but you've been busy, Nola." She widened her stance and folded her arms across her chest. "I'll check into what you said about Debra being at the church, but as for the rest of your story . . . got any proof?"

I shook my head. "No, but—"

"Well then, I've got my own theory I'm working on, and it's based on facts, not a bunch of cock-and-bull ideas about porn writers and blackmail schemes." She unfolded her arms and pulled her mirrored sunglasses from her shirt pocket and tapped them against the book in my hand. "In fact, Nola, I think you need to lay off the readin'. You're starting to get quite the imagination."

I clamped my mouth shut and slowly slid the book back into my bag.

Maudy tipped her Stetson my way and shot me an arrogant wink before putting on her glasses and climbing into her car. "Be seein' ya around, Nola Mae."

Chapter 15

Debutante Rule #014: Good manners, grace, poise and style are the ingredients for a happy life, and friendship is the egg that binds them together. Just make sure y'all aren't mixin' with bad eggs.

I woke up Tuesday morning, still groggy from a late-night conversation with Mama. After leaving the hospital, I stopped by the Pack-n-Carry and picked up a frozen pizza to bring home. By the time I got back to the house, Mama had returned with quite the story to tell. Over iced tea and a few slices of pepperoni and mushroom, she told me all about Maudy Payne's theory. Apparently Reverend Jones confided everything to her after I left the hospital. And was Maudy's theory ever a doozy!

According to Maudy, the doctors began to suspect foul play when they discovered some defensive wounds on Maggie's arms along with scratches and some bruising that appeared around her mouth and on her throat. It looked like someone had tried to force her to swallow the pills and then strangled her. And the sheriff figured that "someone" was Reverend Jones.

Evidently, Maudy heard through the grapevine that Maggie Jones was seen leaving Nate Crenshaw's house the night of Vivien's funeral. I'd already known that, of course. Hattie and I were there when Maggie left Nate's house. Which made me wonder if Hattie hadn't told someone about seeing the preacher's wife at Nate's house. It wasn't like her to gossip, but she *was* really upset over the whole ordeal. Only since then, we'd come to realize that Maggie was there looking for whatever was supposedly inside Vivien's purse, not because she was having some sort of fling with Nate. But in this town, once a rumor got started, it spread like wildfire.

So, Maudy had heard a rumor and jumped to the crazy conclusion that Maggie killed Vivien so she could have Nate to herself. Then, according to her, after Maggie realized what she'd done, she become overwrought with guilt and confessed everything to Reverend Jones. In return, either in a fit of jealous rage or fearing a ruined reputation—Maudy wasn't quite sure which—the preacher staged the whole suicide thing in an attempt to kill Maggie. Of course, I'd had some of my own doubts about the preacher, still did, but nothing that far-fetched. And truth was, I really didn't want to believe that Reverend Jones was capable of killing anyone, let alone his own wife. My only solace was that Maudy obviously didn't have the evidence to back up her addlebrained theory or she would have already arrested him.

Anyway, after running it through my mind over and over, I'd come to the conclusion that I'd better hurry and find the truth before something else happened. The first thing I intended to do was find out if Maggie really was Sindy St. Claire. And I knew the best place to start looking—the Cays Mill Library.

•   •   •

So, later that afternoon, after finishing some work in my shop, I took a break and headed on foot for the library. Back when I was in school, the library occupied a couple spare rooms inside the city building. However, just a few years back, thanks to fund-raising efforts by Friends of the Library volunteers, the library acquired the old brick railroad station on the west side of town, just a block away from the high school. The railroad had long ago deserted the line that connected our little village to the bigger towns up north, leaving behind a sizable station, which now housed over four thousand books—and growing! Of course, the abandoned tracks next to the building made for a bit of an eyesore where the disjointed ties jutted up between splotches of overgrown weeds. Nonetheless, the station itself—maintained by tax dollars and ongoing fund-raising by the Friends of the Library volunteers—was in great shape.

Walking up what used to be a loading platform and past colorful window boxes full of trailing petunias, I pushed through the heavy wood door and into the marble entry. Fortunately, when they converted the station to a library, they left much of the original charm: the black-and-white tiled floor, palladium windows with thick wavy glass trimmed out in dark wood and the old ticket counter, which now served as the library's checkout counter.

The bulk of the building was taken up with bookshelves, but toward the back of the room, a space was set aside for study tables. I spotted Carla sitting at one, books spread around her as she worked. My friend Joe Puckett was also there, sitting at another table with his nose buried in a paperback novel.

Pulling the Sindy St. Clair novel out of my purse, I made my way over to the checkout counter where Ms. Purvis was seated, dressed in her usual lacy collared blouse, buttoned to the neck and secured with a cameo brooch. Her gray head was bent in concentration as her nubby-knuckled finger skimmed over a page of a book. She looked up as I approached, removed her glasses and let them dangle from their chain. "Nola Mae! I haven't seen you in ages. How's your mama doing?"

"Just fine, Ms. Purvis."

"Well, you be sure to tell her I said hello." Her bright eyes twinkled. "And I hear you're opening your shop soon. I can hardly wait. You're selling Della's peach preserves, right?"

"Yes, ma'am. The very same recipe that's been in my family for generations. Mama's chutney, too, and a lot of other family recipes."

"Then I'll be one of your best customers." She leaned in, her eyes roaming to the back of the room where Joe was sitting. "I've been wanting to thank you, Nola, for all you've done for Joe. You've opened up a brand-new world for him."

I briefly glanced at Joe, who was fully engrossed in his novel, his eyes scanning the page as a small grin tugged at the corner of his mouth. "I'm glad I could help," I told her. "Joe's a good guy." Ms. Purvis batted her lashes nervously, a hint of pink rising to her cheeks as she busied herself righting a stack of flyers on the corner of the counter. "Did you hear about Maggie Jones?" I asked.

As soon as the words were out, Ms. Purvis's face sank. I regretted bringing up such an awful matter, but I needed to get some answers. Not just for me, but for everyone involved, including Maggie.

Ms. Purvis stopped fussing with the papers and glanced

away. "Yes, I did." She sighed. "Such an awful thing. Maggie's such a sweet girl." She focused on me again, this time with misty eyes. "You do suppose she's going to be okay?"

"I certainly hope so," I answered softly. "I know my Mama's been calling around to get a prayer chain started."

"You tell her to mark me down, too."

"Of course," I promised, placing the novel onto the counter where she could see it. "Do you carry this series here, Ms. Purvis?"

She placed her readers back on the end of her nose and picked up the book for a closer inspection. Her eyes grew wide, then she handed it back and started working over the pile of papers again. "Sorry. We don't carry that type of romance. Maybe in one of the bookstores up in Macon. Or online, perhaps."

I picked it up and pointed at the author's name. "This book is written by Sindy St. Claire. Do you know if that's a pseudonym?"

She squared her shoulders and looked me directly in the eye. "I couldn't really say."

And she didn't have to. I could tell by her defensive reaction that I'd hit on something. Henrietta Purvis was as sharp as a tack. Nothing got by her. I knew this for a fact. I couldn't even recall how many times she'd busted me over the years for every library infraction possible from sneaking in food to dog-earring book pages. Still, as quick as she was to call foul when it came to library business, Ms. Purvis was discreet when it came to other people's business. I'd never be able to coerce her into betraying someone's confidence.

I noticed her eyes narrow as she glanced over my shoulder toward the door. "Stop right there, young lady!"

Cringing—a knee-jerk reaction from past years of being

on the receiving end of Ms. Purvis's scolding—I snapped my head toward the door, where Carla Fini was frozen in place.

"That book you put in your bag is a reference book," Ms. Purvis accused. "It's not to be removed from the library."

Carla stiffened, clenched her fists and shot Ms. Purvis a dark look. The room fell quiet as the two of them engaged in an ominous stare down. From the back of the room, Joe cleared his throat and broke the trance. Then he stood slowly, homing his eyes in on Carla as he tapped his book against his open palm Clint Eastwood style. And just like that, Carla dropped her tough-girl posture. "Sorry, Ms. Purvis," she said, loosening her fist and extracting the book from her bag. She crossed the room and placed it on the counter. "Won't happen again."

"Let's see that it doesn't," Ms. Purvis said, casting a look of awe toward Joe.

Carla nodded and shuffled back toward the door. I shot Joe a quick wave, bid Ms. Purvis good-bye and hurried out the door.

"Carla, wait up!" I caught up to her outside. "How've you been?"

She kept going, her eyes focused downward as she walked. "Fine," she said, tucking a strand of hair behind her ear.

I did a little skip to keep pace with her. "A lot of strange stuff's been going on around here, huh?"

"I don't know what you're talking about."

"Well, Vivien Crenshaw's murder, and now all this about the preacher's wife. You heard, right?"

"Yeah. Too bad. She seemed like a nice lady."

"That's right. She spent a lot of time here at the library, didn't she? Is that how you got to know her?"

The girl shrugged. "She helped me with my homework and stuff."

"That was nice. Did you happen to know what she was working on?" I probed.

Carla's expression hardened. "Maybe. But it isn't anybody's business but hers."

I noticed her neck muscles tighten as she cocked her head and glanced past me. I was tempted to try to get more information from her, not only about Maggie's activity at the library but about the purse that was found stashed behind the diner. I had a feeling Carla knew something about that, too, judging from her reaction at the diner the other day. But there was no way she'd come right out and tell me. She didn't trust me. Heck, I don't think she even liked me. I decided to change tactics. "Ginny was telling me you like to cook."

She met my eyes, her face softening a little.

I continued, "We could use someone like you to help us at this weekend's Peach Cotillion. We're in charge of the menu, but since Ginny's daughter's a debutante this year, she'll be tied up with all the cotillion events." I thought I detected a slight eye roll from Carla, but I continued anyway. "Hattie's going to help me with transporting the food and setting up for the dinner, but we could really use another set of hands."

Carla stopped walking and faced me, folding her arms across her chest. "Does the job pay?"

I blinked a few extra times. "Certainly," I said, throwing out a number. She upped me by five bucks, which I agreed to before sealing the deal with a handshake. As she reached out, I noticed a tattoo on the upper part of her arm. It looked like a gang marking. If so, I could certainly understand why her mama shipped her down to Cays Mill. Sure, there were a few bad eggs in our town, but nothing like a gang. In fact, the closest thing we'd ever had to a gang was a Friday night gathering at the Tasty Freeze. "And if you're looking for more work, I happen to know that Sugar's Bakery is needing extra help." I remembered what Ezra had said about being overwhelmed with his business.

She narrowed her eyes and shook her head. "No, thanks. I don't plan to be around this stupid town for that long."

"Are you going to leave as soon as school's out?"

"That's my plan. My mom wants me to stay down here, but if I can get enough money together, I'm heading back. I've got friends in Chicago. Cool friends. Not like these prissy girls around here."

Bet that's true. "I understand. But just so you know, the opportunity is there if you change your mind."

She assured me she wouldn't. We talked a little longer, firming up a few details for the cotillion dinner. In the end, she agreed to be at the diner by one o'clock on Saturday to help me with the final food preparations.

After Carla walked away, I stood on the walk trying to formulate my next plan of action. I'd been hoping to track down Debra Bearden, but glancing at my watch, I could see I only had a few minutes before I needed to be back to meet Ginny at the diner for our daily cooking session. Spurred on by Ms. Purvis's compliments on Mama's recipe, I was planning to knock out another couple dozen jars of peach preserves. I had a feeling it might be my top seller.

So, I made my way back down the street, my mind reeling with a checklist of things I still needed to do for my store's grand opening and the upcoming cotillion dinner. Then my thoughts turned to Maggie, and I felt guilty for being stressed over such petty things. What was all this compared to lying in a hospital bed, fighting for your life? Maggie had been robbed of her chance to enjoy such a special time in her daughter's life, not to mention the heartache suffered by Vivien Crenshaw's family. I couldn't imagine who the person was who'd orchestrated all this evil, first Vivien and now Maggie. Could it be Debra Bearden? Had she been running from the church because she'd tried to kill Maggie? I didn't think so—she'd been running like a scared rabbit, not like a vicious predator. I was missing something, but I just couldn't put my finger on it.

I'd just crossed over Blossom Avenue and was about to cut across the courthouse green when I heard a familiar voice cut through the air. Glancing back across the street, I saw a crowd gathering in front of Pistil Pete's Flower Shop. *What could possibly be going on now?* I wondered.

As I approached, I caught bits and pieces of the argument that'd drawn so much attention. "Other woman?" I heard Pete say. "But there's nobody but you, baby."

There was a bunch more bantering that I couldn't quite discern until I heard Hattie shriek, "Don't you dare try to deny it, you lying pig! I know what you've been up to." I pushed my way through the gawkers just in time to see Hattie pick up a nearby watering can and dump it over Pete's head. "Maybe that'll cool you down, you hot blooded, two-timing, son of a—"

"Whoa!" I jumped in, snatching my friend's arm and dragging her away before she turned the air blue. "What's going on?" I asked, pulling her away from Pete and the crowd and heading across the street. I'd decided the best place for her to cool down might be at the diner.

But halfway there, she shook off my hand and veered toward the center of the courthouse green, stumbling to a stop in front of the statue. "Oh my goodness. Did I really just do that?" she asked, plopping down on the edge of its concrete base and rubbing at her temples. "What's gotten into me?"

I sat next to her. "You're upset, that's all. You think the man you love has been cheating on you."

"Think? I know."

"Oh, come on, Hattie. What makes you so sure? One note? That could have been anything."

She stood and started pacing. "Not just the note. Sure, that was weird. But it's been a lot of other things, too. Little things. Like he's always busy. I can't even count how many dates he's canceled lately. Then when we are together, he's so distant. It's like he's off in his own world. Probably thinking about *her*."

I shook my head. "This is crazy, Hattie. Have you even tried to talk to him about it?"

"Talk to him!" she shrieked. "That's what I was doing when . . . when . . . arg!" She clenched her fists in front of her then opened them again, taking a deep breath. "I'd just closed my shop," she started over in a calmer voice, "and was walking home past his shop when he came out and begged me to discuss things." She looked at me. "I swear, he can be so relentless sometimes. He's been calling me constantly."

"He loves you," I interjected.

"And *her*, apparently."

I threw up my hands. "Her? Her who?"

Hattie reached into her bag and pulled out a note. "This her." She shoved a tiny scrap of paper in my face and plopped back down next to me. It said: *I'm ready and can't wait for the special night, Pete. Don't worry. She doesn't have a clue.*

Hattie rubbed at her shoulders, circling her neck to loosen her muscles. "Mercy, but I could use a drink. How about going to the Honky Tonk with me? It's happy hour and tonight's Two-Buck Beer Night to boot. A girl could drown her sorrows cheap tonight."

I shook my head, still staring down at the note. "No, I don't think so. Not tonight. I'm sorry, but I'm supposed to be at the diner now. Ginny and I are working on a couple batches of preserves. But honestly, Hattie. I don't think you have anything to worry about. There has to be a perfectly reasonable explanation for all this." *At least there'd better be*, I thought. Because I recognized the handwriting on the note. I should, after all. I'd seen the same flowery handwriting several times since Vivien's murder. In fact, I was a little surprised Hattie didn't recognize it, too, but then again, maybe she'd been too distracted lately to notice such things. But there was no doubt in my mind that the loopy, feminine script on the note was an exact match for the handwriting on Ginny's suspect list.

Ginny was the other woman.

Chapter 16

Debutante Rule #047: A debutante knows that the only cure for jealousy is to stop countin' other people's blessings and start countin' your own.

"There you are," Ginny said the moment I walked into the kitchen. She waved the latest copy of the *Cays Mill Reporter* in the air. "Have y'all seen this?"

I caught a glimpse of the headline, which read: "Local Woman Found Unconscious in Church." Frances must not have known at the time this went into print that the sheriff suspected an attempted murder. Because certainly, had she known, the headline would have been more sensational.

"Your name's in the article." Ginny slid the paper across the counter for my inspection before going on. "I feel awful about this. Here I was, all worried that it would be my picture on the front page. Especially after Frances snapped all those pictures when I was being hauled out of here by the sheriff." She shook her head and adjusted her apron strings. "I wished something else would upstage any slander Frances wanted to thrust on me in this issue, but not at the expense of someone as sweet as Maggie Jones just dropping over like that. I mean, what an awful thing."

"She was still in a coma last I heard." Mama had been spending time with the family at the hospital and had been keeping me posted on Maggie's condition.

"Oh dear Lawd!" She ran her hands along the front of her apron. "Do you know if anyone's organized meals for the family yet?"

I shrugged. "I don't know, but Mama's got a prayer chain going."

"Tell her to mark me down." She heaved a sigh and headed toward the storage room in the back of the kitchen. She was still going on about Maggie when she came out lugging one of the heavy crates of peaches I'd brought from the orchard that morning. "I just can't believe all that's happened in the last couple of weeks. First Vivien and now Maggie. And poor Belle. Her mama like this and the cotillion's just four days away."

"Speaking of the cotillion . . ." I told her about asking Carla to help with the dinner. "I'm sure Hattie and I could handle things, but it wouldn't hurt to have an extra pair of hands around. Just in case." Especially since I knew Ginny was going to be tied up all evening with Emily's presentation to society. The plan was for Ginny to do the prep work earlier in the day, and Hattie and I would take over the transportation and final preparation of the food.

"That's a fine idea," Ginny agreed. "Carla's pretty handy in the kitchen." She placed a large colander in the sink, and we started filling it with peaches to be rinsed.

"Good," I replied absently, my mind already switching to a more pressing matter. I decided it was as good of a time as any to show her the note Hattie gave me.

I wiped my hands and pulled it from my pocket. "Does this look familiar?" I asked.

Her mouth fell open. "Why, yes. I wrote that. But how'd you get—"

"Hattie gave it to me."

She slapped her hands against her cheeks. "Uh-oh."

I stared at my dear friend, waiting for her side of the story, something simple and logical. Because surely she wouldn't betray a friend like Hattie, not to mention cheat on her devoted husband, Sam. But all I got was silence. "Well?" I prompted.

Ginny shrugged. "What can I say? Guess the cat is out of the bag." She started rolling the peaches around to clean them.

"Ginny!" I couldn't believe my ears. I waved the note again. "What's this all about anyway? Certainly you and Pete aren't . . ." I couldn't even finish the statement.

"Aren't what?" she asked, sorting the peaches.

I caught her arm in motion, and she looked at me with a puzzled expression.

"You know . . . you aren't, well, having an affair with Pete."

Ginny's eyes widened. "Oh, for heaven's sake! Of course not. How could you . . ." She glanced down at the note, and her eyes scanned the wording, her complexion turning red. "Oh my!"

I nodded. "Hattie saw a note last week, too, and she's just sure Pete is seeing someone on the side. Only she didn't recognize your handwriting like I did."

Ginny exhaled and shook her head. "Well, shoot! No wonder she's been so uptight lately. I thought it was all this stuff with Vivien's murder and then . . . well, you know how busy she's been getting dresses ready for the Peach Cotillion."

I squinted. "So what's this all about anyway if it isn't . . . ?"

She threw up her hands. "God's truth, Nola. There's nothing like *that* going on."

I believed her. Of course I did. I hadn't really believed anything like that could ever be true in the first place. But even though I still didn't understand what *was* going on, a few things were starting to come together. "You were with Pete at the time of the murder, weren't you?"

She nodded. "That's right. He's my alibi."

"And the signed statement Ray got to clear your name?" I asked, remembering that Ginny had said Ray came through with an affidavit from a witness.

"That was from a jeweler over in Perry where we were that night. A real nice fellow named Dan something or another."

"A jeweler? You and Pete were looking at jewelry together?" *What's going on?*

She started flitting around the kitchen, grabbing bowls and utensils for making preserves. "Yes, we were looking for a ring for Hattie. Pete's going to propose."

For a second I didn't know how to respond. I'd been so busy imagining all sorts of scenarios, I hadn't even considered the obvious. "When is this supposed to happen?"

"Thursday night. Right after the rehearsal. Oh, he has it all planned out, and it's so sweet." She bit her lower lip and glanced off for a moment, then went back to work, as if nothing more needed to be said.

I blinked a few extra times. "Rehearsal?"

"Yes, Nola." She let out a long, exasperated sigh and put the stockpot on the stove with a *thunk*. "I swear, I don't know where your mind has been lately."

Well, murder, for starters. Then there was my shop opening, the cotillion dinner, my own love life . . .

She went on, "The rehearsal's Thursday night at the VFW. It's for the debs and their marshals, just to go over a few of

the basics." Then, she began ticking items off her fingers.
"There's the Grand March Presentation and the curtsy—all
the girls need to brush up on that, of course."

Of course.

"And the cotillion waltz." Her eyes went a little dreamy
as she rinsed off peaches. "Don't you just love the cotillion
waltz? It's so graceful and elegant."

My brain stumbled over that for a second before I recalled
that the cotillion waltz was that silly dance where the debutantes pranced around in a circle, waving their bouquets. "Yes,
just lovely. But getting back to this note. Hattie thinks Pete's
cheating on her, and she's all worked up about it. You have to
tell her about this."

She stopped and turned off the water. "Are you nuts? I can't
tell her. It's a *surprise*! I promised I wouldn't say a word to
anyone. I only told you because of that note." She nodded at
the now crumpled paper in my hand. "Oh, and I told Sam.
Only because he was so upset over not knowing where I was
when Vivien was murdered." She started removing the rinsed
peaches from the colander and placing them on a clean dish
towel. "And don't think that I wouldn't love to spill the beans,
if anything just to prove my innocence. Half the town thinks
I killed Vivien Crenshaw."

I squeezed my eyes shut for a second and took a deep
breath. I couldn't believe the idea of helping a friend in creating some fantasyland of a romantic moment could supersede
something like being accused of murder and infidelity. "But
Hattie's so ticked off. You should see her. She just emptied a
full water can on top of Pete's head. Right out in front of his
flower shop," I added for emphasis.

"Uh-oh. That *is* bad," Ginny agreed.

I gathered a grater and a large piece of fresh ginger.
Mama's secret to making the best preserves was a touch of

fresh ginger to complement the sweetness of the peaches. "So you'll tell her?"

"No."

I clenched my teeth and raked the ginger across the grater.

"He wants to *surprise* her, Nola. I can't ruin that. It is just so very sweet, so romantic." She started peeling and dicing the peaches. When she spoke again, her voice was softer. "The ring's gorgeous. Pete paid a lot for it."

I noticed a tinge of sadness as she glanced down at her own modest wedding ring—a thin gold band, dull from years of wear and tear. I felt my earlier irritation melting away. Things couldn't have been easy for Ginny and Sam when they got engaged. They were barely out of high school, and Ginny was already pregnant. Sure they had a wonderful marriage, and two beautiful kids, but they'd worked so hard, sacrificed so much. And here she was going to all this trouble to help make her friend's engagement special and memorable. I took a deep breath and managed a smile. "Tell me what he has planned," I prompted.

We continued to work on the preserves as she explained the whole scenario she and Pete had schemed. She told me that since it had been that mixed-up take-out order from the diner (orchestrated by Ginny) that'd brought the two of them together in the first place, Pete thought it would be romantic to put together a candlelight dinner for two at the diner Thursday night—which just happened to be the one-year anniversary of their first date. As soon as rehearsal was done, Ginny promised to lure Hattie to the diner, where Pete would be waiting on one knee in a room full of flowers and candles. It was clear from Ginny's wistful looks and sighs that she was living vicariously through the romance of this planned moment. Not that she was unhappy with her life with Sam, but she obviously missed out on the honeymoon period in her own life, and this was filling that void for her. Pete had even remembered and asked Ginny to prepare the very same take-out meals that'd brought him and Hattie together in the first place. "Fried catfish, hush puppies and coleslaw for Pete. Just some roasted chicken and a side salad for our dear friend," Ginny explained, scrunching her nose. "You know how healthy Hattie always eats. It's no wonder she's skinny as a rail."

I bobbed my head in agreement, thinking how I had to lay across my bed that morning just to get my own pants zipped. "It all sounds very romantic," I said, grabbing a measuring cup and the bag of sugar. "If it still happens, that is."

"What do you mean? Of course it's going to happen."

I shook my head. "You didn't see how mad Hattie was just a while ago. And poor Pete. She pretty much humiliated him in front of half the town."

"Oh pulease! Like that's going to scare him away. I'm telling you, he's so in love, there's nothin' that's going to keep him from poppin' the question," she gushed. "I'd just love to be a fly on the wall when he slides that ring on her finger and asks her to be his wife."

Yeah, well as mad as she is, he might not get the chance.

A similar thought must have occurred to Ginny. She stopped dicing and turned to me. "I guess Hattie's another deal, though. There's just no predicting her." I could tell by the sudden slump in her shoulders that a little of her enthusiasm was dying away as she thought it over. "I guess there's a chance she won't even listen to what he has to say."

As much as I hated to see Hattie upset, I also hated seeing a gloom overtake Ginny's earlier glow. Whether it meant that much to me or not, the whole romance angle meant so much to Ginny. Heck, I had glowed myself just to have a silly lunch on the floor of my shop with Cade the other day. Maybe all women needed at least a bit of romance in their lives even if it was secondhand like Pete's planned proposal. "Maybe I'll pop by tomorrow afternoon, after Hattie's had a little time to cool off, and try to talk some sense into her."

"Would ya?" Ginny perked up a bit. "And I'll talk to Pete. Let him know why she'd been so upset and that you'll smooth things over. But don't give anything away when you talk to Hattie. Pete's counting on it being a complete surprise. You promise?"

I promised.

But the next day, I found out that talking sense into Hattie wasn't as easy as I thought it would be. She had it in her mind that Pete was cheating on her, and there was no convincing her otherwise. "I honestly don't care if I ever see that two-timer again," she said. "And here I thought I loved that man." She slid a stack of dresses back on the rack, checking a list on her clipboard as she examined each alteration ticket. It was around four thirty on Wednesday afternoon, and the shop was empty except for Hattie, Mrs. Busby and me. Oh, and Carla was there, too, doing some odd jobs for Hattie. Currently, she was on the other side of the room dusting a display of accessories. I'd tried to make a little small talk with her when I first arrived at the shop, but she wasn't in a talkative mood. In fact, she seemed downright depressed. I wondered if something bad had happened at school that day.

I lowered my chin and stepped forward, forcing Hattie to make eye contact with me. "You're telling me that you don't love him anymore? Not even a little?"

She flinched. "Like it matters now? It's over. I dumped water over his head in front of half the town." She stopped counting and tossed the clipboard onto the counter with a heavy sigh. "I still can't believe I did that."

"Love will make you do crazy things, no doubt about it," Mrs. Busby chimed in from behind the folding screen where she was working at her alteration table.

"That's right," I agreed with a nod. "Besides, this is all just some weird misunderstanding."

"I don't think so, Nola." Hattie reached under the counter and pulled up a bakery box. I leaned forward and watched her flip it open.

"What's that?"

"Cookies," she replied, snatching one up and taking a quick bite.

I reached over and helped myself to a shortbread cookie dipped in chocolate. The combination of buttery shortbread and deep, rich chocolate was like a party in my mouth. "You're eating cookies? I hardly ever see you eat sweets," I mumbled, my mouth still half full.

"She's a stress eater," Mrs. Busby offered from behind the screen.

Hattie nodded and grabbed one more cookie before replacing the lid and sliding her stash back under the counter. "Anyway, like I was saying. This isn't some sort of misunderstanding. Half the town knows he's having a fling."

"What do you mean, half the town knows? Like who?"

She shrugged. "Like everyone." I could see her hand itching to grab up the box of cookies again, but she refrained, drumming her nails against the counter instead. "Just this morning, Candace from the bank came into the shop to tell me she was sorry to hear of my relationship trouble. Of course, she said she had a feeling about Pete. Saw him giving roses to some woman the other day right out in front of the Mercantile."

I threw up my hands. "He's a florist, for crying out loud!"

"That's what I told her," Mrs. Busby said. I couldn't really see her behind the screen, but I imagined her head was bobbing up and down as she spoke. At least there was another voice of reason in the room.

Hattie waved away our comments and continued, "Then Doris from the Clip and Curl came by. She was telling me that one of her clients spotted Pete driving around Perry last week." She lifted her chin and looked over my shoulder. "Hey, Carla. Would you mind getting those shelves along the backside? The dust is horrible back there." She turned her attention back to me and continued, "Her client didn't get a real clear view, but she said it looked like a woman was in the car with him."

I shook my head, wishing I could tell her the real story and put her mind at ease, but I'd promised not to give away the secret. I was just trying to figure out another approach when the bells above the door jingled. It was Frances Simms.

"Hello, Nola. I've been looking for you." She nodded toward the other ladies. "Mrs. Busby. Hattie." Then she turned back to me. "I'm wondering if I could ask you a few questions about what happened at the church the other day."

I stiffened. I'd taken time to read the article the night before and knew it didn't mention anything about a suicide or the real reason Maggie was in the hospital—attempted murder. "You already had an article about it in yesterday's paper. There's nothing else I can tell you."

Her eyes narrowed. "Oh, I think there's a lot more to the story."

Out of the corner of my eye, I saw Mrs. Busby walk around the edge of the folding screen and root herself nearby, hands on her hips and dark eyes flashing. I sucked in my breath, wondering what Frances had heard. So far it seemed the town's busybodies hadn't caught wind of the fact that someone tried to kill Maggie. Maybe they were too busy with gossiping about Hattie and Pete to worry too much about Maggie.

"I have my sources, after all," Frances continued. "Every good newspaper reporter does." She glanced around the room for affirmation. From whom, I wasn't sure. Did she think we were going to assure her that she was a good reporter? Not a chance.

Frances's beady eyes gleamed as she continued, "I tried to be discreet in yesterday's article, not mentioning anything about Maggie trying to kill herself." All around me I heard little exclamations of surprise. Hattie gasped, Mrs. Busby furrowed her brows and let out a long *hmmmm* sound and somewhere behind me I heard a muffled whimper. That one bothered me the most. From what I had gathered, Maggie had befriended Carla in the library, and I assumed Carla didn't have many friends. I hated the fact that she was hearing this.

"Oh yes," Frances went on, obviously enjoying the drama she was creating. "I knew about the sleeping pills found at the scene. As did you, Nola Mae, being you're the one who found her." Her tone was accusatory. Like I was supposed to rush right over to the newspaper office and report my finding to her. "But I have too many scruples to disclose something like a suicide attempt in my column. For the family's sake."

No one said anything. As for me, I kept my mouth shut, afraid of what I might say once I got started.

"But my source says it wasn't suicide after all," Frances continued. "But attempted *murder*."

A sudden crashing sound averted our focus. Carla had knocked over a display of necklaces. "I'm sorry, Ms. Mc-Kenna," she said, scrambling to pick them up off the floor.

I crossed the room to give her a hand. From over my

shoulder, Frances continued asking questions as I worked to pick up the jewelry. "Was anyone else at the church when you found Maggie?" And, "Did you notice signs of a struggle?" She'd whipped out a notebook and pen as if she actually thought I was going to answer her questions. Carla seemed to become more agitated with every question. Her fingers trembled as she tried to untangle two necklaces that had become knotted together. "Or, did you notice any unusual marks on her body? Scratches? Torn clothing?"

With that, Carla dropped the chain and clenched her fists together. Her face flushed red, and I noticed tears forming along the edges of her eyes. I clamped a hand over one of her fists. "Just calm down. I'll take care of this."

I stood and wheeled around. "Look here, Frances. These questions are out of line. If you really want to know the answers, I suggest you go talk to Maudy Payne."

Frances's head sunk back into her neck, reminding me of a scared turtle. "I did. But she wouldn't comment."

"Well, neither will I!"

Hattie spoke up. "I think it's best you leave, Frances. Your questions are upsetting and inappropriate considering there's a child in the room."

Frances's gaze fell on Carla. "Oh. I'm sorry."

"You should be," Mrs. Busby said, stepping forward and pointing toward the door. The room fell silent as Frances considered her options. Finally, she folded her notebook, tucked it back into her bag and sauntered out.

"Well, I'll be!" Mrs. Busby said, as soon as the door shut. "The nerve of that woman."

While Hattie and Mrs. Busby started chewing over Frances's annoying attributions, I put my hand on Carla's arm and gave her a little tug. "Hattie," I interrupted. "If you don't mind, I think Carla and I might head down the road for some ice cream. I think she could use a break." I glanced at my watch on the way out the door. I was due to meet with Cade in an hour. He'd called earlier in the day and talked me into taking the evening off from working with Ginny and heading over to a small town just over the county line to some new restaurant that had recently opened. Cade had heard they had the best chicken fried steak around.

"I don't really like ice cream," Carla announced as soon as we were outside. She turned on her heel and started walking in the opposite direction. "I'm gonna head home. I'm not feeling so great."

"I noticed that," I said, skipping to keep up with her. "Seems you got that way as soon as you heard someone tried to kill Maggie."

Her tennis shoe snagged a crack in the walk, and she started to stumble forward. "You okay?" I asked, my arm shooting out to help steady her. But she batted it away and kept walking.

I did a little hop and a jog to maneuver in front of her. "My truck's parked right across the square. Let me give you a ride home." She started to go around me, so I shuffle-stepped to block her way. "I insist. We need to talk anyway."

"About what?"

"The purse that was stashed behind the diner. Vivien Crenshaw's purse."

Chapter 17

🍑

Debutante Rule #089: Learn how to cook right. After all, a good Southern meal can make a person forget bout anything.

I'd only driven about three blocks when Carla cracked. It started with a shaky admission: "I know something about Mrs. Jones." My gaze darted across the seat to where she sat, slumped over, tapping her cell phone nervously against her leg. "And I think maybe it had something to do with someone trying to kill her," she added, with a little sob.

Giving the wheel a sudden crank, I whipped into the nearby grade school parking lot and threw the truck out of gear. My quick maneuvering sent the empty peach crates in the back crashing against the side of the truck bed, but I didn't care. Carla wasn't the crying type. Something big was going on, and I sensed she needed help. "What is it, Carla? What's happened?"

"I'm going to be in big trouble." I noticed her bottom lip trembling as she spoke. "I did something wrong."

"Tell me."

She raked her hand through her hair, revealing the silver

studs that pierced the sinewy part of her earlobe. "I was at the library when Tara and her friends came in. They were acting all giggly and talking about cotillion stuff, like they always do. I was sick of hearing about all that, so I packed up my stuff and left. Mrs. Jones was there that afternoon, too. She left before me."

"And then what happened?"

She shot me a sideways glance, her dark eyes angry and untrusting.

"I'm on your side, Carla. Whether you think so or not." I softened my tone and pressed on. "Why is it you think you're in trouble?"

For a second, she seem to detach from the conversation, her eyes staring out across the school's playground with an almost wistful look. I tried to imagine this girl as a young child swinging carelessly on a school playground, laughing as she pumped her legs to propel herself higher and higher into the air. Idly, I wondered what had happened to make her stop reaching for the sky.

"I was taking out the trash at the diner, the day after it happened," she finally said, her voice just a little over a whisper. "And there was a purse in the bin. Just lying there, right on top. A nice purse." She stumbled a bit over her words and began picking at a bracelet tied around her wrist. The edges of the bracelet were frayed and dirty. Looking closer, I could see it was made from braided shoelaces. From her friends back home in Chicago? "There was money in it," she continued. "About two hundred bucks."

"It was Vivien's purse."

She nodded. "Yeah, I didn't know that until later, though. Anyway, someone was coming down the alley, so I pocketed the money and shoved the purse between the crates stacked by the back door. I meant to go back and throw it away again, but I didn't get the chance."

"I don't understand what this has to do with Maggie."

She shifted uncomfortably. "There was something else inside the purse. A little bag. I thought it was a makeup bag and . . ." She let out a long sigh. "I liked it."

"So you took it, too?"

She nodded. "But later I found out it wasn't makeup inside the bag. It was some other stuff. Weird stuff. But one of the things I knew Mrs. Jones wouldn't want anyone else to see."

"Something that proved she was wrote books about . . . Scotsmen?"

Carla blinked a few times. "Yeah, that's right. You know about that?" I nodded, and she continued, "It was some pieces of paper from one of her notebooks. She would handwrite her stories and then type them out on the library's computer."

That made sense. Especially if she was trying to keep her Sindy St. Claire alter ego a secret from her husband.

"Somehow Mrs. Crenshaw must have gotten ahold of it. I figured Mrs. Jones would want it, so I took it to her that day. Then she ended up . . ." She swallowed and let out her breath. "There were a couple of other things, too. One of them was a picture of Sophie's mom."

My antenna went up. "Debra Bearden? What type of picture? Was she naked?" A slew of possibilities ran through my mind, and a compromising picture fit into every one of them. Maybe Debra quit her job at the Honky Tonk because she had another, more profitable, side business. One that didn't involve so much time on her feet. *That* would certainly be fodder for blackmail.

Carla screwed up her face and looked at me like I had a third eye. "Naked? No! Yuck. She wasn't really doing anything.

Just standing there holding a dress. I think she was getting ready to work on it, because she had a pair of scissors in her hand. I didn't think anything of it but showed it to Mrs. Jones, in case it was hers, too."

"Scissors?" My mind flashed back to Vivien's rigid body sprawled on the floor of Hattie's Boutique, a pair of scissors skewered through her throat and a blood-soaked debutante gown wrapped around her cold, lifeless hand. I rubbed my suddenly sweaty palms on the side of my jeans as I pondered this new information. A dress? Logically, I knew it wasn't the debutante gown from the crime scene. The timing wasn't right for that. But what dress? Then I remembered what Maggie had said about last year's Peach Queen Pageant. That Belle had to drop out because of a problem with her dress. That must have been it! Vivien caught Debra in the act of sabotaging Belle's dress and snapped a picture, probably with her cell phone, and was using it to blackmail Debra. "What did Maggie say when you showed her the picture?"

"Not much. At first her eyes got real wide, then I thought she was going to get angry, but all she did was just stare at it for a minute, shaking her head. Then she took it and said she'd make sure Mrs. Bearden got it back. She asked me not to tell anyone else about it. Or about the notebook pages." She quickly glanced away. "But . . ."

I reached over and touched her shoulder. "You've done the right thing by telling me," I assured her. "You said there were a couple of other things. What else?" I prompted.

"A photocopy of some old letter. The writing on it was pretty fancy."

An old letter? A love letter, perhaps. Evidence of a scandalous affair. But with whom? "Do you remember anything it said?"

She sighed. "No. I didn't pay much attention to it. Mrs. Jones seemed surprised when she read it, though. But she didn't say what it was about, just that she'd make sure it got back to the right person."

"Huh. Well, we'll need to tell the sheriff all this, too."

She stiffened and drew away. "The cops? No way!" Her voice became shrill. "You can't tell them. I stole that money. They'll put me in juvie. I've been in trouble before. Back in Chicago. I've got a record."

"Carla, this is a murder case. You know something that could help the sheriff find Maggie's would-be killer. And probably Vivien's killer, too. You *have* to tell the sheriff what you know. What if someone else gets killed? Think how you'd feel then. And Maggie's your friend. Don't you want whoever did this to her to be brought to justice?"

She reached over and jerked on the door handle, getting ready to bolt. I snatched her by the shirtsleeve. "Hold on! Okay," I said, pulling her back into the seat. "Let me think about this. Maybe there's a way we can tell the sheriff without her knowing who you are. My brother's an attorney. I'll talk to him and see if there's some way around this."

"Promise me you won't tell her it was me," she pleaded.

This making promises bit was getting more than a little cumbersome. There were several reasons why I shouldn't make that promise and should instead go immediately to the sheriff and relay everything Carla had just told me. I had an obligation to tell the sheriff, didn't I? But as I looked into Carla's scared face, I felt another type of obligation. I had a feeling trust didn't come easy for a girl like Carla, yet she had confided in me. How could I betray her trust? I sighed and said, "I'll do everything I can to keep your name out of it. I promise."

• • •

After dropping Carla by her aunt's house, I headed back to the farm to change and get ready for my dinner with Cade. I rushed a little on the back roads, knowing I was running late and thinking he was probably already at the house waiting for me.

I was right. Halfway down our lane, I spotted his pickup parked in front of the house. And next to it, Hawk's motorcycle.

My stomach churned as I eyed the bike's black diamond finish and polished chrome, which gave off an ethereal sheen, sort of like a black mamba basking in the late-evening sun— alluring but dangerous. It suddenly hit me that these two vehicles really epitomized their owners' personalities. Cade's truck was sturdy, dependable and built for hard work, while Dane's bike was a lot like him: buffed, polished to a tee and made for fast pleasure. *Did I really just think that?* Well, not *my* fast pleasure, that's for sure. The one time I'd got caught up in all that had changed the entire course of my life. With a quick shake of my head, I put my runaway thoughts in check and parked my own truck: a bit dented, not always that dependable and in need of a thorough clean-out. I shook my head again.

As I started for the house, a bit of anxiety kicked up inside me at the idea of both guys being here at once. First they were sitting by each other at church, now at my own house. But I didn't have long to contemplate the situation, because as I reached the top step, the front screen door popped open and Roscoe skyrocketed onto the porch. He scurried toward me, ears flopping and short little legs propelling him pell-mell across the wood planking. As he made his way, he paused and greeted me with a quick sniff before bounding down the steps and lifting his leg on Mama's petunia bed. One whole patch had turned brown since Roscoe came to visit, but Mama, who was so enchanted with the little fellow, didn't seem to mind a bit.

My eyes drifted from Roscoe back to the porch where Hawk was now standing, arms crossed over his strong chest and blue eyes flashing. Seeing him in my own territory always gave me the flutters. "Hello, Nola," he said, my name rolling off his tongue like liquid velvet. How did he manage to make it sound that way? Or any woman's name, for that matter?

"Hi, Dane."

"Hawk."

"Hawk," I corrected myself and nodded toward Roscoe's favorite spot. "You're going to owe my mama some new flowers." A weird look crossed his face as he looked at the brown spot. "I'm kidding. They're just annuals anyway. Are you here to visit Roscoe?"

He shoved his hands in his jean pockets and nodded. "Yup. Just brought by some extra food for him."

"Great. Thanks," I said, glad he'd left the food and was on his way.

"He might be staying a little longer than I thought," he added, catching me right before my hand reached the screen door. I turned back. "Oh? The job's working out, then?"

His gaze roamed out over the orchards. "It's okay. Keeps me in the area, I guess."

There was only one reason a guy like him would want to stay in this area. I wasn't sure how she did it, but Laney had managed to get him wrapped right around her red-lacquered fingers. Good for her. In my opinion, they were well suited for each other. "Well, good for you," I said, turning and reaching for the door again.

"Can't say I really care for my boss's wife, though," he went on, his voice tight.

I sighed, let my hand drop and turned back toward him.

He continued, "She's always sending me on stupid errands. And she's demanding. Throws a hissy fit when things don't go her way." He shook his head. "Don't know how the congressman does it. I could never be married to a woman like that. It'd drive me crazy."

"Still cleaning out the attic for the cotillion?" I asked, remembering he'd told me about clearing out the plantation's third-floor ballroom and hauling a lot of donations down to the church.

"Oh yeah. That and tons of other crap." He let out a long sigh. "Today, I drove over to Perry to pick up her dry cleaning and a bunch of tablecloths from some rental place, then by some retired Professor Scott's house to deliver something, and then over to the Pack-n-Carry for—"

"Professor Scott?"

"Yeah. You know him?"

"No, I don't," I said, narrowing my eyes. "But I've heard the name somewhere. What did you deliver to him?"

He shrugged. "Just a manila envelope. It was sealed. Why?" He stepped closer, eyeing me curiously. "What is it? You've got a strange look on your face."

"It's the name. Professor Scott. I've heard it recently, but I can't place it." I shook my head and chuckled. "Don't you hate it when that happens?"

He looked down his nose and smirked. "Can't say it ever happens to me."

I was going to laugh, but I wasn't sure he was kidding. Not that it mattered, because Roscoe suddenly appeared at my feet, whimpering and favoring one of his paws. Surprised, both Hawk and I bent forward and reached out at the same time, clunking heads. "Ouch!" I cried, straightening up and clutching my head.

"Sorry about that, darlin'," Hawk said, reaching out to steady me. "You okay?"

Right at that moment, the screen door screeched open and Cade walked out.

I brushed away Hawk's hands and bent back over to get Roscoe. Carrying him to one of the cane rockers, I sat down and examined his paw. He whined and tried to pull it back, even snapped at me, but I was able to see the source of the problem—a tiny rock wedged between the padding on his paw.

I told Hawk, and he immediately squatted next to me, rubbing Roscoe's backside while gently holding his leg steady. "Okay, I've got him. Think you can work it out?"

"I'll try," I said, using my finger to work at the stone. Finally, it came out. "Got it!" Roscoe let out a little yelp and wiggled off my lap, immediately retreating behind the chair to lick his paw. Hawk and I exchanged a look of relief.

I glanced over toward Cade, expecting to see relief in his expression as well, but what I saw was hurt and maybe a little anger, too. I wasn't sure. Regardless, I felt apprehensive.

Hawk must have sensed the sudden tension. "Well, I'd better get a move on," he said, reaching behind the chair to give Roscoe's ear a playful tug. "You're in good hands, buddy." He told us both a quick good-bye and strode back out to his bike. With a final salute and a rev of the bike's engine, he was off.

Cade and I stood together in silence long after the sound of the retreating engine faded away. "I can be ready to go in a jiff," I finally said. "Just a quick shower and change."

He nodded and moved toward the rocker to wait. He let out a long sigh and settled back, kicking out his legs and folding his arms across his chest. Roscoe came out from behind and curled up at his feet. "You know, Nola," he started, his voice catching me as I pulled open the screen door, "watching you and Hawk just now, taking care of Roscoe . . ." He smiled sadly while gently rubbing his foot along the dog's back.

"Yeah?"

"Just got me thinking that you two would have been good parents together."

Time dragged on Thursday. Probably because I spent most of the day preoccupied with everything except my work at Peachy Keen. Truth was, my date with Cade the night before had left me in a funk. After getting a late start, we'd decided to forgo the new restaurant and just grab a couple burgers at the Tasty Freeze, where we ran into Hollis, Ida and the kids. That was okay; I always love spending time with my nieces and nephew, except that particular night I would have preferred some time alone with Cade—if anything just so I'd get the chance to alleviate the damper left by Hawk's untimely visit. Why *did* that man always show up at the most inopportune time? But instead of a quiet romantic dinner, I spent the evening listening to Ida go on about her responsibilities as a cotillion board member and my nieces bantering between slurps of icy neon-colored drinks while I bounced a fussy Hollis Jr. on my knee and cast apprehensive glances toward a broody Cade. All in all, it wasn't a date I wanted to remember.

Although, one interesting thing did come of the evening. Right before leaving the Tasty Freeze, I pulled my brother-in-law, Hollis, aside and asked him what he knew about Nate Crenshaw. Hollis, president of the Cays Mill Bank and Trust, was reluctant to divulge any information about his client's business, but after quite a bit of finagling on my part, and a

reminder of all I did for him last summer—speaking of
extortion—I finally got him to confirm what I'd already heard
through the rumor mill: Nate Crenshaw's business was in dire
straits. A few more months and he'd more than likely be filing
for bankruptcy. So, for sure, Vivien felt desperate for money,
especially considering pending college expenses and all of
Tara's pageantry costs.

At any rate, the residual doldrums over my bad date combined with a haze of confusion spurred by the new facts I'd
learned about Vivien's murder and Maggie's attempted murder made it difficult for me to concentrate on even the tiniest
tasks. Right off the bat, I mismarked a package of preserves
being shipped to an online customer. Next, I spilled an entire
glass of iced tea over a stack of brochures for my grand
opening. Then, to top it all off, I whacked my chin against the
corner of my checkout counter, causing me to drop a jar of
peach salsa, which shattered and splattered orange guck
everywhere. What a mess!

Nonetheless, sometime between answering online inqui-
ries and picking bits of onion and pepper out of the cracks
in the floorboards, I managed to place another call to Ray.
Ever since talking to Carla, I'd wanted to get his take on what
she had found in Vivien's purse. Only I still couldn't reach
him in person. Finally, I ended up leaving a message with
his secretary, who informed me he would be tied up in court
for most of the day.

After leaving the message, I sat with my cell phone in
hand, debating whether or not I should break my promise to
Carla and call the sheriff. I knew the information regarding
the contents of Vivien's purse should be turned over to the
authorities immediately, but how to do that without getting
Carla in trouble? Would the sheriff press theft charges against

her? She did take a couple hundred dollars from the purse. Or she might be charged for obstruction of justice, since she didn't bring the purse forward in the first place. I hated the idea of Carla getting into trouble. Of course, I also hated the idea of *me* getting into trouble. Would I find myself facing the same charge if I didn't come forth with this new information soon? Ugh! I finally decided to give it until the end of the day. Maybe Ray would call back soon.

About the only thing that lifted my spirits and carried me through that gloomy day was Pete's pending proposal to Hattie. It was supposed to happen that very night. I was so happy for my friend! As off track as her emotions were now, I knew she loved Pete, and if she'd give him a chance, they could have a wonderful life together.

Not getting much accomplished, I called it quits around four o'clock. Once again, Ginny and I had canceled our afternoon cooking session. She'd needed extra time to clean up after closing to help Pete get things set up for the big dinner, most of which they'd planned to do while Hattie was busy running the cotillion rehearsal at the VFW. I didn't mind putting off our cooking session, though. Ever since Carla told me about the photo of Debra with the dress and scissors, I'd been planning to pay a visit to the Beardens' house. I had a few questions for Debra. For starters, why was she running out of the church right before I discovered Maggie?

Debra's house was located in an older neighborhood behind the high school. Most of the houses in this part of town were built right after World War II, when a shortage of housing sparked the frenzied construction of prefabricated cookie-cutter homes. Now over seventy years old, some of the homes were being demolished and bigger, more modern homes built in their place. The overall effect was a mixed-up neighborhood—massive new homes with manicured lawns interspersed with one-story ranches with cracked driveways and overgrown landscaping. The Beardens' home was one of the newer builds: two stories of vinyl siding, brick veneer and architectural shingles lording tall over its modest one-story neighbors.

Before I got to the front stoop, the door opened. A tall, dark-haired man stepped outside. "What can I do for you?"

I approached with my hand out. "Mr. Bearden? Nola Harper. I'm looking for Debra. Is she around?"

"I know who you are. And no, she's not here." He started to turn away.

"Excuse me!" I hurried forward, trying to insert myself between him and the door. "When will she be home? There's something I need to talk to her about."

His lips pressed into a thin white slash as he glared down at me. "She's gone out of town for a couple days. Not that it's any of your business."

"Oh," I said, taking a step backward. "Out of town? But she'll be back for the cotillion, right? I mean, Sophie—"

"Look, Ms. Harper," he said, looming over me. Suddenly the front stoop seemed incredibly small. "Debra's got nothing to say to you. And I, for one, don't appreciate you siccing the sheriff on her. She's been upset ever since Maudy Payne came by here asking questions about the preacher's wife." He reached for the door handle again. "Good-bye, Ms. Harper."

I thanked Mr. Bearden, or at least said "thank you" to the door he slammed in my face, and plodded back to my car. I had to wonder if Debra left town because she was upset or guilty. Maybe she did have something to do with the attempt on Maggie's life. Still, I couldn't see Debra forcing pills down Maggie's throat or choking her. She wasn't that strong looking. Then something else occurred to me. Maybe Debra saw something, or someone, at the church that afternoon and now she was running scared. Who could blame her? First Vivien, then Maggie. Maybe she was scared of becoming the next victim. I'd assumed that Vivien was blackmailing several people and one of them had killed her. Meaning they'd all be off the hook for the blackmail if the purse holding the proof of their errant ways went missing. Which it did, except who would throw a purse with both money and evidence in a Dumpster? It was lucky that Carla found it and gave the evidence to Maggie. Only then Maggie also had that damning photo of Debra. She must have realized what it was and called Debra in order to return it, because surely Maggie wasn't going to blackmail Debra; she had her own secret to protect. Could another of the blackmail victims have found out Maggie had the contents of Vivien's purse? Someone who feared exposure enough to have killed Vivien and then try to kill Maggie? But who? The only other item Carla mentioned in the purse, a copy of an old letter, could have been anything. I had too many questions and not enough answers.

I sat in the car for a few minutes, trying to figure out what to do next. After thinking it over, I decided it was time to call the sheriff. I'd do my best to keep Carla's name out of it, but if there was any chance Debra or anyone else was in danger, the sheriff should be informed.

I had just picked up my phone to dial when it started ringing. It was Ray. "Ray! I'm so glad you called."

"Hey, sis. What's going on? I had a couple missed calls from you, and my secretary said you sounded stressed about something."

"I need advice." I went on to explain the whole situation to him, including my promise to Carla. "She trusted me,

Ray. But I'm worried if I don't take this information to the sheriff, someone else may get hurt."

"You did the right thing by calling me. I'll give Maudy a quick call right now."

"But—"

"Don't worry. I'll keep Carla's name out of it for now. But eventually the sheriff will need to talk to her. She might know something vital to Vivien's murder. Just trust me. I've got a lot of tricks up my sleeve. Carla's not going to get into trouble."

I let out my breath. "Thanks, Ray. Oh, and just FYI, you don't have to keep any secrets about Ginny anymore. I know where she was at the time of the murder, and the big event is going down in just a couple hours."

He laughed over the line. "Wish I could be there."

"Me, too," I agreed, before disconnecting. Then I thought, why couldn't I? Well, not there as inside the diner when he proposed, but certainly close by. At night, with the diner lit up, it would be easy to see right through the front windows without being observed. I giggled at the idea. No one would ever know!

Later that night, I parked my car on the north side of the square and worked my way across the courthouse green. The rehearsal was due to finish around eight o'clock, at which time Ginny was to trick Hattie into going to the diner under the ruse of helping her move some boxes of meat out of the freezer to put into the refrigerator for thawing. I thought it would've been easier to simply ask Hattie to the diner for a slice of pie and a late-night cup of coffee, but Ginny thought Hattie might turn down that offer. On the other hand, Hattie would never turn down a friend in need.

I climbed the base of the courthouse statue and went up on my tiptoes, lifting my chin to check out my view of the diner's front windows.

Suddenly, a voice came out of nowhere, startling me. "How's the view?"

"Cade! I'm, uh . . ." I took his hand and let him help me climb back down. "What are you doing here?"

"The same thing you are, probably."

My eyes darted toward the diner, then I caught myself. "What do you mean?"

He threw his head back and laughed. "I know all about Pete's proposal."

"You do?"

"Yup. When Hattie claimed he was two-timing her in front of every busybody in town, I paid him a little visit. No guy's going to treat my sister that way."

My hand flew to my mouth. "Oh no."

He nodded. "Yup. I had the poor guy up against the wall with my fist in his face before he finally came clean. Then he made me swear not to say a word to anyone. Including you."

"Poor guy," I said, taken aback at the idea of Cade threatening anyone. I'd never seen him angry in that way, but with his well-toned muscles from construction jobs and his devotion to family, I found it easy to believe he'd be a formidable force under those circumstances. Admittedly, the idea of such brute manliness gave me a little thrill.

We fell silent, both of us staring toward the dark windows of the diner. A few minutes later, we saw Hattie and Ginny ambling down the street, heads bent together and their conversation interspersed with laughter. When they reached the diner, Ginny stepped ahead and opened the door. At once, a spark of fire pierced the darkness and settled on the wick of a taper candle. Then another and another, until the restaurant glowed softly in a flickering light.

"This isn't going to work," Cade said. "It's too dark in there, and we're too far away." He grabbed ahold of my arm and tugged me toward the street, where we crouched next to a parked car. From that vantage point, I was able to see Pete step forward, his hand outstretched as he approached Hattie. Even with the dim lighting, I could see her body take on a defensive posture. She turned slightly toward the door, and I was sure she was going to bolt. "Oh no," I hissed. But then Ginny stepped forward and whispered something in Hattie's ear, before turning to leave the diner. I held my breath, staring at the window, watching and wondering if Hattie would stay.

"Hey, you two," Ginny said from behind.

I jumped and let out a yelp. "Ginny, what are you doing?"

"The same thing you are, silly. I doubled back to spy on the lovebirds." When our only response was silence coupled with a dumbfounded expression, she added, "What? Y'all didn't think I was going to miss this, did ya? It's not every day that one of my friends receives a marriage proposal."

So we stood, huddled together behind a dusty four-door Crown Vic, spying on our friends. "At least she's sitting at the table," I said, watching as Pete helped her into a chair and poured two glasses of wine. Then he disappeared for a moment in the darkness toward the back of the room. Returning, he carried two covered dishes.

"He wanted me to fix the same meals that'd brought them together in the first place," Ginny said. I knew the story already, but she explained to Cade how, last year, Ginny had purposely mixed up their to-go orders so they'd have a chance encounter. She'd known them both and said she'd felt in her bones—her words—that they were made for each other. "Why, I'm pretty much the whole reason they've come this far," she boasted with a nod toward the window. "Look, she loves it." I turned just in time to see Pete lift the lid on her dish and Hattie's hands fly to her cheeks in delight. Then she tilted her head and smiled, motioning for him to sit with her.

"You see," Ginny stated. "It's always the food that brings people together. Why, good Southern cooking can cure about anything that ails you. Don't y'all agree?"

We did. And for the next ten minutes we watched while the two of them enjoyed their meal, sharing bites of food and sipping wine. "At least it looks like they've worked things out," I said. All three of us were now leaning against the car's bumper, unable to crouch any longer. Not that it mattered. Hattie and Pete wouldn't notice us anyway; they only had eyes for each other.

"Isn't this the most romantic thing ever?" Ginny gushed. In the light from a nearby streetlamp, I could see her eyes glistening with emotion.

"Was your marriage proposal this romantic?" I asked her, noticing that Cade had started shifting from foot to foot.

She folded her arms and shook her head slowly, letting out a tight little laugh. "Are you kidding? My marriage proposal consisted of Daddy telling Sam he could either make an honest woman out of me or become fish bait at the bottom of Hill Lake. Sam didn't care much for the second option, so two weeks later we tied the knot. At least it was a church wedding. Small, but I wore a dress and—"

"Hey," Cade interrupted. "I think he's finally going to ask."

Ginny and I turned our focus back to window, where we saw Pete push back from the table and drop to one knee in front of Hattie. I squinted, wishing the lighting inside the diner was better. I would have loved to be able to see the sparkle in her eye as he opened the case and presented the ring to her. But what I saw was equally amazing. Wiping tears from her face, Hattie nodded while Pete removed the ring from the case and placed it on her finger. Then she leapt from her chair for what I thought was going to be a passionate embrace, but instead she crossed the room and headed for the front door of the diner.

"What the . . ." Cade said, grabbing me and scurrying around the backside of the car. Ginny was on our heels, giggling as she crouched down beside us.

"Hey, y'all!" Hattie's voice cut through the night air. "Come look at the size of this rock Pete just gave me!"

"Oh no," Cade moaned, leaning forward and lightly banging his head against the side of the car. "How'd she know?"

Ginny and I exchanged a quick hug and burst into giggles before jumping out from behind the car. We rushed right over to share in our friends' new happiness.

Chapter 18

Debutante Rule #011: In the face of trouble, keep
your feet on the ground . . . and be sure you're
wearing nice shoes.

I woke up Friday morning still feeling elated about Hattie's
engagement. Her ring, a large solitaire diamond mounted
high and haloed by a circle of smaller diamonds, was as
elegant and stylish as she was. I had to hand it to Ginny: she'd
done a good job helping Pete choose the perfect ring. And we
could all rest a bit easier now that things were on the right
track with the happy couple.

As for the rest of Friday, it flew by in a whirlwind of activity. The morning was spent packaging and mailing my online
orders: a gift basket for a law firm in Macon and a case of
preserves going to an upscale hotel restaurant in Atlanta that
hoped to give their customers an authentic taste of Georgia.
Harper's Peach Products were catching on across the state.
In addition to the online orders, Margie over at Sunny Side
Up Bed & Breakfast phoned in an urgent request for a dozen
more jars of spiced peach preserves. At the last minute, I

decided to throw in one of my new jars of sugar-free jams as a bonus. Hopefully, she'd like it and order more.

Between running errands and squeezing in some odd jobs around the shop, Ginny and I made a run to the Pack-n-Carry to pick up a few last-minute items for the cotillion dinner, after which we spent the rest of the evening in the kitchen of Red's Diner, along with Hattie, precooking as much food as possible and carefully rehashing the plans for the next day's events.

Not that all that planning made much of a difference, as I soon discovered the next day. That old saying: "The best-laid schemes of mice and men . . ." Well, it applied to cotillion dinners. Because as it turned out, no amount of planning could have prepared me for the flurry of chaos I encountered Saturday afternoon. For starters, Ginny had made arrangements for us to borrow the Baptist Church's van to transport the food from the diner to the Wheeler Plantation, which was great, except we'd failed to account for the length of the vehicle—a fifteen-seater mainly used to transport seniors from the convalescent home to church Sunday mornings. As I tried to back it up to the diner's back door for easy loading, I rammed the Dumpster on the other side of the alley, leaving a nice golf ball–sized dent on the bumper. Oops. Then Carla, bless her heart, stumbled while carrying one of the appetizer trays and sent a dozen or more peach salsa and Brie crostini flying through the air. No biggie, though. We had leftover ingredients, and Hattie was able to whip up some more. Nonetheless, by the time we pulled into the back service drive at the plantation, I was frazzled. How did I ever end up roped into this Peach Cotillion deal in the first place?

"Can't you get any closer than this?" Hattie whined as I maneuvered toward the back entrance of the plantation house.

I threw the gear into park and turned off the engine, pulled out the keys and dangled them in front of her face. "Be my guest," I said, shooting her a scorching look.

"Okay, okay. Never mind." She waved away the keys with her newly diamond-studded hand. (She'd been doing a lot of waving since her proposal.) "Geez, you're cranky."

I heard a chuckle from the back of the van and glimpsed in the rearview mirror and caught Carla rolling her eyes at us. She was strapped in the back between several large roasting pans and stacks of trays, balancing a full pitcher of pre-made salad dressing on her lap. I was glad to see at least some semblance of happiness from her, even if at my expense. She'd been pretty miserable since learning that Maggie slipped into a coma. She was also feeling worried about the sheriff tracking her down over the two hundred dollars she took out of Vivien's purse. I'd assured her that Ray had everything under control but reminded her that she wasn't going to be able to keep the ill-gained money. As soon as the cotillion was over, we'd figure out a way to return the money to Vivien's family.

All in all, despite the current chaos and the excitement ahead, regret hung over my head. I'd hoped that Vivien's killer and Maggie's would-be killer would have been brought to justice long before the ball. Instead, one woman's murder was still unsolved, and another woman was in the hospital fighting for her life. "Do you suppose Maggie's kids will be here today? Nash was supposed to bring Emily."

Hattie took her eyes off her ring for a second and glanced over at me. "Last I heard, neither Nash nor Belle would be here. But Belle felt so bad about her marshal being left without a date and Nash not going with Emily that she asked her boyfriend to take Emily. Belle's so thoughtful—like her mama—and at a time like this with their mama so sick and all, well, it speaks of good upbringing."

"You're right," I said, casting another look into the backseat. Carla had returned to looking miserable. "Well, let's get this show on the road, shall we?" I said, wishing I hadn't brought up the subject in the first place.

After a half hour of unloading, we finally had everything inside the kitchen and ready to start heating. The Wheelers' kitchen was specially designed to accommodate large parties. Along the back wall was a double glass door cooler with shelving deep enough to hold large trays of food. The rest of the kitchen was set up with two cooking stations, both with large gas ranges, stainless steel work surfaces and enough pots and pans to stock a culinary school.

"Here's the deal," I said, glancing at the large wall clock that hung just outside the kitchen's spacious walk-in pantry. It was just a little after two. "The roasts will take about three hours, so we've got to get them in the oven now." I set the temperature on the large ovens to preheat. I paused and pulled the instructions Ginny gave me out of my back pocket. "Let's see. It looks like things kick off around five with the presentation followed by a receiving line where the debutantes meet each guest. The guests will be served drinks and appetizers at that time." I looked over my shoulder at Hattie. "We have all the appetizer trays, right?"

She pointed to the row of trays in the fridge. "Yup. There's five trays of the crostini, three trays of prosciutto-wrapped peach slices with Parmesan and two roasting pans full of chipotle and peach–glazed meatballs."

I scanned the directions. "Okay, it says here we should start reheating the meatballs around four o'clock. The crostini only takes a few minutes, so . . . Goodness! Are we going to have enough oven space with the roasts in there?"

Hattie bent down and glanced into the ovens. "I certainly hope so."

"We don't have to serve this stuff, too, do we?" Carla asked, frowning toward the trays.

"No, of course not," I told her. "The Wheelers have hired a waitstaff for this evening."

"And they'll be on hand in plenty of time to start carrying trays of appetizers," Stephanie Wheeler said from the kitchen doorway. She strolled into the kitchen, looking stylish in sleek black yoga pants and a quarter-zip jacket. Suddenly, my own choice of cargo pants and a T-shirt, not to mention my work boots, seemed out of place. I tugged at my shirt and watched as Stephanie started lifting foil on trays and peeking at our supplies. She must have liked what she saw, because after surveying the food, she clapped her hands together and flashed a bright smile. "Everything is going to be fabulous tonight, I just know it!"

I tried to match her enthusiasm, but I barely felt capable of getting the food heated and ready to serve on time, let alone worrying about it tasting "faaabulous," as she put it. Then she started droning on about the evening's schedule and how we should have the appetizers ready by such and such time and please don't forget to make an all-vegetable plate for Mrs. So and So who had just recently turned vegetarian. By the time she finished her checklist, I was feeling like a hurricane of stress had just blown through my life. I'd handled the aftermath of real hurricanes by just sucking it up and pitching in to work. Certainly I could handle a little ol' cotillion dinner. Couldn't I?

"That woman must have us confused with the hired help," Hattie declared as soon as Stephanie excused herself to go get beautiful. "Maybe someone forgot to tell her we volunteered for this job."

"Hawk has told me that she's demanding," I said, reaching into one of the boxes I'd packed. "Look what I brought," I said. At the last minute, I'd thought to bring the old Czar radio from my shop. "This should make working a little easier." I set it on the counter and turned it on. Instantly, the room flooded with the sounds of Johnny Cash's song "I Walk the Line."

Hattie squealed. "Oh yes, Johnny's old songs always make things better."

"Who's Johnny?" Carla asked. "And do we really have to listen to this?"

"Shut your mouth, girl," Hattie countered. "The man's a legend." She started swinging her hips to the tune, filling in here and there with her own high-pitched version of the lyrics.

As it turned out, the local station was featuring a Johnny Cash marathon. So—much to Carla's chagrin—Johnny spurred us on for the next couple of hours. Together, we chopped, mixed and cooked until everything was set for the dinner.

"Pour me another glass of that, would ya?" I told Hattie, who was busy mixing extra punch. While the adults were having cocktails prepared by the Wheelers' personal bartender, Hattie and I were in charge of providing liquid refreshments for the younger set. We'd come up with a sparkling peach punch made from peach nectar, ginger ale and lemon-lime soda. It was good, too. I was already on my third glass.

"Yeah, I think we should all have some," Hattie said, filling up cups for herself and Carla. "With all these ovens going it's hotter than Hades in here."

I took my glass and leaned against the counter, enjoying the cool sweetness of the drink, while I surveyed our progress:

The roasts were ready to come out of the oven, which would leave them plenty of time to rest before slicing. A pot of peach chutney was simmering on the stove, ready to be paired with the pork at the last minute. The salad was chopped and waiting to be dressed, and the appetizers were heating and almost ready to be plated. "Uh-oh," I said, glancing up at the wall clock. "We'd better get the punch upstairs before guests start arriving."

Hattie slid two large containers our way. "Take Carla with you to help. I'll start getting the appetizers plated."

I handed a container to Carla and took the other myself. "We'll take the back stairs, so we don't run into the guests," I suggested, heading to the rear of the kitchen to a large butler's pantry. In the back of the pantry, another door opened up to a short hallway leading to the formal dining room, sunroom and another set of stairs that led to the second and third floors: a common setup for antebellum mansions where back stairways were often used by servants.

By the time we'd reached the second floor, I was breathing heavily, my arm muscles straining with the weight of the pitcher. Too much of Mama's fried chicken and not enough exercise, I thought. Finally, we reached the third floor, emerging into yet another hallway. This one, however, opened up onto a wide landing with inlaid parquet floors and potted topiaries. Over the tall banister to the right, I could see to the bottom of the sweeping stairway to the foyer where several debutantes in flowing white gowns were already gathered with their dark-suited marshals and doting parents. I pressed up on my tiptoes and squinted to see if Emily had arrived, but there was no sign of her or Ginny and Sam yet. I did see the congressman and Stephanie, looking every bit the dashing couple as they greeted their guests and welcomed them into their home. Standing behind them were two tall men dressed in usher uniforms ready to show guests upstairs. "They're getting ready to come up," I told Carla, directing her toward a set of massive carved doors, opened wide to invite guests into the ballroom. "Let's get this inside." We dashed into the ballroom with our containers, stopping short when we saw the magnificent room.

"Holy crud!" I heard Carla mutter.

I agreed. The ballroom, with its historic architecture, crystal chandeliers and floor-to-ceiling windows, was breathtaking. Then there were the decorations. Absolutely stunning, I thought, as I took in the brocade linen tablecloths and straight-backed chairs covered in cream-colored fabric and tied in the back with flouncy peach-colored bows. In the center of each table, a tall brass vase filled with white and peach colored roses and trailing vines was offset by glowing tapered candles. Crystal glasses and gold-rimmed chargers seemed to sparkle in the candlelight, creating an almost magical air to each table.

"How do you like it?"

My eyes snapped across the room to where Pete was standing at the cake table putting the final touches on a large arrangement of roses. "They're gorgeous," I told him after we joined him. "I've never seen anything so beautiful." In the back of my mind, I felt a tiny niggle of regret over having missed my own cotillion. Although I didn't think my cotillion, held in the back room at the VFW, would have been such an elegant affair. For a second, I wondered what Mama would say when she and the others on the governess's board arrived and saw all this. The board always occupied a table of honor at the cotillion, a small way to say thank you for all their efforts to bring such an event to fruition. I couldn't help but think that Mama would be sitting at the head table, eating more than just peachy food tonight. No doubt she'd also be eating her words about not wanting the ball to be held here at the Wheeler Plantation.

Next to me, Carla's eyes widened and settled on the center of the table. I followed her gaze, admiring the three-tiered stand filled with miniature cakes decorated with peach and cream fondant. They were like tiny pieces of art and sure to be the talk of the town all next week. Ezra was going to be in high demand from here on out, that was for sure. I nudged Carla. "The punch bowls are right down there," I said, moving down the table to where two large crystal bowls were surrounded by neatly stacked matching punch glasses. Off to the side, a separate bar was set up for the adults. A bartender was already busy filling wineglasses. "I saw you admiring the cakes," I said to Carla as we filled the punch bowls. "That's the baker I was telling you about. His business is growing, and he's going to be looking for help."

She shrugged. "I'll be long gone as soon as school's out. Some of my friends in Chicago are getting a place of their own. I'm going to move in with them."

I decided not to push it. She seemed dead set against sticking around here. Who was I to argue? I'd said many of the same things at her age. "We'd better get back downstairs. Hattie's probably got her hands full."

Back on the first floor, I took a little detour to the restroom. All that punch was catching up to me. Only when I tried the handle, it was locked. Shoot! I really had to go. Deciding my restroom break couldn't wait another second, I raced through the kitchen, told Hattie I'd be right back and headed for the back stairs again. Halfway there, I realized the third-floor bathroom would probably be crowded with primping debs. My best bet was to find a restroom on the second floor.

I knew it was bad manners to be in the Wheelers' private

quarters, but in this case, urgency seemed to overrule convention. So, I ducked into the master suite and quickly located a bathroom. Thank goodness!

A few minutes later, on my way out of the bathroom, I lingered a bit to admire the master bedroom. Stephanie had wonderful taste, I thought, rubbing my hand along the wood banister of the four-post bed, which was done up in a luxurious gold and taupe covering and piled high with fringed pillows. The entire room was the epitome of understated class with bold white crown molding offsetting neutrally painted walls and tasteful gold-toned accent pieces. The only thing that distracted from the room's elegance was another gaudy oil painting of General Aloysius Wheeler. Man, these people must really think highly of their steely-eyed ancestor. I shuddered. I know I sure wouldn't want to wake up and see those eyes first thing every morning.

From the floor above, I heard the soft strains of orchestra music punctuated by the clicking sound of a microphone snapping to life. I needed to get a move on; the presentation was about to start. But just as I turned to leave, something caught my eye. Something red on the floor next to the nightstand. Blood? I walked over and took a closer look. No, not blood, but a pill. A red pill. The same color and shape as the ones I'd discovered under Maggie's limp body.

I stiffened and shuffled back a step or two, rubbing down the tiny hairs raising on my arms. Then moving forward again, I picked up the pill for a closer examination. I wasn't positive, but they sure looked like the pills I'd found by Maggie. I scanned the stand's surface but didn't see any sign of a prescription bottle, so I opened the drawer a little and peered inside. Nothing. I yanked the drawer open further, letting loose with a couple cusswords when it slid off its track and crashed to the floor. My hand shot out, grabbing a prescription bottle before it rolled under the bed. I didn't recognize the name of the prescription, but the pharmacy directions said take one pill before bedtime to induce sleep. I opened the bottle and peered inside. Yup. Red tablets. Another quick look at the label told me the prescription was filled just a little over a week ago for a three-month supply. But now, there were only a few left. I thought I knew where the rest had gone. Could Stephanie be involved somehow with the attempt on Maggie's life? But why would Stephanie want to kill Maggie? I was more confused now than ever.

In the background, I heard the announcer start to present the debutantes: *"Ms. Amelia Forbes, daughter of Mr. and Mrs. Robert Forbes . . ."*

Hastily, I slid the drawer back on its tracks and started replacing its spilled contents, while my mind reeled with details of Vivien's murder case. All along I thought it had to do with blackmail. But I must've been wrong. What could Vivien possibly have had on Stephanie, or any of the Wheelers for that matter? These people lived a charmed, exemplary life. They were pillars of the community going way back—

"What are you doing in here?" came a voice from behind.

I jumped up and wheeled around, finding myself face-to-face with Stephanie. "Mrs. Wheeler! Uh . . . I just popped in to use the restroom. The one downstairs was locked," I explained. "But I should probably get back down to the kitchen now."

She looked down at the pill bottle in my hand and then to the floor where some of the contents of the drawer still lay strewn on the carpet. Her eyes narrowed into tiny slits. "So you've got it all figured out now."

"Ms. Janie Stanton. Daughter of Mr. and Mrs. Leonard Stanton," the announcer was saying.

My heart pounded as I watched her expression darken with

anger. There was no doubt in my mind now. Stephanie Wheeler was a killer. I grasped the bottle even tighter and started to make my way past her, but as I did, she snatched my arm and jerked me back.

"Give me that," she hissed.

I shook off her arm and pushed past her, breaking into a run as soon as I hit the hallway.

"Ms. Sophie Bearden. Daughter of Mr. and Mrs. Thomas Bearden."

My palm was so sweaty, I could hardly manage to open the door to the stairwell. Glancing over my shoulder, I saw Stephanie coming down the hall, talking into her cell. Who was she calling? The congressman? Was he in on it, too? Vivien's blackmailing tactics may have worked on Debra and Maggie, but she'd crossed the wrong people when she threatened the Wheelers. And if I didn't get out of here fast, I may end up just like her.

Still looking over my shoulder, I stumbled into the stairwell, my foot slipping on the first step and twisting underneath me. Before I knew it, I was sliding down the stairs, each rung cutting into the small of my back. Somehow I managed to snag the railing and stop myself halfway down the sharp wooden steps. Just then, the door at the top of the stairs opened and Stephanie started toward me. "The back stairs," I heard her say. My back was screaming in pain, but I righted myself and kept going.

Reaching the bottom, I burst through the door and collided with Carla. "There you are," she started. "Man, is Hattie ever ticked—"

"Run!" I yelled, pushing her forward. But I was too late. Our path was blocked by a bulky, dark-haired man who I recognized as the other security guard from the Mother-Daughter Tea.

He pulled a gun from under his jacket just as Stephanie stepped up behind us and hissed into our ears, "Scream or make another stupid move and I'll have Franco shoot you." I believed her.

Suddenly, the house filled with music. The cotillion waltz had started. I imagined my mama and sister, seated at the Board of Governesses table, their chins held with a prideful tilt as they watched the culmination of their hard work over the past months. I don't know why I ever thought the cotillion waltz was so stupid. Suddenly, I wanted more than anything to be there with them, watching the belles in their beautiful gowns twirl around their white-gloved marshals.

"I'll be taking this," Stephanie said, snatching the pill bottle from my hand and pushing us toward the sunroom. She was forcing us toward the double doors that led to the back patio. *Then where?* I wondered. *Down to the river?*

"You tried to kill Maggie, but why?" I said over my shoulder, but as we made our way into the sunroom, something clicked in my memory. The photocopied letter Carla found in Vivien's purse—it was old, she said, with fancy writing. I'd seen something like that recently, right here in this very house. . . . My eyes slid over to the wall where the framed commendation from Robert E. Lee hung next to the portrait of General Wheeler. "It was the letter, wasn't it? Vivien was blackmailing you with it." I wondered what was in that letter that would be worth killing for. An old deed to property? Maybe a birth certificate that would upset their pristine lineage?

Stephanie's lips formed a strange sneer as she stared blankly at the portrait of the congressman's famous ancestor. Suddenly her voice took on an eerie monotone. "All these years my husband's been bragging about his famous ancestor, and no one knew Aloysius Wheeler was a traitor."

Oh my!

"Come to find out he sold secrets to the Yanks. That's how he kept all this—" She waved her hands to encompass the room. "It's why every other plantation in the area suffered at the hands of the enemy but the Wheeler Plantation persevered." She shook her head. "Just Vivien's bad luck that she found that letter inside the field desk. Who did she think she was anyway? Trying to extort money from me. That letter would have ruined our family heritage. And this close to the election! I really had no choice but to have Franco kill her. Just like I have no choice but to have him kill you two." She looked toward Franco and nodded her head, giving him the go-ahead to carry out her evil plan.

"It was only a photocopy," I said, thinking hard to form some reason to stop this madness. "The original is still out there. Someone will eventually find it and figure out what you've done."

Stephanie tilted her head back and let out a strange little cackle. Then she leveled her gaze on us, her eyes taking on a dark, menacing look. "I've already taken care of that. Besides, once you two are gone, no one will know about any of this."

Next to me Carla began to tremble with fear or anger, or maybe both. Was she putting it all together in her mind, realizing that Stephanie was the one who tried to have Maggie killed? I eyed the muscles bulging under Franco's shirtsleeves. Now it all made sense. He was definitely strong enough to force those pills down Maggie's throat and then strangle her. He was probably strong enough to plunge scissors into Vivien's neck, too. And he was definitely strong enough to carry out Stephanie's latest orders—killing us!

I reached over and clasped Carla's hand in mine, hoping

to keep her calm. We both needed a clear mind in order to get out of this alive.

"Take them down by the river, Franco." There was no mistaking the undertone of evil in Stephanie's voice as she spoke. "And make sure no one ever finds their bodies."

Chapter 19

Debutante Rule #018: A debutante is more than just a pretty face. Look again. We wear boots under our dresses, and they're made for kickin'.

As Stephanie turned away, Franco grabbed Carla and held the gun to her back. "Here's the deal," he said to me, jerking his head toward the patio doors. "We're going to take a little walk. You're going first, and this lovely young lady and I will be right behind you. If you run or do anything to attract attention, I'll pull the trigger. No one will even hear it over the music upstairs. Got it?"

I swallowed hard and nodded. My legs felt like lead, but I managed to move forward and open the doors. As soon as the familiar smell of fresh-cut grass and magnolia blossoms hit my nostrils, I started to lose it. This had always been my favorite time of year. I remembered many a hot May evening out on the porch, escaping the bottled-up heat of the house. Mama and Daddy would be in the cane chairs, discussing the day's events, maybe even some new strategy about peach growing, while Ida swung on the porch swing with one of her dolls. After a while, Ray and I would grow restless and run out to chase fireflies as they rose from the tall blades of grass along the edge of the orchard.

The poignant memory made my eyes sting, tears blurring my vision. I stumbled a few times and then fell all the way to the ground. "Get up!" Franco ordered.

As I got up, I dared a glance backward. My eyes briefly met Carla's. I knew the look of terror on her face mirrored my own fear. The music had stopped, and the only sound coming from the house was the clinking of pots and pans from the open windows of the kitchen. The cotillion waltz was finished, and the guests would soon be seated for dinner. Hattie must be frantic trying to get everything together by herself. What would she think when we didn't show up? Certainly she would send someone looking for us. Wouldn't she?

"To your right and head toward that building," Franco ordered.

I obeyed and walked toward a barnlike structure. When we reached the side of the building, Franco ripped open a large sliding door and motioned for us to go inside, where he led us to a four-wheel utility vehicle, the type with a roll bar, two front seats and a back cargo area. My senses heightened. I was familiar with this type of vehicle. I'd driven them many times over the years, especially in rough terrain when it was necessary to get medical supplies and water to remote mountain villages.

"See those blocks over there," Franco said, indicating toward a stack of cement blocks. "Load a couple into the back of this vehicle." He stood with the gun trained on Carla as I did what he said. Her shoulders shook as she softly sobbed. "Now get that rope over there on the tool bench."

I knew what he was planning. He was going to tie the blocks to our dead bodies and sink us to the bottom of the river for eternity. Fish bait. Suddenly, I remembered Ginny joking about her own daddy threatening to make fish bait out of Sam. She'd meant it to be funny, but now I was facing that very fate. For real!

I walked slowly toward the workbench, the sound of Carla's sobs echoing around me. I knew I had to do something. I couldn't let this monster kill us. I could try to jump him, but attempting to overpower a man of his size would certainly prove fruitless. Then, I saw my answer. Next to the rope was a utility knife, its razor-edge blade fully extended.

"Move it!" Franco yelled.

I startled and snatched the rope, sliding the utility knife into the side pocket of my cargo pants. Turning around, I carried the rope to the utility truck and threw it on top of the cement blocks. Franco told us to get in the front, then he climbed into the back and positioned himself on top of the blocks, one hand on the roll bar above our heads and the other pointing the gun our way. "The keys are in the ignition," he said. "Turn it on."

I did as he said, starting the engine and slowly backing up until I had enough head room to turn the vehicle around to face the door. "Nice and easy, now," he said. I was acutely aware of the gun trained at our heads as I reached down and put the vehicle in gear. But instead of putting my hand back on the wheel, I pulled out the utility knife, thrust my arm up quickly and sliced it into the meaty underside of the arm holding the roll bar. He screamed out in agony and aimed the gun directly at my head.

I ducked and punched the accelerator, gunfire zinging past my ears. The sudden forward momentum threw him off balance momentarily. I floored the pedal then yelled, "Hang on!" as I slammed on the brake and cranked the wheel as hard as I could. Franco flew forward, hitting the back of the seat. That's when I rammed the utility knife into his shoulder.

This time, he dropped the gun and reeled up, screaming in pain. I punched it again, and he toppled over backward off the vehicle.

"Get out of here!" Carla screamed. But I glanced behind us and saw that Franco was starting to stand. I needed to make sure he wouldn't follow, possibly with a backup gun. So I threw the gear into reverse and pressed the accelerator again, this time ramming Franco with the back bumper. His body flew through the air and landed in a heap several yards away.

"Don't you two come showing your sorry faces around here after all the work is done!" Hattie complained the moment we ran into the kitchen. She was standing amidst piles of pots and pans, crumpled wads of tinfoil and greasy utensils. Two members of the waitstaff were there with her. Apparently she'd recruited help.

"Call the police right now," I screeched. "And stay with Carla. I've got to find Stephanie."

"What's going on?" she called after me.

"Carla will fill you in. Just call the cops, will you?" I started toward the back of the kitchen then halted, realizing I didn't want to chance being on the deserted back stairway again. What if Stephanie was lying in wait for me? Or, maybe she had another goon working for her. Who knew how many of those she had up her sleeve.

After a quick shuffle step, I headed out the other way, sprinting down the hallway toward the front foyer. My feet pounded as I bolted up the steps, slowing a little as I passed the landing between the second and third floors. By the time I reached the top floor, I was sucking wind. Leaning forward, I placed my hands on my knees and took a few deep breaths.

"Is there something I can do for you, miss?" one of the door ushers asked.

I righted myself and held up my hand. "No . . . no, thanks. I'm fine," I managed, trying to slip inside the ballroom.

"Hold on a minute," he said, taking in my ragged appearance. "The waitstaff use that door down there."

Not willing to take the time to argue, I shuffled down the hall and entered through the service door. The door opened up on the far side of the ballroom, near a bank of large potted ficus plants.

I hung close to the back wall and surveyed the room. If circumstances had been different, I would have taken time to really appreciate how elegant everything appeared: sparkling gowns in the candlelight, white-gloved waiters . . . oh, and there they were, the congressman and Mrs. Wheeler, sitting at the head of the room at the table of honor. And about five yards behind them, practically blending into the wall, was Hawk with his arms folded across his chest and his eyes scanning the room of people in front of the congressman. Stephanie was next to her man, of course. And by the looks of it, she was thoroughly enjoying her shrimp skewer. Guess murdering people didn't curb her appetite.

I deliberated for a second then decided my best bet was to stand my ground and keep an eye on her until the sheriff arrived. I stepped to the side, trying to look casual and not call attention to myself. Only my mother, who was sitting at the Board of Governesses table across the room, caught sight of me. She pointed to her dinner plate and shot me two thumbs up. I smiled and shot her a tentative wave, sinking further back into the wall and hoping no one else noticed my presence. But then, Ida, who was right next to Mama, decided to come over and say a few words.

I tried to shoo her away as she approached, her chiffon dress swishing and her heels clicking, but she was a woman on a mission and there was no stopping her. "I just had to come over and tell you how wonderfully tasty the food is tonight. I'll admit, when Mama recommended your assistance to the board as part of the catering committee, I thought she was crazy. Why, the whole family knows you can't cook worth a . . ." I tuned her out, arching my neck to see past Ida's impossibly large hairdo. But when I caught sight of the Wheelers' table again, I saw Stephanie stand and quickly excuse herself. Uh-oh! She'd spotted me and was making her way down the opposite side of the ballroom, making a break for the front door.

What if she gets away? Where is that sheriff anyway?

"And did you see those gorgeous cakes? They're almost too pretty to—"

"Excuse me," I said, starting to break away. There was no way I was going to let Stephanie get away. Except Hawk intercepted me before I could get very far.

"Hey, darlin', why don't you come with me?" He grabbed me by the crook of my arm and escorted me through the ballroom doors, waving away the concerned usher as we passed. Back out on the front landing, he looked down at me with concern. "You're not lookin' so good."

"That's because your friend Franco just tried to kill me," I hissed into his ear.

That got his attention.

I continued, keeping my voice low, "And, your boss is a murderer." I gave him a quick lowdown on everything.

What I said must have induced mental whiplash, because his expression changed from shock to anger and then back to shock again. But when his features finally settled, it was definitely rage I saw. With a sudden lurch, he broke into a full sprint. I took off after him, barely keeping up as he bolted down the stairs and out the front door. We paused on the front porch. There was no sign of Stephanie anywhere. Or the sheriff. What was keeping Maudy?

We were about to head back inside to look for Stephanie when off to the right we heard the sound of an engine firing up. "It's coming from the carport," Hawk said. "Come on!"

He half pulled, half dragged me across the lawn until we reached his bike. I hesitated. "No way, Hawk. I can't."

He snapped his helmet in place and handed me the one from the bike's back rack. "Get on," he ordered.

I shook my head. "I just can't."

"Fine. Stay, then."

I couldn't do that, either. So, abandoning all caution, I buckled the helmet into place and threw a leg over the seat just as he revved the motor to life. Leaning into him, I wrapped my arms around his torso and tightened my grip as we roared into action. The sensation of the engine and the feeling of air as it moved over my face took me right back to that fateful night. For a second, I felt the same reckless abandon I did then, flying free as we tore over the road, scenery flashing by. . . .

"Those are her taillights," Hawk yelled over his shoulder, then accelerated the bike to full throttle. I clung harder, melding against his back as we moved in unison, leaning through each turn and racing ahead toward Stephanie's vehicle. I knew where she was heading. To the freeway. Only at this speed, she was never going to be able to navigate the turnoff. *What is she doing?* She wasn't slowing down a bit; instead she was speeding up. I watched in horror as her car blew past the exit ramp and hit the ditch on the opposite side of the road, the impact sending her vehicle hurtling through the air. In an explosion of metal and glass, the car flipped over and over before finally settling on its roof.

Hawk screeched to a stop and kicked down the stand. Immediately, I slid off the back, shedding my helmet and dodging pieces of metal and glass as I ran toward the decimated vehicle. I could hear Hawk's heavy boots pounding the ground behind me.

Dropping to my knees, I crouched down and peered through the shattered glass. What I saw would stick with me for the rest of my life: Stephanie's head, slumped at an unnatural angle against the steering wheel, blood trickling past her lifeless eyes.

Chapter 20

Debutante Rule #090: A debutante knows that family isn't just blood and relations. It's the people who love you no matter what.

Through the next week, I replayed the vision of that horrible wreck over and over in my mind. Could Hawk and I have done something different? Would Stephanie be dead if we hadn't chased after her? If I hadn't invaded the ballroom to watch her? And surely it was my confrontation with Maggie outside the restroom that day at the tea that tipped off Stephanie and started this whole ugly chain of events. I couldn't shake the fact that I'd contributed to Stephanie's death somehow, even though logically I knew it was her own actions that led to her demise.

As expected, the death of a congressman's wife drew both state and national media. In a matter of hours, our little town was overrun with reporters and camera crews. Not to mention our own duteous reporter, Frances Simms, who stuck to me like white on rice. It seemed everywhere I went, she was there, notepad in hand, staring me down with those beady eyes and firing off questions like a Gatling gun.

Unfortunately, I couldn't answer half of them. Not that I would, but there was still a large part of me that fretted over the loose ends of the case. What was in that envelope that Stephanie had Hawk deliver to Professor Scott? Was the professor somehow involved? Where was that original letter that proved that General Aloysius Wheeler was a traitor? Was it still out there somewhere? Without it, there were still so many unanswered questions. Sadly, there was only one person left who might have the answers—Franco. And that was a problem. Because despite being stabbed and run into by a sport utility vehicle, Franco somehow managed to make an escape. Although, the sheriff was confident that he'd soon be found. I had my doubts.

So far, no charges had been brought against the congressman. He'd maintained that his hands were clean of all wrongdoing, and, of course, to demonstrate his innocence, he'd hired a team of attorneys to design an airtight defense strategy. Fortunately, the one person in all this who really did need a defense strategy was receiving free legal representation from Ray. In exchange for her full cooperation, Ray convinced the sheriff not to bring any charges against Carla. So on Monday, Carla and I spent the entire morning in the sheriff's office, rehashing bits and pieces of the case, including Maggie's secret career as an erotic romance author and Debra Bearden's ploy to eliminate the competition at the Peach Queen Pageant. I had to shake my head every time I thought of Debra's dilemma. Why anyone would go so far to win a pageant was beyond me. But, the fear of the truth coming out was weighing heavily on her, evident by the fact that she'd been spending all her time out of town "visiting relatives." As for the damning picture of her sabotaging the costume, it was still missing along with the other blackmail fodder. The sheriff, Carla and I spent almost a whole day tearing through the junk piled in the church basement, finally coming to the conclusion that Franco must have taken the evidence the day he tried to kill Maggie. Either that, or Stephanie destroyed it all.

Something good did happen midweek, though. Defying the odds, Maggie Jones woke from her coma and was expected to make a full recovery. The news of her "awakening," as the town folk have come to call it, came to us when the bells of the Baptist church started ringing. Since that usually only happens Sunday mornings and after an occasional wedding, it sent a ripple of alarm through town. Within minutes, a large crowd gathered at the church. Expecting the worst, we slid into the pews with downcast eyes and sullen spirits. Imagine our astonishment when Betty Lou took to the pulpit and announced that Maggie was awake. Of course, Mama was just sure it was the power of her prayer chain that led to Maggie's recovery. Maybe she was right. Nonetheless, the news was just what the town needed to banish the dark cloud left over from the shock of so much tragedy.

Thursday evening, I went with Carla to the Crenshaws' house to return the money she'd "found" in Vivien's purse. I wasn't too surprised to find a "For Sale" sign outside the Crenshaws' residence. With the family already devastated by Vivien's death, the realization that she was a blackmailer had about sent Nate over the edge. I felt horrible about the assumptions I'd made about Nate killing his wife. He was broken. My heart went out to him that evening Carla and I visited. I wished there was something I could do to ease his agony, but sometimes there aren't any words. In the face of all his pain, however, Nate managed to do something extremely generous and kindhearted. He promptly turned the money back to Carla, placing it in her palm and covering her hand with his. He insisted she keep the money, telling her to use it for something that would make her happy. I thought I knew exactly what that would be—a ticket back home. Much to my surprise, however, Carla informed me that she planned to send the money to Reverend Jones. She figured they might need help paying all their medical bills since Maggie's hospitalization. I wasn't sure if that meant she'd changed her mind about leaving Cays Mill or not. I hoped she would stay. I was really feeling attached to the girl.

For all the confusion, upset and hubbub of the week, I still managed to pull together the final preparations for Peachy Keen's grand opening. And when I threw open those doors on Saturday afternoon, I found a crowd of friends, neighbors and family gathered outside on the walk. Everyone was there, including Daddy, who'd taken time away from the orchard, something he rarely did during harvest. Mama was there, beaming with pride. And of course, both Ida and Hollis with the kids in tow, and even Ray, who'd popped back over from Perry just for the occasion. In a ceremonious gesture, Ginny and I stretched a long peach-colored ribbon in front of the door, which Mayor Wade Marshall snipped with the town's official ribbon-cutting scissors before running over and picking up his banjo. For the next few hours, the mayor's band, the Peach Pickers, serenaded the crowd with lively bluegrass tunes.

"Well, I'd say that was a success," Ginny gushed later that day after the shop had finally cleared out. She, Hattie and Cade stuck around to help clean up after all the others left. Actually, they'd been there the whole afternoon helping out with everything from ringing up customers to restocking shelves. I'm not sure what I would have done without them. All in all, it was one of the best days ever. And making it all the better was the fact that my friends and family were there to share it with me.

I was just about to turn over the "Closed" sign when I spied Maudy Payne coming down the walk. I held the door, and she sauntered in, an aura of confidence and bravado coming in with her. Once inside, she removed her Stetson and threw it down on the counter, taking a deep breath and puffing out her chest. "We apprehended Franco late last night over in Marion County. Seems he was trying to get to the Alabama line. I just returned from questioning him."

"And?" Cade prompted. The rest of us listened anxiously, waiting to hear if she'd unburden our curiosities or if she'd only stopped by to reassert her position of authority in the case. She'd been a little touchy ever since I'd figured out the murder.

"He was delusional with pain." She nodded my way. "Seems our little Nola here messed him up pretty bad. But lucky for us, he was willin' to talk. 'Course, it's not hard to compel a confession from a man who needs medical attention. He was more than eager to tell us what we needed to know while he waited for his pain meds." Her lips curled upward in some sort of half smile, half sneer. I shuddered. I didn't even want to think about the tactics Maudy used to ferret his confession. Not that I felt sorry for the guy.

"Anyway," she continued, "he maintains that the congressman didn't know anything about the murder or the attempt on Maggie's life."

"Of course not," Cade said. "The congressman is probably going to pay his legal fees."

"Was he the one who forced the pills down Maggie's throat?" I asked. I heard Ginny sigh and looked over to see Hattie put an arm around her.

Maudy nodded. "Yup. Said Stephanie paid him extra

money for all sorts of side jobs. Trying to kill Maggie was just the tip of the iceberg. Luckily, Debra came by and interrupted him before it was too late. But get this . . . right after the cotillion, he was planning a little trip up to the hospital. Stephanie was concerned that Maggie may make it out of her coma and start pointing fingers. They were planning to finish her off."

"What a coldhearted witch," Hattie exclaimed. We all nodded in agreement.

Maudy shook her head. "Yeah, Vivien really underestimated Stephanie. She must have figured the Wheelers would pay a fortune to hide a letter that proved General Aloysius Wheeler was a traitor, but she met her match when she went up against Stephanie."

Ginny let out a little whistle. "General Wheeler a traitor! No matter how many times you explain it to me, I still can hardly believe that's true."

I glanced her way. "I have no doubt that it's true, but we still haven't been able to locate the copied letter that Carla said she gave to Maggie." Or the other blackmail evidence, for that matter. "There must be an original of the letter somewhere, but where? Without it, no one can really prove that General Wheeler was guilty of treason."

Maudy shook her head. "No, we may never find it." She glanced over at me. "By the way, I followed up on that envelope Hawk said he delivered to Professor Scott. Surprisingly enough, the professor's neighbors said he packed up and left town late last week, supposedly on a European vacation. No one's really sure which country, though."

"Payoff money to keep quiet," I surmised. "I bet that's what was in the envelope Hawk delivered."

"To keep quiet? What do you mean?" Cade asked. He'd gotten in late on the explanations I gave Ginny and Hattie last night, so he hadn't heard how the blackmail letter had ever surfaced in the first place.

"When Vivien was sorting items for the church bazaar, she found an old Civil War field desk; that's where she found the letter. The desk was delivered with some other donations from the Wheeler Plantation. Carla said she'd seen Vivien at the library, reading books on the Civil War. She'd assumed Vivien was helping her daughter with that huge project due soon."

Ginny nodded. "It's a big one. Practically worth fifty percent of their grade."

I went on, "Only I think Vivien was trying to learn more about General Wheeler and the letter. When she couldn't figure it out on her own, I bet she turned to our local expert."

"Professor Scott," Hattie threw out.

I nodded. "Yup. I even remember Maggie telling me something about Vivien getting the field desk authenticated by the professor. She probably showed him the letter at the same time."

"So, how did Stephanie know about the professor?" Cade asked.

"Probably, Vivien mentioned that she'd had the letter authenticated. In a town this size, it wouldn't take too much to figure out who would have been best suited for that type of job."

"Okay, hence the payoff," Cade cut in, nodding. "But Vivien only carried a photocopy of the original with her. That means that either she hid the original somewhere for safe-keeping or gave it to the professor. Either way, it'll probably never show up again."

I tended to agree with his theory. Shaking my head, I said, "Sadly enough, with Stephanie gone, we may never have all the answers about the letter. But at least with Franco's confession we've got some answers about Vivien's murder."

"That's right," Maudy said. "Franco said Stephanie mas-terminded the whole thing. She was the one who used a throw-away cell to cancel the appointment to get Mrs. Busby out of the way. Then, she had Franco break into the shop, unlock the front door and lie in wait to murder Vivien. She also told him to plant the purse outside the diner to frame Ginny."

"Only Stephanie must not have known Vivien carried the blackmail evidence with her in her purse, or she cer-tainly would have had Franco remove the letter."

Maudy chuckled. "Franco mentioned something about that. He said after Stephanie overheard some conversation you had with Maggie at the tea, she realized Vivien might have been carrying a photocopied letter in her purse. She sent Franco back to the diner to retrieve it from the trash, but it was already gone."

"Carla had shoved it between the crates," I commented absently, because my mind was stuck on the fact that the confrontation I had with Maggie outside the restroom that day of the tea sparked this whole sequence of tragic events. I sighed and continued, "Only before she discarded it between the crates, she found a pretty little makeup bag inside and took it. Later, when she looked inside the bag, she found something that belonged to Maggie."

Maudy held up her finger and butted in. "And things that belonged to the other two ladies, only Carla didn't understand what she'd found. But Maggie did. As soon as she saw the other items in that bag, she realized she wasn't the only one being blackmailed. Being the nice lady she is, she called up the other gals to come meet her at the church so she could return their items. That's how Stephanie knew Maggie had seen the copy of the letter. And she couldn't take the risk of anyone else knowing about it."

The room fell silent for a while as the tragedy of it all sank in. Ginny finally spoke up. "You know, Stephanie worked really hard to frame me for this whole thing: timing the murder for the evening after Vivien and I had that big argument, tossing the purse in the trash can behind the diner. . . . But how'd she know about my argument with Vivien in the first place? She wasn't even in the shop when the fight broke out."

"I think I know the answer to that," Hattie said. She glanced at Ginny and then looked down toward the floor, a small blush creeping over her face. "She feels just awful, and she didn't mean for anything like this to happen, but I'm afraid it was Mrs. Busby who told Stephanie about the fight. You see, I left Mrs. Busby in charge of the shop and left early that afternoon. I'd had a bad day. . . ." She looked my way. "You remember, with the dress mix-up and all. Then that fight between Vivien and . . . well, you know." She sent an apologetic look Ginny's way. "Anyway, I left early and went down to see Pete, just to vent, you understand." She took a deep breath before going on. "Well, while I was at the flower shop, Stephanie Wheeler stopped in to pick up her alterations. It seems Mrs. Busby told her all about the things that transpired that afternoon, including the argument. I'm afraid she does like to dabble in gossip now and then."

There it was again—gossip. The cause of so much destruction. "So, after hearing the story about Ginny and Vivien's argument, she must have decided it would be the perfect opportunity to take care of Vivien," I said.

Ginny splayed her hand across her chest and shook her head. "And to think, all these years I've served on committees with Vivien and I never would have suspected her to stoop to something as low as blackmail." She shot me a sly glance. "You still haven't said what exactly Vivien had on Debra and Maggie. I imagine it must be something downright shameful."

Maudy's bushy brows shot up her forehead, and she pressed her lips into a thin line, waiting to see, I supposed, if I was going to disclose the whole truth. The rest of the room fell silent, everyone hanging on the edge of suspense. I knew that the congressman had pulled a lot of strings to bury Stephanie's involvement in the murders as deep as he could, so it was very unlikely that the full details of Vivien's blackmail scheme would ever see the light of day. "I don't think that's really relevant," I finally said. As far as I was concerned, Debra and Maggie could keep their secrets.

Hattie slapped her hand down on the counter, startling us all. "Enough with all this talk of murder and blackmail. This is supposed to be a joyous occasion." She signaled toward Cade, who disappeared into the storage closet for a second, returning with a white cake box in hand.

"I had Ezra make something special for today," he said, opening the box's lid to reveal one of Ezra's hand-designed cakes.

My hands flew to my face as I stared down at the perfect replica of the sign that hung outside my shop. The one Cade had designed. I looked up, happy tears pricking along the edges of my eyes. "This is too pretty to eat."

"No cake is too pretty to eat," Ginny said, reaching under the counter to pull up a bag full of paper plates and napkins. That's when I realized they were in cahoots, planning this little surprise all along.

Hattie reached back under the counter, this time pulling out a bottle of champagne, a corkscrew and a bag of plastic champagne flutes. "And don't y'all forget that we'll be needing a little something to wash it down with," she said, with a mischievous grin.

The sheriff started to don her hat. "Guess it's about time I headed back to the office."

"No, don't go, Maudy," I said, smiling warmly. "I'd like it if you stayed."

A hint of color rose on her cheeks as she tossed her hat back down. "Well then, don't mind if I do."

Cade stepped forward, taking the bottle and corkscrew. "Let me do the honors," he said, popping the cork.

I watched the champagne bubble up and overflow the rim of the bottle, thinking I felt exactly the same way—bubbling and overflowing with joy. I could hardly believe all the blessings I'd incurred since returning to Cays Mill: my family's business was slowly getting back on track, Cade was back in my life, my best friend was engaged to a wonderful guy and now, my first day in business had been a success. Most importantly, though, the trials and challenges I'd overcome since returning home had taught me something—family and good friends are life's truest gifts.

"To Peachy Keen," Hattie said, lifting her champagne. "Many years of success."

I tipped my own glass and smiled. "And here's to good friends."

Recipes

Ida's Peach Cobbler Cupcakes

Cupcakes

> 1 box yellow cake mix plus ingredients as listed on
>   package
> ½ cup applesauce
> 1 15-ounce can diced peaches in heavy syrup
> 1 teaspoon cinnamon

Frosting

> 1 stick butter, softened
> ⅓ cup diced peaches
> 1 teaspoon vanilla extract
> 2 cups powdered sugar

Reserve ⅓ cup of diced peaches and set aside for the frosting. In a large bowl, combine the yellow cake mix ingredients according to the package instructions. Add ½ cup of applesauce, the remaining peaches with syrup and 1 teaspoon of cinnamon. Mix well. Line a cupcake pan with cupcake foils and fill each approximately ⅔ full. Bake at 350 degrees for 15-20 minutes or until baked through.

Frosting

Using a hand mixer, blend 1 stick of softened butter, ⅓ cup of diced peaches and 1 teaspoon of vanilla extract until creamy. Slowly add 2 cups of powdered sugar, mixing as you add. Mix on high until the frosting becomes light and fluffy. Frost the cupcakes once they are cool. Leftover cupcakes (if there are any!) are best if stored in the refrigerator.

Yields 24 cupcakes

Ginny's Peachy Pecan Salad

1 head Boston Bibb lettuce, washed and dried well
3 fresh peaches, peeled and diced, or 1 cup of canned
    diced peaches
1 cup chopped pecans
3 ounces Feta cheese

Dressing

¼ cup extra virgin olive oil
4 tablespoons apple cider vinegar
1 shallot, finely chopped
Salt and pepper to taste

Peel and dice 3 fresh peaches. Chop washed lettuce and place into a large bowl. Add peaches, 1 cup of chopped pecans and 3 ounces of crumbled Feta cheese and toss.

In a separate bowl, whisk together ¼ cup of extra virgin olive oil, 4 tablespoons of apple cider vinegar and 1 finely chopped shallot. Add salt and pepper to taste.

Best if dressing is added to the salad immediately before serving.

(For a little something extra, add crispy cooked bacon. Yum!)

Yields 4-6 servings

Sparkling Peach Cotillion Punch

64 ounces peach nectar (chilled)
4 cups lemon-lime soda (chilled)
4 cups ginger ale (chilled)
1 cup lemon juice (chilled)

In a large punch bowl, mix 64 ounces of peach nectar and 1 cup of lemon juice. Slowly add 4 cups of lemon-lime soda and 4 cups of ginger ale. Serve immediately.

(According to Hattie, peach punch, mixed with a little schnapps, is the perfect libation for a hot Georgia day.)

Yields approximately 16 cups

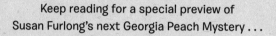

Keep reading for a special preview of
Susan Furlong's next Georgia Peach Mystery . . .

War and Peach

Coming soon from Berkley Prime Crime!

My Southern mother's life is bound by rules. Rules she believes are key to raising strong, confident children who cherish tradition, know hard work, have good manners, and above all else, treasure family. For as long as I can remember, she's been doling out these regulations in hopes of turning me into not only a proper, polite and oh-so-polished woman, but a woman who's independent, strong and indestructible.

Over the years, depending on the situation, she's called these rules different things: Southern Belle Facts, Debutante Rules and even Southern Girl Secrets. Most of these little gems of advice are the same bits of advice mothers everywhere have handed down to their daughters. Of course, my mama always adds her own peculiar slant, but nonetheless, I've come to treasure her quirky tenets. I've also learned that no matter how far I travel from home, if I remember my mama's rules, I'll be okay. Because simply put, I've been blessed to be raised by a woman whose well-maintained exterior is only exceeded by her dogged determination and unsurpassable inner strength. And by passing on her special codes of living, she's taught me how to tackle life with just the right blend of toughness and kindness.

Mama has always told me that one day I'd thank her . . .
and I do—every single day.

—Nola Mae Harper

Southern Girl Secret #045: A Southern gal never
starts a fight, but she sure the heck knows how
to finish one.

"I do say, this election business has folks as divided as the
states during Mr. Lincoln's war," one of the Crawford sisters
was saying. I glanced from one gray-haired sibling to the
other and stifled a chuckle. The Crawford sisters were old,
but not *that* old. Although, I had to agree with them. Our
little Georgia town was definitely divided.

"And did y'all read the latest issue of the *Cays Mill
Reporter*?" her sister asked. "Seems the paper's predictin'
an excitin' debate. You're going, aren't ya, Nola Mae?"

"Of course," I replied, putting on my best shopkeeper's
smile as I passed their bag of peach preserves across the counter. "Wouldn't miss it for the world." When our esteemed
Mayor, Wade Marshall, announced his plans to leave his political office to launch a back-road bar tour with his blue-grass
band "The Peach Pickers," the political scene in Cays Mill
exploded. In the aftermath, two candidates emerged: Clem
Rogers, a local peach farmer who quickly won the support of

the agricultural community and Margie Price, owner of Sunny Side Up Bed & Breakfast, and the favorite contender of local business owners.

The sisters exchanged a sly glance before narrowing their eyes on me. "Town folks are wondering just which side you're on," said the older sister, thumbing toward her sibling. "Sister here says that since you own this new shop and all, you'd be for Ms. Price. But, I'm bettin' you're going to stand by your peach farmin' roots and cast your vote for Clem Rogers."

"Uh . . . well," I stammered. "I'm still undecided."

"Undecided?" they asked in unison. The younger sister clucked her tongue and shook her head. "What would your daddy say, if he heard you talkin' that way?"

Oh, I already knew what he'd say. I'd been hearing it all week. The election had been a point of controversy at our house. Daddy, of course, was all about supporting Clem Rogers, one of our own. Clem had rallied support amongst most of the local farmers by promising tax cuts for local peach producers. Unfortunately, he planned to engineer those cuts by raising municipal retail taxes. A prospect that business owners, like myself, worried might send shoppers to nearby Perry or down to Hawkinsville, maybe even up to Macon, to save a few bucks. Still, I was surprised by Daddy's vehement support of Clem Rogers. The two of them had a contentious history that went way back when. I'd never quite known what started their rivalry, but whatever it was, Clem Rogers had been a thorn in Daddy's side ever since. Still, Daddy was backing his candidacy and expected all the Harpers to follow suit. I just wasn't entirely convinced yet that Clem was the man for the job. It was one thing to run a successful farm; another altogether to handle the politics of even a small town like Cays Mill.

The older sister tugged at her sweater and shook her head. "How anyone can vote for an outsider is beyond me. I'm castin' my vote for Clem. He may be ornery as an old bulldog, but least we know what we're gettin' with him."

"That's right, sister," the other agreed. "Ms. Price isn't one of us. How's she supposed to know our ways?"

A few years back, Margie Price, owner of the Sunny Side Up Bed & Breakfast, had moved from somewhere up north and bought a neglected, dilapidated antebellum home over on Magestic Boulevard. She'd spent over a year painstakingly restoring every inch of the three-story home to its original glory and was now running a successful inn. To me, she'd more than proven herself an asset to the community, but to many she'd always be considered an outsider—or worse yet, a Yankee.

"Well, maybe someone with a fresh perspective would be a good thing for our town," I offered, struggling to maintain my smile. I knew what it was like to feel like an outsider. After more than a few youthful indiscretions, I had fled Cays Mill and embarked on a career as a humanitarian aid worker. My job took me to some of the most remote areas of the world and immersed me in cultures so different from my own southern roots that I often felt like an outsider. I'd felt that way again, more recently upon my return to Cays Mill, as I struggled to reinsert myself into this tight little community. Sure, Cays Mill was a wonderful place to grow up, but the people here, my own family included, were so rooted in culture and tradition, they were sometimes slow to be accepting of others.

"What on earth are you talkin' about, Nola Mae?" the older sister asked. "Fresh ideas? Why, everything's been just fine the way it is. There's nothing around here that needs changin'."

"Could be," the other sister jumped in, "that all that traveling Nola's done has made her forget her roots and what's important."

I shook my head. "Now both of you know that's not true. I've always been grateful for my raising. I came back, didn't I?" I waved my hand through the air, taking in the expanse of my shop with its rustic country charm and displays of peachy products. "And I opened this place to help my family."

The sisters exchanged glances and nodded. "That's true, dear. But you've always been one of us. You understand how it is 'round here. Just like Clem Rogers does. Why, that boy's been livin' here his whole life."

"That's right. Livin' here his whole life," her sister echoed. "I was good friends with his grandmamma, rest her soul. She made the best peach pie. Always said it's best to use yellow peaches. Not white peaches. The white ones are too sweet. Did you know that, Nola?"

I breathed a sigh of relief, glad the conversation had shifted from politics and my apparently inflammatory, too-worldly concept of "fresh perspectives" back to something neutral—peaches. "Yellow peaches, for sure," I nodded, recognizing a sales opportunity. "Which is why, being that it's November and all and since there aren't any fresh peaches available for pie, I put up some of the best canned spiced yellow peaches you'd ever want to taste." I came out from around the counter and directed their attention toward the far wall of shelves which held several straight rows of bright yellow peaches in sparkling jars. "We always heat them and serve with a dollop of vanilla ice cream. My nana's recipe," I added in a conspiratorial whisper, which garnered an appreciative smile from the women.

"Then they must be good," the older sister said, reaching back into her bag for her pocketbook. "We'll take a couple of those, too. Then we better get going. We want to have time to get some supper before the town hall meeting tonight."

My focus quickly shifted out the front windows and across the street to the courthouse lawn where I noticed a man unloading folding chairs from the Baptist church's minibus. They must have needed to borrow extra seating for the meeting. "Looks like it's going to be a big crowd," I said, ringing up and packaging their additional purchase. "Hopefully, people will remain civil tonight." I was referring to the last debate held in conjunction with the Chamber of Commerce's monthly luncheon. After several rounds of heated bantering about who should carry the tax burden, the farmers or the business owners, Doris Whortlebe, the owner of the Clip & Curl Salon, got so mad she stood up and chucked a chicken leg across the room at Harley Corbin, who in retaliation slung a spoonful of potato salad her way, and on and on until a full-fledged food fight was underway. What a mess!

The oldest Crawford sister leaned across the counter, an unmistakably mischievous glimmer in her blue eyes. "Don't bet on it, Nola. Rumor has it that Clem Rogers is going to drop a bombshell tonight. Something that's goin' to change everyone's opinion about Ms. Price."

"Really?" *What could that be*, I wondered. Margie was an honest business woman and always willing to lend a helping hand to those in need. I couldn't imagine what Clem would have to say that could possibly change everyone's opinion of such a wonderful person. "Who told you about this?" I asked.

The older sister dipped her chin my way. "Why everyone in town is talking about it, dear. Supposedly it's something that has to do with Margie's past. She's from up north, ya know."

"And," the other sister added. "Haven't you ever wondered what brought Ms. Price all the way down here in the first place? She doesn't have any kin in the area."

I shrugged. "I just assumed she'd stumbled upon a good business opportunity with the bed and breakfast."

The sisters harrumphed in unison. "Not likely," one of them said. "There's more to that woman than just business. And whatever this bombshell is, it's going to be big. Why, even Frances Simms said she thinks it's going to be big news. She's plannin' a special edition this week."

Now I did roll my eyes. Frances Simms was the editor of the *Cays Mill Reporter*, our town's one and only source for breaking gossip, oops, I meant news. Normally, the paper released every Tuesday and Saturday, but something really big might spur the printing of a special edition. Although, I only remember it happening one time before and that was when Bobby Tindale picked the winning numbers for the Georgia Power Ball Lottery. Thanks to the *Cays Mill Reporter*, the news of his eleven million dollar win spread so fast the poor guy couldn't walk down the street without someone holding their palm out. Finally, he ended up packing it in and leaving town. I certainly hoped Frances would exercise more prudence this time around. Of course, Frances wasn't known for her prudence, a fact I'd learned the hard way: once when she published a series of innuendos that almost resulted in a life-long prison term for my brother-in-law, and another time when she published a completely biased story that turned my good friend Ginny into an overnight social outcast. "You certainly don't believe everything you read in the newspaper, do you?" I countered. Especially not the *Cays Mill Reporter*.

The sisters exchanged a glance. "Well, of course we do," one of them said, giving me an incredulous stare. "It's the newspaper, after all." Then she turned to her sister. "Come along, sister. If we don't get home and get supper fixed, we'll miss that meetin'. And it's supposed to be the biggest barn burner this town's ever seen."

The enticing smell of Mama's cooking wafted through the screen door and greeted me as I mounted the steps of our front porch. As I do every evening, I paused and leaned against one of the posts, letting my eyes wander over our farm. Autumn was one of my favorite times of year. Summer was behind us, along with the hard labor and pressures of the harvest season, the fruit long ago packed and shipped. Then, late summer brought the Peach Harvest Festival where we celebrated our successes, and often times placated our losses, in the company of good neighbors and family. Now, in November things had finally settled down, the cooler night air bringing relief to the burdensome heat of summer and the heavy workload of the previous seasons. Of course, there was still a lot to be done: mowing, pruning and fertilizing, planting new trees, record keeping, and strategizing for the next season, but for the most part, life on the farm had slowed to a manageable pace. A time to catch our breaths and count our blessings.

Blessings were something I'd had plenty of lately. We'd enjoyed a bountiful harvest, punctuated by a surge in peach prices which resulted in enough to cover our operating costs, plus some to sock away for harder times. And my new shop, Peachy Keen, was experiencing success beyond my imagination. Not only had foot traffic picked up in the storefront, but online orders had almost doubled. With Christmas quickly approaching, I was hoping to see even more sales, especially with the addition of a new line of peachy gift baskets.

And to top it all off, my personal life was on the upswing. Just recently, my friend Hattie asked me to be the maid of honor for her upcoming wedding to Pete Sanchez, love of her life and owner of Pistil Pete's Flower Shop. They were perfectly suited for each other and I was so happy for them! Best of all, my relationship with Hattie's brother, Cade, was blossoming. After working through a few minor hitches last spring, we started seeing each other on a regular basis. With all the excitement over Hattie's wedding lately, I couldn't help but dream a little about the day Cade and I might . . . well, maybe I wasn't ready for all that. But I was happy. In fact, the past year or so since my return to Cays Mill had proven to be one of the best times in my life. Except for the murders, that is. I shuddered, squeezed my eyes shut, inhaled the smell of wood smoke, probably a neighbor burning off his recent pruning, and exhaled the unpleasant memories of the murders that had occurred over the past year, one right here on Harper land.

"Nola Mae? Is that you?" The sound of my mama's southern drawl cut through my thoughts. "Come on inside. We're waitin' supper for you."

"Coming, Mama!" Inside I found my parents sitting at the table, three red and white checked placemats already set with plates and silverware. In the center of the table rested a large platter of chicken fried steak, flanked on either side by a bowl of greens and a nearly overflowing gravy boat. Mama was pouring from a sweating pitcher of iced tea. I leaned in and gave Daddy a quick peck on the cheek, inhaling his familiar scent of spent cigars and perhaps a touch of peach jack whiskey, before settling into my spot. "Looks good, Mama." Of course, if Mama made it, it was good. For as long as I could remember, people had been talking about my mother's skill as a cook. In fact, it was her famous peach preserve recipe that inspired and made Peachy Keen the success it was today.

"How'd things go at the shop, hon?" she asked.

"Busy. I'm going to need to make a few more batches of preserves if I'm going to cover my online orders and the extra business in the shop. Chutney's selling well, too."

"It's the cooler weather," Mama commented. "Ladies are making more pork roasts. Y'all know how well peach chutney goes with pork."

I nodded, casting a glance toward my father. "You're quiet this evening, Daddy. Everything going okay?"

He grumbled, but didn't bother looking up from his plate.

"Never mind him," Mama said, reaching again for the tea pitcher and topping off her glass. "He's had a bad day."

I put down my fork. "What happened? Something with the orchards?"

"No, nothing like that," Daddy said, pushing his own food around his plate. "A problem with Snyder's."

"Snyder's Fruit Stand? I don't understand. What's going on?" The Snyders ran one of the largest produce stands in the county. A couple seasons back, Daddy negotiated a sweet deal with Jack Snyder—he gave Daddy a higher percent of profit than we'd normally get at other stands on all the bushels of fresh peaches we could provide. In exchange, the Snyder's stand got the best of our crop. It was an exclusive deal and we were his only supplier, which meant a sure-thing market for our highest quality peaches, plus we didn't have to pack and ship. Which saved even more money. Rumor had it that Jack hoped to open other stands in nearby counties as well, though so far it was just a rumor.

From across the table, Mama let out a long sigh. "Raymond, is it really necessary to talk business at the dinner table?"

Daddy waved her off. "Seems Clem Rogers stole the contract out from under our noses. Snyder said Clem offered a better deal—ten percent less retail than we've been getting. I'm not even sure how Clem can afford to do business that way."

"I don't either. Sounds like he deliberately undercut you."

Daddy shoved his plate away and leaned back in his chair. "Wouldn't surprise me. Clem Rogers bears a grudge."

"For what? What ever happened between the two of you anyway?" I asked.

Mama and Daddy exchanged a quick look, but offered no explanation. I sighed. For as long as I could remember there had been contention between Clem Rogers and my father. And most of it coming from Clem, in my opinion. Once, he cut off our water supply by diverting the small branch of the Ocmulgee River that ran through our property and provided our irrigation water. Thank goodness my brother Ray, a local attorney, was able to talk some sense into the man, but not before some of our trees were damaged. Then there was the time Clem ousted Daddy for the coveted role of General Lee in the local Civil War reenactment. Didn't think Daddy would ever survive that disappointment! He did so love to ride into battle on Traveller, the horse, and scream the rebel yell. Now, this thing with the Snyder's Fruit Stand. Just one more of Clem's dirty deeds.

"Did you try talking to Snyder again? To change his mind?" Mama was asking.

"Yes, but he wasn't around by then. But I couldn't let it rest, so I stopped in at Clem's. Just got back from his place a while ago. We had a few words. None of them good, I'm afraid."

She shook her head. "I just can't figure that man. So bitter. And to think you've been supporting him in his race for mayor."

Daddy shrugged. "Who should I support? Some city slicker with big ideas?"

"You're not being very nice, Raymond," Mama admonished. "Margie Price may not be from this area, but she's a very nice woman. Why, I was just at her place yesterday for afternoon tea and it was quite pleasant."

Daddy placed his elbows up on the table and waved his fork as he spoke. "All I'm saying, Della, is that Clem's a farmer, like us. We want someone in office who'll protect farmers' interests. I don't think your friend, Margie, is the best man . . . *woman* for the job."

"Yeah, but what about *our* interests?" I wanted to know. "Clem's definitely not supporting us. Sounds like he wants to put us out of business."

"It's just one small fraction of our distribution list, Nola. It's not like it's going to hurt us all that much. Besides, there's other fresh fruit markets out there. I'll get another deal going with one of them." He sighed and started pushing his chair back from the table.

"Where are you going?" Mama demanded. "Sit back down and eat something." She glanced over our plates. "Both of you need to eat. All this good food's going to waste."

Daddy stood and looked back. "Sorry, dear. 'Fraid I don't have much of an appetite right now. I'm going to look over some paperwork in my den for a while. Call me when it's time to leave for the meeting." I watched as he retreated to the safe haven of his den—a place where he stored his worries right along with a full box of cigars and a bottle of Peach Jack. I imagined he was going in there now to relieve some of this latest stress with a quick tip of a shot glass.

I turned back to my own plate, speared a piece of meat and slid it through a smudge of gravy before popping it into my mouth. Guess we all have our special ways to mollify stress. Daddy's was partaking in libations, while I preferred to drown my worries with gravy, grits or any other southern delish Mama cooked up. "The gravy is perfect tonight, Mama. And there's a little kick to the chicken fried steak. Did you do something different?"

She smiled with pleasure at the compliment. "Added a little Cajun spice to the flour."

"Well, I love it." I was about to spear another piece when we heard the sound of sirens coming down the road.

"What in the . . ." Mama popped out of her seat and ran out to the porch. I followed on her heels, the screen door slapping shut behind us. "Sounds like fire trucks," she said, scanning the horizon. We couldn't see the main road from our house, so there was no telling which direction the trucks were heading. "I don't see any smoke, do you?"

The screen door screeched open again as Daddy joined us. "See anything?"

The early evening sun was quickly setting, making it difficult to see much of anything. "No," I answered, still searching. Then I spotted it. A small plume of black smoke rising above the peach orchards. "There! I see it," I cried, pointing north.

For a few seconds, we all stood frozen, staring at the cloud of smoke in silence, before Daddy jumped into action. "Looks like it's coming from Clem Roger's land. Come on, let's go."

I held on tight as our farm truck roared down the gravel drive and turned out onto the main road, dust and pebbles flying out from under the wheels. "You don't suppose it's Clem's house, do you?" Mama asked, her brows furrowed with worry. The Rogers had settled in this area even before the Harpers, and their home, built in the early 1800's, had survived the Civil War. "What a shame if that beautiful old home caught fire."

"Let's just hope no one's hurt," Daddy said, taking a wild turn off the main road onto the country lane that ran between our properties.

"Maybe he's just burning off some old wood scraps, cleaning up the place," I said, hopefully. But as we neared Clem's land, those hopes were dashed by the bright red and orange flames licking the air like a hungry lizard. Thankfully, they weren't coming from Clem's house, but his barn.

Mama's hand flew to her mouth. "Oh, no! What a shame. Looks like the whole barn will be lost."

We got out of the truck and squinted through the smoky air. I watched the water from the firefighters' hoses as it arched across the sky in a seemingly futile effort to quell the angry flames engulfing the structure. Next to me, Mama was pointing and saying something, but her soft voice was drowned out by the popping and crackling of burning wood and the roar of the oxygen hungry fire. Not that it mattered. Because the only thing I could hear were the words playing over and over in my own mind. The very words I'd heard one of the Crawford sisters say earlier that day when she referred to tonight's debate—*a real barn burner.*

FROM BESTSELLING AUTHOR
Susan Furlong

PEACHES AND SCREAM

A Georgia Peach Mystery

**In the first Georgia Peach Mystery, when murder
threatens her family's orchard, Nola Mae Harper is ready
to pick out the killer and preserve the farm's reputation…**

To help run the family peach farm during her parents'
absence, Nola Mae Harper returns to her childhood home
in Georgia. But she soon discovers that things back at the
farm aren't exactly peachy when she stumbles upon a local
businessman murdered among the peach trees. With suspicions and family tensions heating up faster than a cobbler in the oven, this sweet Georgia peach will have to
prune through a list of murder suspects—before she too
becomes ripe for the killer's picking…

"Ms. Furlong's turn-of-phrase is delightful, her characters
are endearing, and the mystery will keep readers guessing
until the very end. Loaded with Southern charm, sassy
characters, and tantalizing recipes—a pure delight!"
—Ellery Adams, *New York Times* bestselling author

"Georgia belles can handle anything—including
murder—as Susan Furlong proves in this sweet and
juicy series debut."
—Sheila Connolly, *New York Times* bestselling author

Includes Recipes

Available wherever books are sold
or at penguin.com

1754

Searching for the perfect mystery?

Looking for a place to get the latest clues and connect with fellow fans?

"Like" The Crime Scene on Facebook!

- Participate in author chats
- Enter book giveaways
- Learn about the latest releases
- Get book recommendations and more!

facebook.com/T